the guy on the right

AN UNDERDOG LOVE STORY

KATE STEWART

The Guy on the Right
Copyright © 2019 by Kate Stewart

1st Line Editor: Donna Cooksley Sanderson
2nd Line Editor: Grey Ditto
Cover by Amy Queau of Qdesign
Formatting by Champagne Book Design

the guy on the right

Strike One-My mother named me Theodore after her favorite chipmunk.

Not cool, Mom.

I've spent most of my life answering to Teddy because I couldn't make Theo work.

Except for here. College. The place where all bets are off, and I've managed to redeem myself.

There's only one problem, my new roommate, Troy, is football royalty and looks like he stepped off the set of an Abercrombie shoot.

Doesn't matter, I cook a mean breakfast for his panty parade, and we get along well.

And anyway, this year I got the girl. And she's perfect.

That's right. Theodore Houseman, former band geek, now marching band rock star has finally landed the girl of his dreams.

Everything is perfect.

That is, until Troy takes a good look at her.

I'm not going down without a fight. As a matter of fact, I'm not going down at all. As glorious as these days may be for my all-star roommate, Laney is my end game. I may not know much about play strategy, but I've been the good guy my whole life. I've been listening, and I know exactly what women want. Framed in a picture standing next to me, Troy may seem like Mr. Perfect, but he's underestimating the guy on the right.

Spoiler alert: In this story, the underdog is going to win.

For my new pillar, Kathleen, thanks for laughing with an outstretched hand. And for all my other rocks who never became rolling stones, I couldn't do this life without you.

one

THEO

OLLEGE STATION, TEXAS, POPULATION 113,564 AND I'VE
finally got a match. It's not something I'm used to, but
my luck's been changing for the past few months, and
seemingly for the better. It only took a few hours for my online
profile to go live, and now that it has, I can freely admit I'm
enjoying the ego boost.

> TJGrand: How's it going?
> BlueBelle2001: Good night so far, you?
> TJGrand: No complaints here. Just got home from the game.
> BlueBelle2001: Me too. I thought that might be you.
> TJGrand: You know who I am?

I can't hide my grin as I look over her profile pic. She's a
bombshell and out of my league. But second guessing myself is
not something I indulge in much anymore.

> BlueBelle2001: Of course, I know who you are. I look for you at every party on game night.
> TJGrand: I'm flattered.
> BlueBelle2001: I can't believe I just admitted it. So, I'm new to this. How do you want to do it?
> TJGrand: Do it?
> BlueBelle2001: You know (winking face emoji)

The loud clink of beer bottles jars me from where I sit on the couch, and I look up to see Troy has just tapped Kevin's bottle, forcing him to down it or it'll overflow. It's going to be another long night. Too stunned by the bombshell matter at hand, I stare at her last message, unsure of what to say. Is this girl really propositioning me so soon? It can't be this simple. It happens all the time, random hookups through an app. It's not news. But this would be my first time, *literally*.

TJGrand: What are you thinking?

That's perfect, Theo, let her think she's in control. But don't give her too much.

BlueBelle2001: I could come to you.

"You have got to be shitting me."

"Sup?" Troy asks, walking over to where I sit on our couch.

Adrenaline spiking, I can only shake my head before I look back at the screen, incredulous. In seconds, my phone is yanked from my hand.

"She's hot," he mutters, "and she wants to hook up."

Charging from the couch, I manage to snatch my phone away just as he finishes typing our address and hits send. Glaring at him, I push at his chest. "You dick, I might not be interested."

"She wants it. You need it. What's the issue?"

"The issue is, I don't want herpes. What if this is her MO?"

Troy shrugs. "So, wrap it tight. Everybody's doing it."

"Everyone? Your mom on here?"

That earns me a deserved glare, but I match it before he smirks. The app is a little less risky than the average global randomness. It's set up for campus students only. Not that that protects me from much. I never thought I would be the guy to use an app to get laid, but desperate times. And CampNookie by title alone is clearly not a dating app.

"You've got to get over this shit and make a move," Troy says, tossing back a shot of Patrón. By shit, he means Nora, the girl I dated and waited for through two years of high school and another year and a half semester at Grand. She'd rewarded my patience by sleeping with some guy she met at a party. I've been bandaging that burn for the last year. I'd been patient, I'd been everything she needed me to be, and it wasn't enough. One night with some random and she'd given him everything I was promised. That fact alone was enough to make me consider BlueBelle2001 a little more seriously.

BlueBelle2001: This isn't a campus address.

TJGrand: We just rented a house.

BlueBelle2001: Send me a current pic.

She seems cautious, smart enough to look out for herself, which eases my anxiety. I scroll through my photos and pick out the best, most recent shot and send it to her.

BlueBelle2001: Hot.

I can't help my grin.

TJGrand: Thanks.

BlueBelle2001: Love that shirt.

I'd worn my favorite rugby-style shirt that day.

TJGrand: Thanks, it's my subtle salute to Harry Potter. You a fan?

BlueBelle2001: Who isn't?

My smile elevates before the bubbles rapidly start to pop up and disappear.

BlueBelle2001: Wait, which one are you? This is Troy Jenner, right?

All the air leaves my puffed chest, and I keep my groan inward.

TJGrand: No, I'm the guy on the right. Troy's my roommate. I'm Theo.

The bubbles again pop up and then disappear...for a solid minute.

BlueBelle2001: But Troy's your roommate?

TJGrand has left the conversation.

I take a better look at my new profile pic and see I used the same damned picture. I judged it on my smile, but by the two hundred or so matches I've gotten in the last hour, I can see the mistake of using my short name—first and middle initials—and Troy's, whose are the same. The picture I chose displaying the two of us equally, only adds to the confusion. To any outsider, it might look like I'm catfishing.

Way to go, Theo.

I delete my profile and then the app and run my hand down my face just as Troy passes me a beer. "Dude, heard you guys killed it tonight."

"Thanks, you didn't do so bad yourself," I say, downing the cool suds.

Troy clinks bottles with me. "Guess you won't come to the party since you've got someone coming?"

"Nah," I kill the screen, "didn't work out, she's too eager." *For you.*

"Grab your shit then," he flashes me his all-American grin. "Let's get you laid."

Standing, I grab my keys off the coffee table and study myself in the entry mirror which hangs below the *Live Nudes* neon sign that Troy brought in to even out the Feng Shui.

Prepping for the night, and a better outcome than my first fail, I run a hand through my wavy hair and grab my light, black sweater from the lip of the couch.

"Yeah," I counter, eyeing him through the hole of my

sweater, "because it's that easy." Six years of striking out, end-less hand jobs and a half-drunken blow-all from my ex later, I'm still trying to break the seal. "And can we not make my sexual status a public service announcement?"

Troy gives me a pointed look while he gathers our empty bottles from the coffee table. "Sorry, bro, but you're picky."

"Standards? You mean, I have standards." Which I was will-ing to push aside for BlueBelle2001 just to rid myself the burden of being a twenty-one-year-old virgin. Heading to the kitchen for a glass of water for preliminary damage control, I grimace when I open the cabinet to see the waiting Smirnoff Ice.

"Damnit!"

"You're too predictable, Houseman." Kevin chuckles be-hind me. "Take a knee."

I've been *Iced*. No one really knows who started this tor-turous ritual, it just is, like a lot of other Grand traditions. The trick is to hide it cleverly and stand in wait for the bottle to be seen. If you're caught, no matter the time of day, you kneel and drink. Taking a knee, I twist off the cap and toss it back with a groan.

Troy towers over me, satisfied with my chug until it's drained. Even when I'm on my feet again, he's got me beat standing 6'3 to my 5'11. He grins down at me with the smirk that's incinerated half of Texas Grand University's thong popu-lation. "I have a feeling about tonight."

"I did," I mumble before I follow him out the door with Kevin hot on our heels. Kevin's of similar build, a hulky-look-ing linebacker and not much for mincing words. Luckily for me, tonight he's decided to pipe up and kick me when I'm down.

"There's a girl at this party, I know she will take you on," Kevin adds as a means of shitty support, totally oblivious to the insult.

"No thanks," I mutter while locking the door to the house. The house is an older, light blue two-story on a mostly quiet residential street, fifteen minutes away from campus. It's what anyone else would call a fixer-upper, but it's my sanctuary. I secured the rental a month before school started in an attempt to live the full college experience. Though I didn't want to be stuck in a dorm anymore, I didn't want shit to do with fraternities either. I take my education and personal space seriously, so instead, I opt to attend their parties.

Troy is a wide receiver for the Rangers and was the first to answer my ad for a roommate. In the beginning, I considered myself lucky because he secured the invites to said parties and attracted attention of the female sort. The decision to let him have a room has turned out to be both a blessing and a curse. My other roommate, Lance, rarely comes out of his room, and we can never tell if he's home because he doesn't drive. As if reading my mind, Troy speaks up.

"Is Lance asleep in there?"

I lift a shoulder. "No clue. He's on your team, not mine. You don't talk to him?"

"Not really," Troy says. "He hangs with a different crowd."

Kevin speaks up next. "He's always hanging out at that coffee shop with Dorman, but at home, he's like the dude in… what's that movie?"

"No idea," I say, knowing damn well what movie he's referring to.

"*Half Baked*," Troy supplies.

"Yep, that's the one," Kevin says with a toothy grin. "Guy's either eating or asleep."

"So far he's quiet and pays his rent on time," I say, tossing a look at Troy, who drops the side of his mouth in a frown. "I don't give a shit what he does in that room."

"I told you I'd get you next week," Troy mumbles clicking his fob to unlock his truck before tossing his backpack onto the seat behind him. "I did spot a blonde creeping out of his room last Saturday."

Once inside Troy's king cab, we collectively stare up at the dark window in curious silence.

Troy's the first to break it. "It is kind of creepy how he's always sleeping."

Kevin spouts off pensively from behind us. "Maybe he's got necrophilia."

Troy and I burst out laughing.

"What?" Kevin leans in from the back seat, his mammoth hands gripping our headrests. "That shit is real. I know someone who has it."

"He wouldn't be able to play if he had *narcolepsy*, dumbass," Troy corrects for the both of us. "Necrophilia means sleeps with the dead."

"Wouldn't that just mean he's dead too?"

"No dude, as in *has sex* with dead people," Troy states with an exaggerated sigh. "Seriously, Kev, how did you get into this school?"

"Eat shit, Jenner. I just mispronounced it, that's all."

"Do yourself a favor and read a book, read several," Troy advises, starting the truck. "Or Google. Just as educational, less time-consuming."

I groan, in protest. "Yes, because the internet is nothing if not factual."

"Still more of an education for him," Troy mutters, hitching a thumb behind him. That's the thing about Troy, he's not a typical jock, he doesn't really fit the stereotype like the company he keeps. He's a decent guy. We get along. We talk about more than sports and women. On most levels, he can get deep.

He has the looks, the king cab, and he's built like an ax-wielding Viking ancestor. I have a little respect for him, and most days I don't mind being the guy on the right.

Everyone has a Troy, very few are lucky enough to be Troy. But Troy himself will tell you he doesn't have it so great. With his status comes a shitload of pressure. I might admire the amount of attention he gets, but I don't necessarily want it for myself. I've seen what that pressure does to him from time to time, and it's not pretty. At times, he drinks too much and spends the rest of it playing catch up on his studies. He's not a frat guy either, and he does the *work* along with the *play*. But as I study him when he pulls away from the curb, I can't help but wonder how good it must feel to be king.

Two

THEO
Four hours later...

S HE'D SCREECHED...IN THE WAY OF A MONKEY. NOT EXACTLY
the throaty and appreciative moan I was hoping for. That's
my first thought when I come to. The room is spinning,
and I can't find my boxers in the dim light. Another pound on
the door has me scrambling for clues as to how I got here.

How many shots had I done?

Shots *and* keg-stands, my brain answers as I wipe the sweat
from my forehead.

Bile burns my throat as the aftermath hits me. My chest
is shredded, and I can feel the evidence when I pull down my
sweater.

What in the hell happened?

Grimacing, I stand and stretch. Either I blacked out and
got into my first fight, or I just lost my virginity in the way of
American Pie band geek sex. The pile of hair and limbs on the
bed snoring below me confirms it was something close to the
latter. I feel like I've just been on a safari that went horribly
wrong.

"Think, Theo," I mumble as I foot on my jeans and stumble, hitting the bed. Terrified, my head snaps up and I monitor
the sleeping hair to see if I've disturbed it.

I'm not well-versed in sex, but I'm pretty sure I could press charges for what went down. Every muscle in my body is screaming, along with my pounding head. I'm still drunk, but unbearably too sober to face what happened. I'm pretty sure I still have splinters under my fingernails from the door frame I clung to before she pulled me inside. I'm going to fucking kill Troy. Tonight. While he sleeps.

I didn't have to participate, and I'm certain, in a way, I didn't. Too terrified to see what slumbers in the small bed with TGU logos embossed all over the comforter, I pull on my chucks. If I had sex, there has to be a condom.

"Evidence. Where's the evidence?"

I search high and low for used latex, not for proof it happened, but for proof we were safe and don't see one.

"Come on, Theo, think." I rip at my hair as I use my phone flashlight to navigate my way around. I'm clueless as to whose room I'm searching. The pounding at the door stops as the bass coming from below clues me in.

"Party, you're at a party."

I'm in desperate need of a shower, and a possible lobotomy. I wince at the images that break into my psyche like horror film flashbacks every few seconds.

The flash of teeth.

The ripping of skin.

The snarling.

The screams...all mine.

Nothing about this experience is meant to be remembered. I'm sure of it. Procreating with a rabid armadillo was not on my agenda tonight. Maybe I should be thankful I can't recall much. "Condom. Find the condom," I mutter, lifting strewn clothes from the floor. "Please God, let there be a condom."

"We used a condom," I hear uttered in annoyance from the bed. "You tossed it into the toilet and flushed it."

Wracking my brain, I nod in agreement. It's the one memory that comes in clear.

Thank you, God.

Cool, fear-induced sweat slides down my back. "Okay, you uh, want something to drink?"

"No, I want you to stop talking to yourself, it's freaking me out."

I stand there staring at her form on the mattress, unsure of how to proceed. I can't, for the life of me, remember her name. It goes against everything ingrained in me. I'm not this guy. What in the hell was I thinking?

"Should we exchange numbers?"

"No, we shouldn't."

She doesn't have to tell me twice. Still, I feel like I have some male obligation to assure her, of what? I'm not sure. I stand there, gaping at her with a hooked mouth as she lifts the comforter over her head and groans. I'm seconds away from curling into a fetal position.

"Have a good night." I shut the door with a quiet click behind me and fly down the stairs like my ass is on fire in search of my traitorous roommate. I've just screwed up in a major way by treating my virginity like it was a nuisance. Nothing about what happened will be savored for a later date.

"There he is," Troy salutes me with a Solo cup as I make it to the back porch.

Charging toward him, his eyes widen with his smile when he sees my agitation.

"What the hell, man?!"

Troy chuckles. "She's a tiger, right?"

"I don't have any skin left...anywhere!" I feel like I'm

bleeding in places one should never bleed. Acid creeps up my throat.

Troy regards me with a shit-eating grin. "It's time to celebrate." His eyes light as he barks out orders to the two guys standing next to him manning the keg. "Houseman's next."

"No," I begin to back away, palms up in front of me just as I'm seized. Troy is too far gone to see how pissed off I really am. Then again, what kind of guy willingly subjects himself to the Tasmanian devil to lose his virginity? Me, I'm that guy, and I'm partially to blame for a percentage of it. Desperation is a disease. Lesson learned.

Theodore Houseman's Colossal College Mistake #1–losing my virginity to a heat-seeking demon.

After a torturous minute upside down while consuming vast amounts of Keystone Light—the last resort keg when the good shit goes dry—I stumble into the yard freshly buzzed. Seeking quiet refuge, I find a soft patch of lawn to land on in front of a dividing hedge. Surveying my person for damage, I'm just about to lay back in the grass when a voice sounds on the other side of the bush.

"No, you don't get it. I just don't want this anymore, with you. How many ways do I have to say it?" Silence. "I'm sorry, really, I'm... Oh, well, now you're just being a DICK!" Her next words come out like an alarm. "DICK! DICK! DICK! DICK!"

Laughter threatens to burst from me, and I cover my mouth to stifle it, but there's no point because she, whoever *she* is, is on a tirade.

"Oh, well, that's rich. You really going to go there?"
More silence.

"Okay, that's one word. Here's another, clitoris, learn how to find it and then worship it, because it may save you some relationship miles." I can hear the aggravation on the other side of the line. She's close, maybe three feet away and has no idea I'm sitting here, but I'm way too entertained to speak up.

"Because I'm bored. And I don't like your friends. They all stare at me. And who in the hell asks a woman for a rain check to play Fortnite? I will not play second-fiddle to a video game."

My lips turn up due to the twang in her accent as she rants about his treatment of her. She feels overlooked and under-valued. It's the same shit I've heard day in and day out since my sisters started dating. Their collective complaints were the first to give me the heads-up on how to treat my ex, Nora. As much good as that did me. The stranger's voice cuts through my thoughts.

"How dare you! Fine. Nope. Nope. Eat shit, Patrick, you're disgusting. I knew better. Yeah, well, I loved you too until about five minutes ago. Bye."

The sound of a phone hitting the fence a few yards away jars me out of my thoughts. "Two months!" She says, pacing the yard. "Lort, I just lost two months to a guy I had to lend gas money to! Damnit," erupts out of her right before vomit hits my shoe.

"This night just keeps getting better and better," I laugh at the shadowy figure of the girl who just shit on her boyfriend, only to turn and spew on my favorite chucks.

"Er mah globd!" She manages through the acid barreling out of her mouth.

"Don't speak, this can only get worse," I order, before standing and sliding my shoe against the grass while I pull her hair back. She jumps at my touch but relaxes when she senses I'm not a threat. The smell of sickly-sweet regurgitated fruit permeates the air making my nostrils flare. It's all I can do to keep from gagging with her.

"Awesome," I mutter as she wretches an ungodly amount

of liquid from her body. "If this were a sport, you would take gold."

Her back jumps as if she's trying to laugh. When her tank is finally empty, she wipes her mouth and turns to me, keeping her head down to spare me her breath. "What were you doing eavesdropping?"

"Eavesdropping? Are you kidding? The neighbors two streets over heard *that*."

"Did I get anything on you?"

"Just my shoe, I think. I'll survive. Hold on a second, I felt a hose somewhere near where I was sitting." I let go of her hair and step back. "And since I have absolutely no desire to go back into that house and you're sure to be thirsty after depleting the liquid in your body, I say we multi-task."

"K," she says, her hair shielding the majority of her face. It's not like I can see her anyway, it's so pitch-black in this part of the yard we can barely make out each other's silhouettes.

I search through the prickly bushes and twist the knob earning myself a few pricks along the way. "Why in the hell would anyone plant prickly bushes around a hose?"

"Can't find the spicket?"

I chuckle. "You mean spigot? Who says spicket anyway?"

"Me, because that's what it is."

Turning the knob, I let the water run briefly over my shoe before offering her the hose. She takes it and eagerly drinks.

"Take it easy, we don't want a repeat of your impression of a fountain."

"Har, har. To hell with this night," she says between long gulps. "How long were you sitting there listening to me?"

"Uhhhhh," I run a hand through my hair. "Like right before DICK, DICK, DICK?"

"You should've said something."

"And interrupted that rant? No, thanks. I prefer to keep my limbs. Besides, I was here first before you came walking up with your drama."

She ignores that statement. "Well, he is a dick."

"I believe you." Head still spinning, I reclaim my seat a safe distance from the newly-drunken bush.

"Why?" She asks, turning off the faucet and jumps back when the bush bites her hand. "Ouch."

"Told you."

"You're right, it's masochistic. Why even plant these things? They're ugly anyway."

"Agreed."

She dusts her palms off and takes a seat next to me. "Why do you believe me? That he's a dick. How do you know *I'm* not the dick?"

"Just being agreeable. I'm treading lightly. I've seen your bad side, it's not pretty. Sisters, three of them," I grumble. "All older."

"Shit," she laughs. "Yeah, you are well-trained. Well, I have a feeling neither of us is living our best life tonight, so do you mind if I sit with you a minute?"

"Not at all." I scoot over, giving her room on the safe side.

"Who are you hiding from?"

"Can't really say."

She slinks down next to me with a sigh. She smells clean, aside from the acid lingering in the air, like mint and citrus. "You don't know who you're hiding from?"

"No. Really I don't. Girl, brown hair, blue eyes. The details are still fuzzy. I smiled at her, she smiled back, another shot, the next thing I know…" I look back at the house, "never mind, it's nothing."

"Doesn't sound like nothing," she says, her finger pressing into my neck before I find motor skills enough to jerk away.

"Ouch, what are you doing?"

"As dark as it is out here, I swear that I can see she leeched your neck."

"You're kidding?"

"No, and it's not the size of a quarter either, that's an appetizer plate hickey."

"Jesus." I bury my head in my hands. "I never thought I would say this again, but I need a drink."

"Didn't go well?" She asks with an uplift to her voice I'm all too familiar with. She's teasing me.

"Look, I don't mind you sitting on my patch of grass, but this is no joking matter. I seriously screwed up. There is no do-over."

Instantly, I regret my words through the awkward silence that follows.

"Because you have a girlfriend?"

"What?" I realize then why she got quiet. "No, I wasn't cheating. I don't have a girlfriend."

"Oh, well, sorry," she says on a sigh. "Your drama, my distraction. I'm trying not to freak out I just broke up with my boyfriend."

"I'm trying not to freak out that I just lost my virginity and may need a rabies shot."

What in the hell, Theo?

"You serious?"

"As a velociraptor attack," I say, wishing a meteor would be decent enough to strike me dead.

"You want to talk about it?"

"No."

"Obviously you do, or you wouldn't have told me."

"Slip of the tongue."

"That's not what slipped."

"This isn't funny."

"You're leaving yourself wide open, partner."

She's inching closer, and I'm too embarrassed to study her. The mid-September night air is welcome, cooling my burning skin. I'm enjoying the temporary snap of fall before Texas weather rears its ugly head and goes back to only one of two seasons—summer or winter.

"So, it was really your first time?"

"Yeah."

"Can I ask why you waited?"

"Long story."

"I'm not going anywhere. And I don't know your name, and I can't really see much of your face. I'm pretty sure that raspberry Bacardi I guzzled has made it impossible to identify you in a lineup, so this is as safe a confession as you're going to get."

Finally, I glance her way. She's right, it's too dark, even close up to get a clear view, the bushes block out all of the light of the back porch. She's wearing dark cowboy boots and a dress, that much I can make out, but the rest is pretty much a mystery. Though I admit, her scratchy voice is appealing. Blowing out a breath, I decide why the hell not? I could use some perspective, even if it's from a drunken stranger.

"It was my first time because my ex-girlfriend made me wait three and a half years, only to give her virginity to some random."

"You should have quit her year two. She was never going to give it to you."

"So I've been told."

"You're still hung up on her?"

"No, I've just been busy. I'm in a band, it takes up a lot of my time." It's mostly true. The rest of that truth is that it's not exactly easy for a guy like me to get the girl because of the Troy's of this world. He seems to be the standard. Even when presented with the opportunity, it never feels right, and I've been hesitant to pull the trigger. I've been holding out for something other than a drunken hookup, until tonight.

"Would I have heard of your band?"

"Maybe. We sell out every Saturday."

"Hmm, maybe I should get a better look at you, just in case I'm getting confessions from someone famous."

"Nope, not in the rules."

"We have rules?"

"Yes. This is confession. No faces, dates, or names."

"Okay, so," she says, plucking at some grass, "you dedicated yourself to a heartless bitch who never delivered?"

"Basically, yeah. But that's not the worst part."

"No?"

"I really loved her. I know it's stupid to think you'll stay with your first love, but I really thought she was worth it."

"Sorry."

"Yeah, well, learn and grow."

"Yeah, but it still sucks."

"I don't disagree," I rub at the place on my neck, uncomfortable with what she can painstakingly see in the pitch dark that I can't. "Let's turn the mic around, what happened with the dick?"

"He's just not for me. In the last couple of weeks, I kept ticking off a list of things I didn't like about him while we were on dates. And you heard the rest."

"But you told him you loved him."

"For a while, he was decent to me, so for a moment there, it felt right. He had a pretty face, pretty body, and we got along. I said the words, but they proved empty as soon as he did. Make sense?"

"It does. Plus, he's bad in bed."

"Yeah, there's that. I'm not proud of myself, I stooped low."

"At least you knew his name."

"You didn't catch her name?" There was clear insinuation with her question, but I couldn't argue with it. And I shouldn't have left her there without at least getting her name. I could get it from Troy if I really wanted it, but I lack the desire. And whether I like it or not, I let it happen. I took part.

"I freaked out. I don't think I have any skin left…anywhere."

"Damn."

"I just…" I sigh, running a hand through my hair. "I wanted it to be different."

"How?"

"For starters, I want to *want* to remember it."

"I get it. Really," she assures me only making me feel more like a needy douche. "So, if we're not going to exchange names but bare our souls to the other, I say I go steal a bottle and come back out."

"Sure." I roll my eyes. "I'll wait here."

She pauses on her knees, her silhouette impossible to trace with my double vision. "Did you just roll your eyes at me?"

"There's no way you saw that."

"I felt it."

"All I'm saying is you don't have an obligation to come back here."

"And I don't feel like I do. I'll be back." She treads through the murky yard, magically retrieving her phone by sense alone just as a few guys stumble onto the grass, blocking my view. She's small in stature, that much I gather. Minutes later, I'm on my back, staring at the starless night sky when she returns.

"All I managed to get was a bottle of banana rum because no one drinks this shit."

"I'll take it." I draw from the bottle as soon as she passes it to me and re-cap the lid. "Blech. It's warm."

"Beggars and choosers," she says before taking a long drink. "So, what year are you?"

"Junior, you?"

"Senior. Home stretch."

"Plans for after?" I ask as casually as I can muster with the ill-feeling of warm liquor coating my throat.

"Easy, take over the world," she giggles.

"Good plan."

"You?"

I shrug though she can't see it. "An idea."

"Listen to us, talking like a couple of adults about our future."

"Scary," I say, taking the bottle. The second sip goes down easier.

She sighs. "Nothing scarier than running your own life. Whatever shall we do when we're not told what to think or when to eat or sleep? In my opinion, college doesn't really give you all that much freedom."

"I disagree by circumstance, I have three sisters, remember? Trust me, this is freedom."

I can feel her smile as she lays back to look up into the vast nothingness above.

"I still live at home, so I guess that's my issue."

"You grew up here?"

"Yeah. Well, in Polk. It's a small community on the out-skirts. And I mean small. I'm leaving when I graduate. At least for a little while."

"Where are you going?"

"Not sure yet."

Silence follows before she speaks up.

"So, why did you do it?"

"I don't know," I say through a frustrated groan. "Guess I felt like at this point I needed to get it over with because I'd waited long enough."

"Mission accomplished. Look, if it makes you feel any better my first time sucked too. And my second. Sex doesn't get good until you practice with someone you have real chemistry with. It stays awkward until you get a sense of what the hell to do."

"Yeah. I get that. But at this point, I've pretty-much mastered foreplay. Trust me when I say abstinence does not a saint make."

"Then you've mastered sex already, at least from a woman's perspective."

"Good to know."

"Huh," she says so low I can barely hear her.

"What?"

"I don't mean to burst your bubble, but how good can you be if you didn't seal the deal with the ex?"

"Ouch."

"I'm just sayin'."

"Point taken. But in my defense, she *always* got off. Always. And more than once."

"And you?"

"Rarely."

"So, she was selfish."

"Very. I was too passive with her. Catered too much. I know that now."

"You were a stepping-stone."

"Yeah, well, I like to think I killed that guy."

"Good on ya."

We settle into a comfortable silence that only two drunk strangers could manage.

"What are you thinking?" she asks sometime later.

"Of how badly I want to kick my roommate's ass."

"Oh?"

"Yeah, this is mostly his fault. The problem is the last fight I got into was with a girl."

"Do tell."

"My sister, Courtney, she wracked me in the balls, and I wracked her back when I recovered. I was eight."

A giggle bursts out of her, and I turn my head to try to capture her likeness and fail. "You wouldn't think that would hurt a girl, but she went down like a sack of potatoes."

Her laughter bubbles around us, and it's musical. I can feel the light tickle of her hair on my arm.

"My mom was laughing too hard to punish me."

"Hey, it's still a foolproof way to bring a man to his knees."

"Truth," I say, smiling. Something I thought I was incapable of tonight. "Hey, thanks."

"For?"

"Talking me off the hedge."

"Cute."

"So, what about you? You okay about your breakup?"

"Oh, yeah. That had to end. I didn't want to lead him on. Just sucks because...well, as long as we're being honest, can I tell you something?"

"Of course."

"I've lied to some of the guys I've dated. I've never felt what you felt for your ex. Like I've gotten butterflies and stuff but nothing more. When they say I love you, I say it back out of obligation, but I don't think I've ever really meant it."

"Heartbreaker," I jest.

"I know that's horrible. I know you should save those words for when you mean them. I just feel terrible when I don't say it back. And then we break up and it doesn't matter if I've said them or not because it's over. I think I'm done."

"Dating?"

"Yeah. At least for a while."

I nudge her with my shoulder. "So, the right guy hasn't come yet. It'll happen."

"That's what I hoped too, but...what if it's me? I've dated a lot. What if I'm just not built like other girls."

"You are."

"You don't know that. You don't know me."

"I've gathered you have a mind of your own and you won't settle. So at least, in a sense, you know what you're looking for."

"Maybe."

"Just give it more time."

"I'll be twenty-two in December. I just feel like maybe I won't get a first love."

"Nah. Have faith."

"Says the guy who just lost his virginity because he felt he had hit his time limit."

"Touché."

"Truth hurts, and we're being brutally honest here."

"Right. So, what bothered you about your ex?"

She uncaps the bottle with a sigh. "For one, he was ridiculously lazy. I work and study hard. My gran used to tell me not to respect or fall for a man who isn't doing as much as me."

"It's good advice."

"Yeah, it is. And I'm ashamed to admit I think I've been letting my eyes do all the leading. He was pretty, but not enough to ignore the red flags."

She leans up enough to take a pull of the bottle. "Damn, this is disgusting. Only bananas taste like banana."

"Ironically, true."

"Anyway, I've been letting my eyes dictate what's right for me, giving into the butterflies. But I think it's about time to give the pretty boys a rest, you know? At least until one of them can prove themselves enough to be worth my time."

"Sounds like a good decision."

"Well," she says, passing me the bottle, "all is not lost. At least tonight I gained a new friend."

"Yeah," I take another sip, "with no face and no name."

She sits up fully and looks back down at me. Suddenly I'm cursing the dark Texas sky and the lack of moon. I want a good look at her. She seems to be thinking along the same lines because she leans down briefly in an attempt to get a better look at me.

"This is ridiculous. Let's de-mask," I suggest.

"No." I can sense her wheels turning, "let's keep it a mystery. Maybe we'll run into each other again."

"Alright." I agree, though I know it's not likely to happen.

Her phone lights up in her palm, and it's too brief to see anything.

"Shit, it's late. My mom is gonna pitch a bitch."

I can't help my chuckle.

"What?"

"Your accent. It's pretty thick."

"Yeah well, you're obviously not from around here."

"Not that far at all."

"What can I say? I was raised in a vat of Texas-grown."

"I'm not criticizing. I like it."

"Damnit, I really have to go, but I hope we run into each other again sometime. Preferably when we're livin' our best lives."

"What does that even mean anyway? A two thousand calorie day including all food groups and a four-mile run? The perfect yoga beach pic on social media?"

"Right?" She snorts. "More like living our best *lie*."

"Exactly. Maybe if we ever hang again, we'll do it while living our *realest* life."

"I love that."

She lifts to sit on her knees, facing my direction. "You know, this is probably the most truthful I've ever been with any guy in my entire life."

"I can honestly say the same. And I'm flattered it was me."

"Why do we do that with the people we're with, hide what we're really thinking?"

"Maybe because it's safer than being alone."

"You know what, stranger?" she drawls out. "I think at this point I'd rather be honest and alone."

"Welcome to my level. It sucks here."

We're both smiling. I can tell.

"Okay, I'll go first."

"You aren't driving, right?" I ask, concerned.

"Nope. Bottle is all yours. Be careful."

"You too."

I feel her pause. "This was actually kind of fun."

"It was."

"Houseman, where the hell are you, man?" Troy calls from the porch.

"Shit," I mumble. "I have his keys. I was supposed to be DD."

"Better get an Uber," she warns.

"We will."

"So, you're Houseman, huh?" I can hear the smile in her voice. "Fair is fair, I'm Laney." Her hand finds mine on the grass between us, and she squeezes it briefly. I move to grasp her somehow and end up clutching her fingertips. She laughs. "See, *awkward*. Well, Houseman, I'm so glad I met you."

I grin and rest my forearms on my knees. "Same here."

"Thanks for holding my hair."

"Anytime."

Troy manages to block her out as she retreats into the party. Dusting myself off, I join him on the porch.

"Where the hell have you been, man? We've been ready to go a hot minute."

"I'm not driving," I say, eagerly glancing over his shoulder. "Did you just see the girl who walked inside?"

"No," he barks, uninterested. "Give me the keys, Kevin is good to drive." I look past him to see Kevin on bended knee.

"He's just been iced." Troy turns his head and sees Kevin guzzling the bottle.

"Shit. Okay, I'll order an Uber."

"Do that," I'm distracted, still searching the party for any sign of her and coming up empty.

Much like the rest of my night, it just wasn't meant to be.

Grannism—The world is full of assholes,
don't be one of them.

three

LANEY

"WHERE WERE YOU?" MY MOTHER ASKS, SCARING the piss out of me just as I clear the front door.

"Momma, you scared me," I say, turning to see her perched in the kitchen in wait. Annoyed, I let the screen door slap closed behind me.

"I guess we're even then."

"I told you I would probably be out late. Breakup...had to be done." Sitting on the couch, I pull off my boots and stretch my toes.

"I thought you liked this one?"

"This one? His name was Patrick, and he wasn't for me."

"What happened?"

"He wanted too much for too little."

"Well, it's three a.m. A text would have been nice." Though she works nights, she looks exhausted, and guilt kicks in. I'm a fun-sized replica of my mother, with dark hair and olive skin we inherited from Gran. My mother is beautiful, but I can't remember the last time she put on anything other than her work uniform or a robe. She's only forty-four but has already aged herself well past her years with presentation alone.

"Sorry. I was going to come home earlier and got sidetracked."

"Oh, and what was *his* name?" She sips her coffee at our old wooden breakfast table. The table Gran used to make home-made biscuits on. The image of her nose dusted with flour as she cuts the dough tugs at my heartstrings.

"Mom, geez, I'm not ready to move on."

She raises a skeptical brow.

"All I know is his last name is Houseman. I didn't even see his face."

She chokes on her coffee as her eyes widen.

"Not like that! Ugh, forget it. You're basically accusing me of being fast. I'm going to bed."

"You need to be careful with your body and who you spend time with."

It takes everything I have not to roll my eyes. "You swore to me if I stayed with you through senior year you would give me some room to make mistakes."

"I just don't want you repeating *my* mistakes. Be patient, you've got to wait for the right tide to test the waters."

"Not this again."

And then she's up on her feet, and ready for a fight I'm too tired to indulge her in.

I lift my hands palms up, in surrender. "Let's not go down this road."

Balled fists planted on her hips, she cocks her head. "You can barely afford to pay tuition with what your loans won't cover. Stop acting like you're doing me a favor by staying here. This is half your home, but I'm still the one paying the bills."

"And I'm thankful. So thankful. That's why *I* paid the water bill and bought you some coffee this morning."

She bristles where she stands. She's not mad at me. She's mad at herself. She's always hated she hasn't been more of a provider for me, she just can't put words to it.

"I love you, Mom. I don't want to fight. I hear everything you're saying. I just have to do my own thing, and you have to trust me."

She scrutinizes me carefully for sincerity and finds it before she dips her chin, and her shoulders relax.

"It's late. You should go on to bed."

I nod. "You aren't coming?"

"No. I'm restless, I'm going to make it work for me and make you some biscuits."

I round the table and hug her to me. "You read my mind. Thank you. Love you."

"Love you, too."

I pull away and see the worry I've caused. "I'll text next time. Promise."

"I'd appreciate it."

"You know, Momma, it wouldn't kill you to get out there and have a little fun yourself."

She nods, absently pulling some ingredients from the cabinets. We're a lot alike in some ways and nothing alike in others. Truth is, I got along with Gran a lot better, and she served as sort of a buffer between us at times. Since she passed away in February, our relationship has been a bit strained.

Worn out, I make my way down the hall of our ranch home and click my tongue. Our ancient basset hound, Max, reluctantly follows, but not before giving me a grunt that translates to something like, 'it's way past our bedtime, hoochie.'

Max is the man of the house and the only one I answer to. Even if he is half blind with cataracts and I'm forced to lift his fifty-plus pound ass into my bed each night, he's dependable.

The other men in our family have never lasted long.

My grandfather died in Vietnam when my mother was only a year old. And my dad, well, he moved on to greener pastures after I turned three. Years ago, College Station was half its size. It was never, by any means, a small town, but if you've lived here long enough, it can feel that way and become oddly predictable. Especially in Polk, and Jimmy Cox never wanted or planned to settle here. The first time Gran got sick; my mother decided she was right where she belonged. They parted amicably, but my mother held a grudge once he stopped coming around. Dear old Dad is now some high-ranking executive in Houston who sent us an annual sum up until the day I turned eighteen to remain his mistake. The checks were a consolation for being his false start.

My mother is determined not to have me make the same mistake. She doesn't want me settling for promises that won't be kept.

She's always encouraged me to keep my guard up. She just isn't a current fan of how much I've taken that advice to heart. I guess I am a bit of a 'serial dater'. I haven't slept with every guy I've had an inkling about, but she is right. I need to respect myself a little more and be practical about who I decide to spend my time with.

In the hall, I pause at a picture of the four of us—Gran, Mom, Max, and me—that we took on the porch a few years ago.

"Max, you were a handsome devil."

His reply is a cold-nosed nudge to my ankle. "Okay, okay."

Though the house is old, I love every nook and cranny. Every memory that makes me up is tucked in some corner of this ranch home. Gran had signed the title over to the both of us the first time she got sick. She died knowing her daughter and granddaughter will always have a place to call home. It was both her legacy and parting gift to us. Mom says she'll sign it over to me once I figure out what life I want.

That's a question I've never been able to fully answer with certainty.

Circling my bedroom, I glance at the packed suitcase in my closet collecting dust. It's been packed since the day I started college. I know its contents. Seven pairs of underwear. Seven dresses with the tags still attached. Seven pairs of light socks. A swimsuit. Four sweaters, three pairs of jeans. I swore to myself once I collected my diploma, I would use it. I am only two semesters away, and I still have no idea where I am going, but I am going.

I've never once factored a guy into any of my plans. It could be why I'm hesitant to keep one longer than a few months. Life is hard enough making decisions for one.

Dressed in my pajamas, I brush my teeth for the second time thinking about my conversation with the guy who'd made me laugh, despite the shitstorm my night had turned into. I can't help my foam-filled smile. He is holding out for something different himself, and it gives me hope. Not about a future with him, odds are good I'll never see him again. But his quest is like my own. But first, I need to take a break, and a good hard look at myself. Scrutinizing my reflection, I decide to cut down on Doritos. Satan made that chip specifically to ruin my thighs.

"Max," I line my brush with more paste as I spot him in the mirror behind me. He lifts his head and tilts it. "We're going to do better. Do you hear me? We're going to get more exercise, forget about the other hounds for a while and concentrate on our goals." Max sighs and drops his head to rest on his paws. I can feel both his dread and judgment.

"As soon as I figure out what those goals are," I whisper around my brush.

We're natural survivors, my mother and me and we grew

up with enough love from the female side not to feel cheated. I have no plans to follow in my father's footsteps, personally or otherwise, and sit in a corner office ignoring life. I want more than that, I just haven't put my finger on what yet. I figure my gypsy heart will let me know.

four

THEO

"**W**HAT IN THE HELL HAPPENED TO YOU? IS THAT from last night?"

Kevin gawks at my newly-cleaved chest from the kitchen to where I stand in our pantry/laundry room with a massive hangover. It's everything I can do to keep my head up as I stuff my dirty clothes in the washer.

Troy catches sight of my back while lifting the orange juice carton to his mouth and bursts into laughter. "Damn, man, did you not get one swing in?"

"I'll kill you both," I mumble, adding detergent, "I swear to God."

Troy guzzles down the juice and crushes the carton before tossing it into the trash. He's a tidy roommate, I'll give him that. "Hey," he says in reaction to my hate stare, "you needed the help."

"I asked for no such thing!" I stab an accusing finger in his direction. They both erupt into more laughter, and Troy shakes his head before reading my expression.

"You're really pissed, dude?"

"Yeah, *dude*, I really am."

Troy nods toward Kevin. "Give us a minute."

"I'm on the X-box," Kevin says, making his exit to the living room while Troy crowds the space.

"That bad?"

"I really don't remember much, but I'm positive I enjoyed little of it."

"I'm sorry, man. I really was just trying to help."

"In the future, don't. Do me no more favors."

"No one put a gun to your head."

"I know."

He paws the top of the pantry door, blocking me in and lifts one shoulder. "Didn't have to do it to make Papa proud."

I raise livid eyes to his, and he grimaces. "Sorry, that was a dick thing to say, but seriously, why do it?" He eyes my chest and winces. "I don't remember her being that rough."

The fact that he's slept with her makes me cringe, but I should have expected it. I scan his solid frame. He's got at least fifty pounds of muscle on me, so of course, he wasn't shredded like a man toy. He probably had her purring like a kitten.

"Troy, get in here, we're about to start!"

"He doesn't live here, you know," I snap. "He ate all my cereal and took a deuce in *my* bathroom this morning that could gag a rat."

Troy grins. "I'll get him out of here early."

I nod, shutting the lid to the washer, and he leaves me to my sulking when my phone rattles with an incoming message.

Brenna: Hey bro. What are you up to?

I move to answer and groan when I realize it's a group text and my sister, Courtney has decided to answer on my behalf.

Courtney: Laundry day. Right? So predictable. Teddy, you're boring.

Jamie: He's probably watching Harry Potter. There's an all-day marathon on.

My fingers are itching to type I'm hungover and scratched up from last night's activity but for one—I'm not proud of it, a lion was not born last night, and two—having three older sisters is equivalent to having three extra mothers.

Courtney: We can see you read the messages, you little shit.

Annoyed, I type out a reply.

Teddy: Mom should have drowned you the minute you started screaming at your baptism because it's proof you're inherently E V I L.

Jamie: Whoa, easy tiger. Courtney, don't get butt hurt. You deserved it.

Courtney: Someone's in a mood.

Brenna: Can't you ever be nice, Courtney? You just told me yesterday you missed him.

Courtney: I did not.

Brenna: She did, Teddy. We'll be coming down soon.

My whole body tenses.

Teddy: Don't come, I'll be there for Thanksgiving. I'm busy. Gotta study.

Courtney: While you do laundry?

Brenna: I just wanted to show you how much Courtney looks like you with the new Snapchat filter.

A picture comes through of Courtney looking like the twin version of me and in no way can I un-see it. I fight the urge to hurl into the washer.

Courtney: You can all burn in hell.

Jamie: OMG THEY LOOK LIKE TWINS!

Brenna: Well they might as well be, they're only eleven months apart.

Teddy: I will never forgive you for that.

Jamie: I'm going to make this into a pillow.

Brenna: OMG. I'm dying. I want one. Oh, make one for Mom too. CHRISTMAS GIFT!

Jamie: Done.

Teddy: Don't you guys have anything better to do?

The replies come immediately.

Jamie: No

Brenna: No

Courtney: You know what? I'm better looking as a man than Theo is.

Teddy has left the conversation.

Sighing, I close the pantry and tuck my phone in my shorts. Heading through the living room, I pass Troy and Kevin who strain to see through me at the screen. Courtney is all about the tough love. And some of it may stem from the fact that she's the one and only girl I've ever stood up to–physically. Through the haze of morning, I almost forgot the retelling of that story to Laney in the dark last night. My scattered thoughts collect as I remember the feel of her hand on mine, the sound of her laughter. I'd been at ease in a haze of booze and took comfort in the fact that I didn't regret a single one of my confessions to her. It was unlikely I'd ever see or speak to her again. The thought of that sucks, and momentary regret cloaks me as I make my way down to the basement.

five

THEO

PACING THE AISLES OF THE GROCERY STORE, I CHECK THE LIST Troy gave me and double back for a tomato with his crumpled twenty in my pocket. As usual, his demands exceed the chump change he gave me. I knew when he moved in, he was penniless. He has yet to pay his rent in full and his IOU's are stacking up. I don't mind doing the grocery shopping, because he does the yard work. I'm also the cook and adhere to his dietary restrictions. This doesn't bother me either because I need to stay in shape myself for my own time on the field. Granted, I don't deadlift the weight of my teammates.

I'm halfway back to produce when I hear a familiar voice utter some magic words.

"He's a dick. I got tired of him. Total dick. Yeah, I know. Well, I had to figure it out for myself. Shut it right the hell on up with the, 'I told you so'. Devin, you're starting to sound like Momma."

Stopping in my tracks, I redirect all my attention toward the woman pacing an aisle over.

It can't be. Catching sight of her, my eyes trail down to the cowboy boots, just as she turns the corner and awareness prickles.

It's her.

Frozen behind my shopping cart, I look down at my clothing choice. I'm wearing my PBS shirt, dark jeans, and Converse. I can't remember if I gelled my hair before I left the house, which could be disastrous. Without a second thought, I follow as she spouts off on her phone.

"Yeah, okay. I'll meet you there."

I'm smiling at her back while she pushes her squeaky cart. She's small but curvy, her dress flaring out a little at her hips. Toned calves peek out through a knee-length slit as she saunters down the aisle with purpose. Dark-brown hair flows past her shoulders swaying with her movement. Intrigued, I follow her into the next aisle as she gazes at the various pickle jars like they have some secret she's straining to hear. She chooses kosher dill, my favorite, as I try to get a better look at her profile. Pink glossed lips protrude as she bites one of them and scans the rest of the shelves. It's when I push forward for more inspection that she turns to look directly at me. All words fall away when I get my first real look at her.

"Need some pickles?"

"Sure," I say with a grin, stepping forward and taking the jar out of her hand.

Her mouth parts as she watches me put them in my cart.

"Is your back broken, buddy? Or are you just desperate for pickles?"

"Uh huh."

"Wow, *okay*, enjoy." She gives me wide eyes that scream 'weirdo' before she grabs a replacement jar and wheels away.

Shaking off my shock, I turn the corner to announce myself and slam into her waiting cart as she blocks the next aisle.

"Why are you following me? And choose your words carefully, or I will make a scene like you would never believe. You're creeping me out right now, and I'm pretty sure I can take you."

I chuckle and shake my head.

"Sorry, that was a dick move taking your pickles."

She narrows hazel eyes at me. *Adorable.* "Yes, it was. Doesn't answer my question. *Why* are you following me? I assure you whatever is in my cart, they have more of it here." I peruse her stash.

"How about some rum?"

"Come again?"

"Rum."

"Ugh, look, I can see that you're high…or something. But this is the grocery store." She jerks her head. "Liquor store is down the street."

"I'm not high."

"You sure? 'Cause that would explain a lot."

"Banana rum?"

"Fascinatin'. Look, no habla whatever the hell language you're attempting to speak to me. I'm thinking you might be a danger to yourself and others for the moment. You might need to find some bubble wrap to protect yourself with."

I bark out a laugh. "Laney, it's me, Houseman."

She tilts her head before realization dawns, and a smile upturns her lips. "Houseman?"

Nodding, I return her smile as her eyes trail down, taking me in. I can't decipher what she's thinking.

"So, this is you?"

"Yep. This is me."

"Well, you're lucky I remembered. I was about to end you."

"Yeah, it's pretty funny you think you could take me."

"Oh, I can," she says confidently. "How did you know it was me?"

"I heard you on the phone."

"Forever an eavesdropper, huh?"

"Forever having disturbingly private conversations in public, huh?"

She smiles. "Got me there."

"Your accent is pretty unmistakable. Especially when you say the word *dick*."

She lifts a brow. I lift one back.

"So, you all healed up?"

"Mostly." I palm my chest, "there's still emotional damage."

She reaches in her cart and extends a bag of Twizzlers toward me. "Here, you need it more than I do."

"I'm good. Wouldn't want you to miss the only fruit in your cart."

We grin at each other a beat longer before she sighs.

"So, you live around here?"

"No, I was running errands and decided to stop here instead of the store closer to home. Crazy coincidence, right?"

"Yeah."

We spend a few minutes circling the aisles while I observe everything she tosses into her cart and it's *all* junk. Doritos. Doritos. Doritos and one bag of sour cream and onion chips for variety.

"Having a party?"

"No. Why?"

"No reason," I say, biting back a smile. "You might want to get another bag."

"Don't judge me. I'm post breakup."

"If memory serves me correctly, you're the one who did the heartbreaking."

"It's still a breakup," she admonishes.

"I'm just trying to save you from clogged arteries."

I lift my hands from my cart in surrender as she peruses its contents. "Leave it to you to be so disciplined."

"Eh, I have food allergies, like, if I eat a peanut or most any nut, and there is no EpiPen around, I die. I rarely eat out. And I live in a house full of athletes with zero percent body fat."

"Not cool," she says with a sigh, "you know I'm trying to cut down on those."

"Sorry, if it helps, they're both acting like fuckboys at the moment."

"It does help, thanks."

"Anytime."

We grin at each other.

"I'm glad we ran into each other again," she says. "You know it's only been a week, but I've made good on my oath."

"Going to need to do better than a week to impress me."

"You seem hard to impress."

"Nah, just giving you shit," I focus on the delicate curve of her slender neck, the full, dark lashes that dance over her cheeks as she scans more junk. She radiates playful energy that's hard to ignore.

"Well, I'm giving up fuckboys for food. So, it shouldn't be that hard to stick to."

"I guess I should start a bad habit to keep up?"

She turns to me with two boxes of Famous Amos cookies and hands me one. "You'll thank me later."

"I could thank you now. That is, if I woke up this morning and thought, 'today is a good day to die.'"

"Oh shit, these have nuts in them," she says, scanning the ingredients. "I may just be too dangerous for you to know."

"Nah, I can handle you."

"Think so, huh? Challenge accepted. Shop with me."

It's the longest grocery store trip of my whole fucking life. Snails have a faster pace than Laney with a shopping cart.

She literally weighs every decision she makes for ten minutes, and not only that, an aisle after a decision is made, if she finds something she wants more or a better 'steal', we have to double back to put it back exactly where we got it because she was taught better. I run my hands through my hair so many times, I feel like I'm balding by the time we make it to frozen foods. But it's her smile and her laugh that keep me from bolting. It's the energy I'm feeling that keeps me with her, though I'm fairly sure everything I have is hot and wilted.

When we finally roll out of the store, she turns to me.

"Well, what now?"

I shrug. "Beats me. You're the one popping up everywhere I am."

"Bound to happen." She chews her lip in thought. "Maybe we're supposed to be friends."

"Maybe."

"Give me your number," she says, unlocking her phone before handing it to me. I type my number in, and she looks at it. "So, Theo?"

"Yeah."

"As in Theodore?"

I grimace. "Unfortunately."

"As in Teddy?"

"Absolutely not," I say with such authority, I'm rewarded with a giggle that strikes me right in the throat.

"Fine, I'll stick with Houseman. Where you off to?"

"To knit some bubble wrap."

"Sorry about that, my mouth can get away from me sometimes."

"No, *really?*"

"Smart ass, believe it or not, I'm shy at times around people I don't know."

"Not. I don't believe it."

She grins, shaking her phone in my direction, "I'll hit you up, soon. We can hang out," she smiles back at me as she rolls away, "and live our realest life."

"Sounds good."

We exchange curious back glances as we walk away. I'm so not her type. I can tell, and if I'm completely honest, though beautiful, she doesn't seem like mine either.

It doesn't matter in the least. Some part of me wants to know her, and I can tell by the way she looks back at me before she disappears behind a row of cars, she feels the same.

Six

THEO

"**S**UP, THEO?" MY NEIGHBOR'S SON, DANTE YELLS FROM HIS porch as I check my mail.

"Hey, Dante."

"I'm not allowed to get off the porch."

"What did you do this time?"

He grins over at me. "Nothing."

The screen door rattles on its hinges as his mother pokes her head out.

"Lying," she says, looking at me with an eye roll. "He broke his X-box in a fit and lied about it. The boy is only five years old and lies as easy as he takes a breath."

Dante shakes his head. "This is my time to reflect on my bad decisions, Mom. I need to be alone."

Clarissa and I share a grin. "Manipulative too. He gets that from his father."

"I don't have a Daddy," Dante spouts, "he's dead."

"BOY! What in the world?! Your father is not dead."

"Well, he never comes over to see us!"

Clarissa pauses, and I can see the embarrassment on her face before she steps off the porch shielding her eyes from the sun.

"This child is going to be the death of me. How are you doing, Theo?"

"No complaints," I say, meeting her between our yards. I met Clarissa and Dante the week I moved into the rental. I made it a point to ask her that if me or my roommates made too much noise to let me know. While we aren't a frat house, I like and play my music, *loud*. Clarissa is beautiful, with long auburn hair and icy blue-colored eyes. I place her somewhere in her mid-to-late twenties, as is most of the neighborhood. It's why I chose the area. Since I've moved in, Troy and I do little things for her, like watch Dante so she can have an hour to herself to get her nails done. Troy mows her lawn when he does ours. We have the same landlord with the same strict rules, so I figure we're sort of in it together. And I think Troy has a soft spot for single mothers, due to being raised by one himself.

She glances toward my house with interest. "So, what's up with the quiet one? He's got that serial killer vibe."

I laugh. "Lance? He's harmless. He's on the team with Troy."

"Oh? I might have to bring Dante to a game soon. He needs to be involved in something. Maybe I can get him excited about football."

"I hate football," Dante speaks up from behind her.

"Hush, Dante, you hate the air you're breathing right now. Get your butt inside and straighten your room."

"This house is a prison!"

I can't help my laugh. "Someone has been watching way too much *Step Brothers*."

"Tell me about it. I busted him watching it on regular TV while I was grading papers. He's a sponge, and I was too late. He told the pastor he was going to have a 'Boats and Hoes' birthday cake after church on Sunday."

"Oh no."

"Oh yes. And I found out last week he started his own YouTube channel."

"Scary smart, huh?" I look over at Dante.

"It's called The Legit Life," Dante puffs up with pride. "You should give it a like."

I can't help my laugh as Clarissa covers her face with her hands before mouthing 'Help Me.'

"Theo will let me play his X-Box, won't ya, Theo?"

I shake my head. "Not until you clean your room, Mom's rules."

He raises his chin and squeaks at me. "Punk."

"Dante!" Clarissa shrieks, eyes bulging. "You apologize right now!"

"Sorry," he says, opening the door and looking back at me before flashing a devilish grin, "so sorry I ain't sorry!"

Dante slams the door as Clarissa sighs.

"Of all the sperm, *this* is the one that made it? This one? Really? I know we're not supposed to question God, but I might have a few for our good Lord once I get there. And if I go early, I'm taking this kid with me. There's your free wrap it *tight* warning for the day. See you, Theo."

I chuckle as she makes her way back to the porch. "See you, Clarissa."

She twists the knob expecting it to open and slams into it when it doesn't budge. "Oh, this boy wants to die today! Unlock the door, Dante!"

Grinning, I unlock my own door thankful for the welcome slap of AC that greets me. My phone buzzes in my pocket as I dump Troy's mail on the entry table. A moan stops me in my tracks when I step inside and I pause, trying to locate the direction of the source. When the house goes silent, I slam the door in fair warning and make my way into the living room thankful the coast is clear. My smile is immediate when I see who's texting.

Laney: What are you doing?

Theo: Just got home from band practice. What are you doing?

Laney: Ignoring coffee orders to text you.

I grin.

Theo: Are you a barista?

Laney: Yep. Amongst other things. So, when do I get to see you play?

Theo: Up to you. I can get you a ticket for this weekend.

Laney: A ticket?

Theo: Yep.

Laney: This is exciting. I would love that.

Theo: Give me your email.

She texts her email, and I send her a couple of student tickets.

Laney: You ass. So, you're in THAT band. What do you play?

Theo: Not telling, I have to leave something to mystery.

Laney: Then how will I spot you?

Theo: Guess you'll have to figure it out.

Laney: I suppose I'll rough a game for you.

Theo: Not a football fan?

Laney: Meh. Not my favorite. BRB. I'm gonna have to go milk a cow for this lady's order.

Grinning, I pocket my phone and scramble to the kitchen for a drink. I can still feel the residual sun on my neck and scalp. A steady thump above has me hustling across the living room in retreat. Troy isn't exactly discriminate on when he decides to bring his conquests home. The girls he 'dates' aren't my type, though with some, I can see the appeal. Escaping to the basement in lieu of a moan-infused shower, I sprawl out on the couch and spread out my books. I may have to share the house, but I'll never share my basement. It's a house rule.

I'm about to crack a book when my phone vibrates.

Laney: Why do guys think it's okay to stare freely at my tits. Why? Tell me!

Theo: No clue. I'm not the spokesman.

Laney: Ninety or nineteen, doesn't matter the age, they ALL do it. It's disgusting.

Theo: Think of it as a compliment?

Laney: I'm going to pretend you didn't text that. And I'd rather drop half a chocolate Ex-Lax into their coffee. (devil emoji)

Theo: That's wrong on so many levels. Caffeine is already a natural laxative.

Laney: That's me being merciful. Which reminds me, I'm almost out. Mind running to Rite Aid to bring me some? There is a free cappuccino in it for you.

Theo: Absolutely not.

Laney: Fine. Want to meet up after the game?

Theo: Sure.

Laney: Okay. Meet you at Harry's?

Theo: See you there.

It's not a date. She said friends at the store. Aside from her drunken confessions, and grocery shopping insanity, I barely know this girl. Besides, she told me herself she's done dating for the moment. But was she specifically talking about the 'bash-and-dash' type of guy? Or men altogether? I reread the texts and decide there's no use mulling over it. She said friends, so friends it is.

The front door closes, and I know Troy's company has just left. Or maybe it was Lance's latest.

I'm surrounded by womanizers.

Something I do know is that eventually, they're going to learn the hard way. The thing is, they both know it, and they're going to fight it until it happens. I, for one, damn sure don't want to be around when it does. It doesn't take a genius to figure out the bigger the ego, the harder they fall.

Laney: Ugh. I really need that Ex-Lax.

Theo: Use your words, Laney.

Laney: I get fired for that.

Theo: How many jobs have you had since you started school?

Laney: Quite a few. I have this plan. I heard once that five to seven lines of income do a millionaire make. I just have to keep enough jobs to get that going. It's my goal.

Theo: How many do you have now?

Laney: Three and a half. I deliver auto parts on Saturdays. It's a half job.

Theo: And how many have you had?

Laney: Does this include summers?

I chuckle.

Theo: Sure.

Laney: Sixteen. I admit that's a lot. I'm working on my people skills. I'm going to need them with my degree.

Theo: What's your major?

Laney: Don't laugh.

Theo: This should be good. *rubs hands together*

Laney: Communications and PR.

I spit my water out and full-on belly laugh.

Laney: In hindsight, it was probably a bad idea.

Theo: You think?

Laney: Damnit, I'm pleasant! ←said in my best Ouiser voice.

Theo: Who's Ouiser?

Laney: One of my heroes. You have much to learn.

Theo: Apparently. And I can't believe you chose PR, you're about as subtle as a bullhorn.

Laney: I consider that a good thing. Bold is better. Gotta go. There's a man who won't come out of the bathroom.

Theo: I wonder why?

Laney: (all teeth smiling emoji)

Grannism—God invented sports for women to save them from hair loss. The older you get, the more you'll realize it's true and thank Him for it.

Seven

LANEY

THEO MANAGED TO GET ME SOME DECENT SEATS, AND I MUST admit I'm enjoying the game, well mostly because I brought Devin with me, and partly due to the three shots of apple pie hooch I took before we got here.

"Aww man, it's so good to be out of the house," she says, sipping her beer. "But I can't believe you're dating a guy in the band." She nudges my shoulder. "Talk about pulling a one-eighty."

"Not dating, hanging out. And thanks for coming. I would have felt weird sitting here with no one to talk to."

"Hate to be the one to break it to you, but you don't *hang out* with guys."

"Sure, I do."

She harrumphs. "Name one."

"Garret."

"*Lie*, you totally made out with him!"

"What's with all the women in my life calling me out for being curious?!" I say, throwing up my hands. Hearing two distinct deep-throated chuckles, I look to my left where two guys are eyeballing us with shit-eating grins.

"Mind your business," I snap at them before glaring back at Devin.

She, at least, has the gumption to look remorseful. "Sorry, but you did."

"I don't even remember."

"Right after graduation."

"Fine, well, I'm turning over a new leaf. I'm done with Batman."

"What?"

"It's a syndrome. A type. I'm done."

"Oh, this should be good." She swivels in her seat to face me.

"I'm serious."

"Oh, I believe you believe it."

"Think about it, Batman is the booty call superhero. Sexy-half face, looks amazin' in the uniform, BUT, he only answers to the signal, at night. He never takes off his mask and only reveals his true colors once he's already bedded the girl. I've been dating nothing but Batmen."

"You're unreal, you know that? You've spent real time thinking about this, haven't you?"

"I really have, and my tastes are changing, my friend."

"What's the new one look like?"

"Theo? A little taller than me, lean build, ear length brown hair, brown eyes, trimmed beard. Adorable."

She smirks. "Scrawny."

"No, he's not," I defend. "Not at all. He's just right."

"You like him?"

"I do, but not that way. I don't think. He's not my type really, but you know he's…appealing. Fun to talk to. We met and just clicked. I talk to him like I do you. Put it like this, if there were a family-sized bag of Doritos in the room, I would eat the whole thing in front of him."

"That close?"

"It happened fast. We shared trauma."

"So, you would show him your Google history?"

"Pshhh, girl, please. I would rather walk buck naked in the grocery store during bush-week winter than let anyone ever see my browsing history. Not even you are privy to that information."

"Should I be worried about being replaced?"

"Hell no. You know better," I say, giving her the side eye.

"Okay, so if you're just friends, what do you need him for? Why not just hang with me?"

"Because I love you, but all you do anymore is plan your weddin' and make me craft favors when I come over. I have thousands of glue gun burns to prove it."

I cringe when I see her reaction.

"Sorry, but seriously, you know you do."

She shrugs, the grudge leaving her face. "Fine, I do."

"Not long now," I say, motioning to the rock on her finger.

"Seven weeks, I'm so excited."

"Me too," I tell her sincerely.

Devin's always had a mapped-out life. Her dad owns a sporting goods chain and the minute she graduated high school she assumed her position on the administrative side while taking night classes at a junior college. I could say she was born into the gravy boat, but she's been working in her father's stores since she was a tween. She earned her place. Even her fiancé, Chase, landed in her lap in a sense. He's an asst. baseball coach and went in the store one day to place an order and came out with her phone number. Some days I envy her, most days I wonder if the life she's planning will be enough to hold her. Then again, it could be my hang up. She seems happy, content, and that's all that matters.

"You think I'll get bored," she says, reading the bad half of my thoughts.

I gape at her as she stares on at the game.

"No, I was just thinking about how happy you are."

She cuts her glare my way calling bullshit.

"I have no objections. None. Chase is perfect for you."

"You know, not all of us have 'grass is greener' syndrome. You've been dying to leave since we graduated," she whisper yells, as the stadium rises to their feet cheering on a wide receiver who just scored, putting TGU in the lead.

"Dayum, I love my man, but he's hot," Devin says, looking up at the jumbotron. I glance to where she's transfixed and see why she's fish mouthed. There's a picture of the player on the big screen, along with his impressive stats.

"He's pretty," I agree, turning my attention back to her to address her accusations. "And you know I'm happy here at home."

"I know," she replies, but only to be agreeable.

"Nothing wrong with wanting a little world experience. But Texas will always be home for me."

Another nod.

"You can't get sore about it yet, either. I've still got a lot of months left, and I have no idea what I'm going to do."

"I just have this feeling that once you see what's out there, you won't want to come back," she says softly. "I know that's selfish of me. I'm sorry I said it."

"I love you too, *Devil*."

Devin and I have been attached at the hip since grade school. I think in some way we envy each other. Her life is set, and mine is the complete opposite.

"Your new guy is up," she says as half-time commences, and the band takes the field. It's useless to look for Theo, there are too many of them. It's not my first game, but I must admit I've never paid too much attention to the band. And when it comes to school spirit these days, I often find mine at the bottom of a bottle.

"Suddenly, I feel like a sad excuse for a fellow Ranger. Maybe I should get a new T-shirt."

"You could have, at the very least, worn your school colors," she says all high and mighty in her Grand T-shirt, a TGU emblem on her cheek. She glances down at my flowered sundress, cardigan, and boots.

"What? I went through this ritual my first couple of years, it's not my first rodeo. And besides, garnet and mustard dry me out," I say in poor excuse just as the whistle is blown and the fight song begins. Glancing around, I catch the stare of the guy sitting next to me on my chest.

"Eyes up here, buddy," I say throwing a two above my nose.

"Just admiring the flowers," he says with a shrug, "and the display."

"Yeah well, they aren't paw and sniff," I retort dryly.

"Want to test that theory?"

"Please don't start a fight," Devin sounds up, her snarl directed at him. "I just got my nails done."

He looks at us like we're insane but averts his eyes. Nothing like showing your crazy to scare a feisty penis back into its shell.

The band begins to play "Thunder" by Imagine Dragons and Devin and I watch on in mild surprise.

"Not bad. I feel terrible I've never paid attention," Devin says, breaking me from my thoughts. "I'm usually with Chase, so it's always the game itself I'm interested in, you know? Half-time is usually when I get more beer and pee."

"Same here."

We both watch stunned as the Grand Band pulls off some

pretty mind-blowing hat tricks which include spreading across the field to form a stick man who starts flossing.

"Oh my God," Devin says through a laugh. "That's awesome."

"You know Theo's here on scholarship," I keep my eyes on the show. "He must be really talented."

"I'll bet," she says in a tone that has me rolling my eyes rather than acknowledging her. "What does he play?"

"He won't tell me. Isn't that weird?"

"He's going to make you work for it, huh?"

"Man, they must have to practice like crazy to nail this stuff," I say as the crowd roars in appreciation. "I can't believe I've never really noticed them before."

"Me neither," Devin's clearly impressed. "First time for everything." She turns to me, carefully reading my expression. "I'm calling it, you'll be dating Grand Band Man by my wedding, and dumping him before Christmas."

I fist bump her tit, and she has the audacity to look miffed. "His name is *Theo*, and that's a horrible thing to say."

"Hey, if we're going on track record alone, I'm spot on with the timeline. But I'll reserve judgment until I meet him, how's that?"

"Better, though the sarcasm negates any good intent on your part. And like I said, we're just friends."

Devin regards me skeptically. "I guess we'll see."

eight

THEO

I ARRIVE AT THE BAR A LITTLE OVER AN HOUR AFTER OUR GAME AND spend a few minutes circling the crowd for Laney. I find her toasting another girl and am surprised at the relief I feel that she didn't bring a date. Laney spots me and waves me over with a grin and a waiting beer as her friend joins the line on the dance floor.

"It's a little warm," she yells over at me. "I expected you sooner."

"Sorry about that, it took a lot longer for me to get home and get changed."

"Don't worry, we've been fully entertained," she grins at her friend, who is shaking her ass in a small circle with a few other women. In the darkly-lit bar I scan Laney, she looks hot in a sundress and a sweater that accentuates the cleavage I refuse to acknowledge for fear of poisoning. A minute of silence passes, and I can feel her eyes on me. I scan the crowd and the dance floor. "Good to see the two-step is still alive and well."

Laney guffaws. "You mean to tell me, you don't like country?"

"Not especially, no."

"Well, that's just sad," she says, shaking her head. "I happen to love it."

I shrug. "What can I say, I grew up in the burbs listening to other stuff. I don't own boots. It's so cliché anyway. When out of towners came to visit my family, they were always surprised when no one dressed and spoke like Yosemite Sam and our front yard wasn't full of rolling tumbleweeds."

"Ever been to West Texas?"

"No."

"Well then, there you go." Laney slams her beer on the table in afterthought. "I'm so disappointed in you, young man, where is your Texas pride?!"

"I have pride. Not all Texans have to wear boots and two-step." I give her my best smirk, surveying her dress and boots. "And what do you have to say for your lack of school spirit?"

She grins over at me. "Well played. I'll buy your next beer—"

"You bought my first one," I counter, taking a sip.

"You didn't let me finish. I'll buy your next beer *if* you'll two-step with *me*."

"No."

She raises a brow in challenge. "Don't know how?"

"I do."

"Then come on, Grand Band Man, live a little."

"He just got here," the friend says breathlessly, scanning me before jabbing Laney in the ribs with her elbow. "Let him have one beer first."

"Shut up," Laney instructs before our introduction. "Theo, this is my best friend, Devin. Devin, this is Theo."

Devin is the opposite of Laney, a platinum blonde with pale skin to Laney's dark complexion.

"Nice to meet you." She yells something else I can't decipher, and we clink glasses and drink. The Rangers lost tonight, but there are no mourners in this crowd. And the place is crawling with TGU-covered alumni.

Devin's eyes dart back and forth between us as I sip more beer.

"So, you two met at a party?"

"Yeah," I offer, setting my beer on the high-top table.

"And then ran into each other at the grocery store?"

"Uh huh," Laney says just as clueless as to where Devin's going with her line of questioning.

"I'd say that's kismet in a school your size."

"That's coincidence," Laney reasons to keep us both comfortable.

"Well, my money is on kismet," she subtly bumps shoulders with her best friend.

Laney not-so-subtly pinches Devin, who jumps.

"How long have you two known each other?" I ask to break them up.

"Since she stole my boyfriend in first grade," Devin supplies in jest.

"Dirty Dustin," Laney says, rolling her eyes. "I did you a favor. He stunk."

Devin tosses back a shot and doesn't flinch. "Puh-lease, don't act like you haven't been boy crazy even *before* you got your first starter bra. And I saw Dustin at the store the other day, he gave me the eye." She tilts her head and gives Laney wide eyes, and it looks so ridiculous we both crack up.

"Well, not like that exactly, but he did," she insists, wobbling out of her seat. "I'm going to the restroom." She looks between us conspiratorially, and Laney shakes her head in warning before Devin saunters off singing Jingle Bells at the top of her lungs.

"How much has she had?" I ask, nodding toward the way she went.

"Not enough to knock her out, unfortunately," she mutters

annoyed while trailing Devin's retreat over her shoulder before looking back at me. "She's curious because I spoke so highly of you. I apologize."

"Don't worry about it. I like her. She's your other half, right?"

Laney bobs her head. "Oh, most definitely."

I can tell she's mildly buzzed.

"I had a friend like that back home."

"Yeah? Where is home?"

"Houston."

"Ah, big city boy," she says, casting her eyes down.

"Not a fan of Houston?"

"Sure." She licks her lips.

"Why don't I believe you?"

"Meh, my dad lives there. We don't talk much."

"Oh, sorry to hear that."

She shakes her head in annoyance. "Let's not let this get weird, okay? No matter how hard Devin tries to rile us."

"Fine with me."

She raises her foamy beer. "To living our *realest* life. Cheers."

"Cheers."

We finish our beers, and I head to the bar to order more. When I get back to the table, the girls are warding off the advances of a group of guys. I nudge my way in and pass out our beers.

"Thanks," Laney spouts loudly, "but, you can go, we're all set." I meet all inquiring eyes and see the confusion in each of their faces. I shrug in a 'what can I say?' way.

"You're serious? You're with *this* guy?" The taller of the milk and grain fed three—who all have my height beat by a considerable amount—asks, scrutinizing me with clear skepticism.

"No offense taken," I salute him with both my beer and stretched middle finger.

"I can guarantee he's got several inches on you," Devin joins in snidely, "and I mean horizontally." She stretches out her hands in length for demonstration and gives me a wink.

I wink back.

The clueless dick leans in while snaking his arm around Laney. His hand slides dangerously close to her ass, just as she lifts a book of matches from the unused ashtray on the table.

"You ever seen a match burn twice?" she asks him with a sickly-sweet voice.

I bite my lips to keep from smiling as he leans in with a "No."

She strikes a match studying it as if it has some mysterious power and he leans in watching it with her, oblivious and gullible to her charms before she shakes out the flame and presses it to his offensive hand. He jumps back with a curse.

"And now you have. Now kindly get your paws off me before I show you my next trick."

"Whatever," the guy grumbles before he lifts his chin in signal and the three of them stalk off.

"That's right, boys, fuckoffsky!" Devin yells at their retreating backs.

She giggles and Laney rolls her eyes, grinning up at me. "She's ten sheets. We're going to have to call it an early night."

"Oh no, you don't! I'm living it up tonight. My fiancé will come fetch me when I'm damned good and ready. You will not police me, *Elaine Cox*."

"I'm not babysittin' you, either."

"Lordy woman, you're like the damn Hitler against happiness these days." Devin raises her finger beneath her nose to make a fingerstache. "Is dat a smile, Fräulein? No smiling, Fräulein! Nech bin doust nech plaque!" she spits between us.

Laney jumps back and dramatically places a hand on her chest. "I'm pleasant. Damnit! I saw Drum Eatenton this morning at the Piggly Wiggly, and I smiled at the son of a bitch 'fore I could help myself!"

I look between them, both confused and entertained, as they crack up.

"Inside joke," Laney snorts, gauging me. "It's from a movie."

"Blasphemy! It's not just a movie, it's the southern woman's bible!" Devin proclaims, raising her beer to toast Laney.

"Amen."

They both drink as the music changes, morphing into a steady thrum of bass and Devin's eyes widen. "Oh my God, we need to dance, now, right now."

"Because a minute from now is too late?" I ask, egging her on.

"Such a smart ass," Laney grins at me.

"I love it!" Devin proclaims before turning to Laney. "I like him so much."

"You love everyone right now, Devil. They don't call it Jesus's Juice for nothing."

Devin facepalms her and grins at me. "She said you were adorable," her head wobbles on her neck as she begins to slide down the side of her chair. "And I must agree."

The foot-long dick I just gained by word of mouth shrivels up as I avoid Laney's eyes while she hoists Devin back up in her chair, sitting her upright and snatching her beer.

This is most definitely not a date, not if the word 'adorable' was used when she described me.

Adorable translation—my penis will never enter her vagina. But she will use me at her leisure, like a stuffed animal. I'll be there for comfort on long, lonely nights; and she will drag my ass around by the arm until I'm filthy, my limbs are ripping apart at the seams from neglect, and my insides are coming out.

I've most definitely been friend-zoned, or in my case, Teddy'd.

"I meant that in a good way," Laney explains after weighing my expression. I chew it over for a second.

"You know, I thought the same thing about you when I first saw you." It's the truth. I did think she was adorable. And I'd thought the same tonight when I saw her. It's just far more flattering on her side of things. For me, it's the kiss of fucking death.

For the next half hour, I watch as Laney stomps on the foot of any guy who gets within a few inches of either of them. I'm mildly entertained but feel like I'm a third wheel. While I watch, I try so hard not to memorize her movements, but it's proving impossible. I'm so in tune with the way she works herself that I have to adjust my junk twice. She is far more than adorable, but I refuse to let myself fixate.

Laney is the first to make it back to the table, lifting her hair to wave a hand beneath the sweaty strands. "Whew, hot."

It's on the tip of my tongue to agree, but that's flirting. And I shouldn't be flirting, because I'm adorable.

Fuck.

It occurs to me then, that on some level I had hoped it was a date.

She looks over to me and thanks me for the water I gathered while they were grinding on air. "I only came here because she loves it. She doesn't get out much. I got over this place after a few semesters at Grand."

"Is she a student?"

"Part-time at Junior, her dad owns Hardin Sports. She works at the headquarters here."

"Ah."

"So, if you need a discount on balls, I'm your gal."

"Thanks."

"Anytime." More silence ensues as we both observe our surroundings. I can feel her eyes on me. "You talked a whole lot more in the yard, and at the grocery store," she sips at her water.

"I gave you a lot to work with."

She lifts her palm, moving it in a circle as she speaks. "And now you're being all *mysterious.*"

I shrug. "No good can come from showing your full hand all at once."

"Hmmm. Going to make me work for it? Okay. Well, you're going to have to be the one to suggest the next…" she twists her lips, weighing her words, "place we go."

"Am I?"

She nods.

"Alright."

She gives me a smile that steals the breath from me. I'm having a hard time not imagining the tickle of her hair on my skin. We both move to speak because, despite our pact to keep it light, it's becoming awkward.

"You owe me a dance—"

"I should probably go."

She frowns. "Really?"

"Yeah, make it a girls' night. I don't want you to feel obligated to cater to me. I'm wiped anyway. I'll text you."

"Well, okay."

I turn to leave and catch her watching me with disappointment. I give her a wink and take my leave. I'm not in the right frame of mind to be the adorable new friend. Mere steps out of the bar into the cool night air, I jump when I feel her latch on to my back and let out an "ugh."

"Theeeeoooo," she says on an exaggerated breath.

Chuckling, I stand uncomfortably with my keys halfway out of my pocket.

"Yes, Laney?"

"Don't turn around," she whispers fiercely.

"That would be kind of impossible."

"Right. Well, I appreciate you. I just wanted you to know that."

"Are you okay to get home?"

"Yes. Devin's fiancé is coming for us. I just sent the SOS." She loops her arms around my waist and squeezes tighter as a few passersby give us odd looks. I couldn't give a shit. I smell the mint and citrus, and instantly I'm back in that yard. My head goes fuzzy, and it has shit to do with the beer I drank. My chest restricts just a little when she sighs out an, "I like you, Theo."

"I like you too, Laney."

I place my hands on hers and wait as she talks to my back. "Your band is amazin'."

"Thanks."

"I promise to always watch you, instead of getting more beer or peeing."

"O-*kay*."

"I mean that. Just because I'm buzzed, it doesn't mean I'm not sincere. And I will collect on that dance eventually."

I feel the weight and imprint of perfect tits on my back and remain mute while clenching my fists to keep me from embarrassing myself. "Night, Theo," she whispers, just before letting go. I turn back in time to see the toss of her hair and swish of her skirt just before the door closes.

nine

THEO

I HAVE THIS THEORY THAT MEN WHO SCORE EASILY WITH THE ladies don't put in enough effort in the sack. Case in point, Bethany. She sits at our cheap folding kitchen table swallowed by one of Troy's T-shirts with her head in her hands, while I pour pancake batter. This is not a woman who has been sexually blissed out. If so, she wouldn't be cloaked in morning-after regret. As a guy who's been sexually deprived most of my adult life, I have no intention of making these kinds of mistakes.

Laney's words strike me then. She told me it's awkward until you find the right chemistry.

The second half of my theory is sex is the Olympics for the sexually underprivileged, and I've been in training for quite some time. I've got way too many pent-up fantasies in my arsenal for the girl I find the chemistry with. I might practice my P's and Q's out of respect for the ladies, but I've got a smut-filled brain, no doubt due to the deprivation.

And there's no way in hell I'll ever let a forlorn sigh, like the one sounding out behind me, come out of the mouth of any woman I bed, the morning after.

Well, except for that one time.

CLICK, DELETE.

"Coffee?"

"Please," she says softly.

I greeted her when she hit the bottom of the stairs to try to put her at ease. She had no bounce in her step when I lured her into the kitchen, and her smile hasn't reached her eyes through any of our exchange.

Troy's either underperforming or they've had some non-committal morning-after chat. But since he's into avoidance, I assume it's a bit of both.

"You don't have to cook for me," Bethany says softly behind me where I stand at the stove.

"I was cooking anyway, it's no trouble," I assure, looking back at her with a smile before flipping a perfectly golden cake. I hate the skittish look in her eye. It makes me just as ill at ease as she is. I didn't start out cooking breakfast for the house conquests, it just kind of happened. They aren't all this sullen when they come down, but Bethany is different; and I'm sure Troy noticed on some level, but it didn't stop him. Then again, it didn't stop her either.

"So, I'm thinking I'm not the first girl you've cooked for."

This is the part where I resent my roommates the most. I'm not good at the bullshit, it's not my job to placate them, but I'm typically the one stuck making the excuses. "I have two roommates on the team, so there's always someone to cook for."

"I'm sure." The snark in her voice isn't for me.

"It's all up to you," I plate up the fluffy cakes and set them on the table in front of her.

She zeroes in on her plate and then looks up to me. "What do you mean?"

I shrug. "I mean, you can leave here hating yourself for something you wanted to do, or you can own it and move on."

"Well," she says with an ironic chuckle, "that answered my next question."

"Which was?"

"Have you ever cooked for the same girl twice?"

"You want the truth?"

"By all means," she says, grabbing her fork.

"No, no repeats, and I don't think that's going to change anytime soon."

She nods and grabs the juice in front of her as I lean in on a whisper when it's halfway to her lips. "You're still the same girl you were before you walked through that front door. It's not you, it's him."

"That's original."

"It's the truth."

She swallows a lump I know is forming in her throat and nods before sipping her juice. "So, you've been in the same position?"

"Used to the point of feeling violated? Ironically, yeah, it was recent, and I have the battle scars to prove it."

"You're nothing like him."

"He's not so bad. Just…oblivious for the moment."

She pulls the chair out next to her and gives me a smile that reaches her eyes. "Eat with me, Theo."

"You ever going to settle on one?" I ask, tapping out a text to my sister as Troy comes into the kitchen after showing Bethany out.

He stills in front of the coffeepot. "Now, no. Later, maybe."

"Not one of these women does it for you?"

"Are you seriously lecturing me?" He turns to me, coffee in hand, his shoulders going tight as I look up to him from where I sit at the table.

"Nope. Just curious."

"You going to the bonfire?"

Avoidance. All play, no pay.

I flip his tactic. "You should be pre-law."

He grins, taking it as a compliment. Like he does everything else.

"So, you going?"

"Not sure."

The bonfire is the annual 'be there' party and takes place in the outskirts of town. I'd gone my first two years with Nora. She gave her virginity away the second night, to the guy who took her home.

"Supposed to be good. I'm going to help set up."

"I'll think about it. Toss me some ice, would you?"

He nods, opening the freezer where I have a Smirnoff waiting on him in plain sight.

"You fucker."

Groaning, he twists off the cap and kneels as I shoulder my backpack and smirk down at him. "Bethany is a biology major and an only child, but she has two cats, Frick and Frack that she considers siblings. She's a vegetarian and a Virgo. Her favorite book is *The Handmaid's Tale.* She's pretty sure she's into kink but hasn't trusted anyone to explore it with her yet. Oh," I say as he finishes the bottle looking like he's smelling burnt hair as I pull out my phone, "she gave me her number and left you her breakfast dishes."

I make it to the door as Lance bounds down the stairs making a rare appearance in nothing but mesh shorts. "Sup, Lance?"

He nods. "Sup," before passing me at the foot of the stairs.

Troy barely acknowledges Lance, arms crossed as he regards me curiously from the kitchen.

"She left her number for me?"

"No. Because you didn't ask her for it."

"And you did?"

"No," I shrug. "I didn't ask her for it either. Later."

ten

THEO

Laney: Let he who is without hangover cast the first stone.

Theo: *throws rock* Did you feel it?

Laney: Just your judgment.

Theo: Still hungover from Saturday?

Laney: I may have indulged in too much hair of the dog. I will say church was far more entertaining this week.

Theo: That's just wrong.

Laney: I'm sure I got points for showing up. Where are you?

Theo: Grand Lounge.

Laney: Didn't you tell me you have a house?

Theo: Sad isn't it?

Troy had decided to invite some of the team to watch Monday Night Football. I wasn't in the mood to argue. I threatened him if anyone went near my basement.

Laney: Mind if I join you?

Theo: I'll save a seat for you.

Laney: On my way.

The Grand Lounge is the common area for TGU students. It's considered the Rangers' living room, consisting mostly of lounge chairs and couches you can kick back and nap on.

Plugging in my earbuds, I mimic the keys of the song I'm learning on my jeans and get lost. Sometime later, I come out of my daze as a set of well-worn cowboy boots comes into view, slowly bringing me back into the present.

"Were you sleeping?"

"Not exactly," I run a hand through my hair. She takes the seat next to me, her now-familiar scent filling my nose. Her lengthy hair brushes my forearm when she plants herself on the couch next to me.

"So, are you done studying since I saw you catching flies when I came in?"

"I was up most of the night, wondering how many times the Lord could be summoned before He made an appearance in the middle of some shameful fornication."

She chuckles and ruffles my hair. "Poor baby."

"Sad part is, it was the quiet one doing the damage this time."

"The quiet one?"

"Lance. Most of the time, I can't even tell he lives there. He rarely comes out of his room."

"Weirdo?"

"Who knows. We've probably exchanged ten sentences since he moved in."

"And the other roommate?"

"Troy. He's the opposite."

She glances around the room. "I haven't been here since freshman year when I had to dorm. My roommate was horrible. She kept stealing my clothes. Tamara. She was such a bitch. She dipped into my Vaseline. Do you know how scary that is? Like what did she need it for? I know what I use it for, and it's *not* chapped lips."

"TMI, Laney."

"For who?"

"For this half of the living room." I gesture to the heads turning our way.

"Oh," she giggles. "Well, I was only too happy to move back home. We did *not* bond. But I do think bondage is in her future, if you know what I mean." She waggles her brows and elbows me, and I roll my eyes.

"Clever."

"Such a smart ass. So, you done here?"

"No," I glance at my tablet. "I've got about an hour left."

"Before what?" We've never been this close in the light of day, and I'm finding it hard to keep my eyes from roaming every inch of her. Instead, I take her in doses as she turns to survey the room. Perfectly arched dark brows hover over amused brown eyes speckled with green. Her flawless olive skin is a shade darker around the thin spaghetti strap of her dress. Tiny moles dot her shoulders below her slender neck. And then there's the dip below, a valley where a gold feather necklace rests between mouth-watering cleavage. I gather all this in a sideways glance doing my best to ignore the threatening stir below.

"Earth to Theeeooo," she says still waiting on my answer, turning her eyes back to mine.

"Before I'm done."

"Oh, it's like that?"

"What can I say?" I hitch a shoulder. "I'm disciplined in my studies." The thing is with new friendships like this, boundaries must be set, especially by me, *the Teddy*. Dropping everything for her will send the wrong signal. It will tell her that I am, in fact, at her disposal. I'm not that guy anymore. No matter how good she smells.

"Fine, I'll wait." She pulls a ten-ton bag covered in sunflowers from the floor.

"Please tell me there are books in there."

"What do you think I am, a monster? Course there aren't any books in here. This bag is Kate Spade."

"Then why are you here?"

She grins, and I'm forced to focus on the quarter-sized birthmark on top of her left hand. "To see you, of course."

"Lucky me."

"Why yes, you are."

"Alright, QT."

"Cutie?" She says with a lift to her voice.

"No, Q-T as in quiet time," I nod toward the silent students in the room.

"Oh yeah, okay."

I lift my tablet and resume my reading.

It takes only a minute for her to break the silence. "You're really going to make me sit here an hour?"

"Yes," I say without looking up.

"Fine."

"Glad we're on the same page."

"Such a smart ass."

After a few minutes of sighs, I hear the rustling of a notebook and glance over. "Ah, you did bring something to study."

"Yes, well kind of, I'm trying to come up with a concept for my media class."

"Concept for what?"

"It's my grad project. I have to come up with a social presence and attempt to make the brand trend."

"What are you thinking?"

"I have no idea."

"It will come to you."

She smiles, and I pretend not to be affected by the pink gloss on her shiny, plump lips. She's a second look kind of girl.

The first look at her is for simple appreciation for the stunner she is. The second look is a realization of what an idiot you were for not looking longer the first time around.

I can't think of Laney this way because she doesn't want or need me to. I shouldn't look at Laney this way because it will lead me back to square one.

And so, I won't.

I've hung out with plenty of girls over the years I've been attracted to. I convinced myself, when Nora dragged me by the balls through razorblades while sprinkling salt over her shoulder, that I would never let myself be friend-zoned by any woman I had real feelings for. If the attraction wasn't mutual, I had to move on. But Laney is different in the fact she's been completely upfront. No mixed signals. We met at the same crossroads and that, in and of itself, makes her valuable to me as a friend more than anything else. I push all those self-sabotaging—Laney is hot as hell—thoughts away and get immersed in my reading when I smell the sunshine on her skin and feel the heat of her face next to mine. "So, what are you reading?"

I jerk my tablet away, just as she takes a closer look and narrows her eyes. "Oh my God!" She jumps from the couch, pointing an accusing finger at me. "You jerk. You do not take your studies seriously! You're reading a Jack Reacher book!"

"And now everyone knows it." I swallow audibly and stand as eyes from every direction turn our way and laughter follows. "I had ten pages left, no big deal, but, hey Laney," I widen my eyes, "we can go now." I grip her arm, while I shoulder my bag before escorting her out of the room. "You ass. You're an ass. A total ass!"

"Better than being a *DICK*," I mutter, trying to hide my grin.

######

I got to finish those ten pages, well actually Laney read them to me as I drove. I have to say with her thick twang narrating, it was by far the most interesting ending of a Lee Child book I've ever experienced. When she declared favor for favor and insisted we go to 'Monday Church', I had no choice but to obey.

Shaking my head, I stare at her as she douses her taco with more sour cream *and* a ketchup packet she'd pulled out from her purse.

I can't hide my grimace. "That's not right."

"Look," she says, licking the ketchup/sour cream combo off the side of the taco as I try to hold my gag, "don't knock it until you've tried it."

"Hear me now. I will *never* try it."

She rolls her eyes and mmm's with exaggeration as she takes a mammoth bite.

"So why is this Monday church?"

"Dorito shell tacos, the Lort sent these to me," she proclaims over a mouth full.

"The Lort?"

"Lor-t," she repeats slowly, as if it will give me some clarification.

"Ah, got it now," I spout with pure sarcasm.

She ignores it. "Of course, you do, because we're meant to be friends. You *get* me." She leans in with a sinister grin. There's that word again. I make it a point to stop any notice of my unexpected attraction to her then and there.

"You don't scare easily, do you, Theo?"

"No, I don't scare easily."

"Good," she says, swallowing the last of her taco. I have to admit the woman has eating down to a science. "So, I have an idea for my project."

"Yeah?"

"We make a dedicated page being completely honest and see if it trends."

"What do you mean *we*?"

"We," she says, pointing between us, "meaning you and me."

I cross my arms. "No."

"Already started it while you were reading Jack."

"Are you serious?"

She shrugs. "Yes. It's all set up. The handle is @living-myrealestlife. Technically it's your idea, so I can't take all the credit. I already texted you the login info."

I lean back in my seat. "You are serious."

She shrugs. "I'd follow it. It's worth a shot."

"Why *we*? Why can't you do this solo?"

"Because it makes more sense and will attract more followers if it's done from both a male and female perspective."

"Pass. Find another male."

"Nope," she says, tossing her napkin beside her tray. "No need, I've found him."

"Laney, I'm in the Grand Band on *scholarship*, I have a code of conduct to follow."

"Then we'll keep it PG…13ish."

"I'm serious."

"So am I. So, you'll help me, right?" I open my mouth to speak as she continues. "You really won't try ketchup and sour cream on a taco? Oh, I forgot to ask what your major is."

"Woman," I say exasperated. "I don't know which question to answer first or in what order."

"All of them," she mumbles around the ketchup packet she's tearing with her teeth, just as she unwraps another taco.

"This is ridiculous," I spin the wheel and put my left foot on green.

"It's honest," she pants, "we don't do yoga, but we both do Twister. And this is the perfect backdrop. Devin, you gettin' this?"

"Oh, I'm getting it," she says through a laugh angling the cell phone to take more pictures.

"It's not honest, if it's contrived," I point out in a huff.

"I get that, and some of it's going to have to be a little contrived because it's a school project and we have to make it interesting," she grunts, twisting her body as her skirt rises another inch. I move to turn my head, but my dick refuses to let me look away.

"Tell you what," she says, spinning the disk. "From now on, we try to keep it as true to name as possible without tarnishing the whole point."

"I'm not that interesting," I say with a groan as her ass comes into view an inch from my face when she plants a booted foot on red.

"I'm going to need a little more enthusiasm on your part, Houseman. This is an adventure."

"I've been suckered, no, *manipulated* into this because I'm a nice guy, so you will get no such thing."

"You're breaking my heart here, buddy, and you aren't so nice. I see you looking at my ass. Besides, I thought you meant what you said in that yard." Her breaths are coming fast as we struggle to keep upright.

"I do believe what I said."

"So, let's do this. Go all in. We can make fun of ourselves and help further my education."

"How convenient, for *you*."

"I think you've met your human bullshit detector, Ms. Cox," Devin coos as she watches us struggle to reposition.

Laney's face comes into view when her hand lands next to mine, her head bent, her hair blowing in the breeze.

For fuck's sake.

"Come on, Theo. It's only the world wide web."

"I don't give a shit what anyone thinks."

It's the truth, for the most part. A single and shitty act from the girl I thought was my dream destroyed any pretense I could ever again try to come up with about myself. Trying to be perfect for her had turned me into more of an imposter than I could ever live comfortably with. It's always hindsight that delivers the biggest bitch slap, even when the hurt has been dealt with. I'll never stray that far away from myself again. If that means being honest over nice, then that's what I'll be.

Laney prods as we end up completely tangled on the plastic and gives me a pointed look.

"Prove it."

She's so close that I can practically taste her and it's making this test even more unbearable.

"Fine, but there needs to be something in it for me."

"Like what?"

"I'll need to think about it."

"Deal."

"Oh my God, that's it!" Devin bursts into laughter. "This is the best picture I've ever taken. I think I've got it, Laney."

"Great." I collapse in a heap and wipe the sweat from my brow. Laney rushes toward Devin and throws her head back with a laugh before snatching the phone and bringing it to me.

Surveying the picture, I have to admit, with the setting of the park and the sunset in the background, it screams heart-hands sunset pic, but it's the ridiculous angle we're twisted in that totally debunks any notion of romance. I give a deserving nod. Not bad.

"Oh, you know damn well, this is hilarious. Hold your grudge, I'll figure out a way to make it up to you," she says, thumbing her cellphone at warp speed. "In three, two, one, and @living-myrealestlife is now live! Hashtag twister ballet, hashtag new best friends, hashtag karate in the basement, hashtag suck it yoga."

"Jesus," I shake my head, biting my smile.

"This is too cool," Devin squeaks. "I'm following. Now, are we all done here? 'Cause Chase is going to kill me. I'm late for our date night."

"We're good. You can go, bridezilla."

"Later, hooch," Devin says, walking toward her monster truck. "Bye, Theo!"

"See you, Devin," I mutter, climbing to my feet as Laney gathers the game and stuffs it back into the box. "You don't think this is a little lame?"

She scrunches her nose. "I mean, yeah, maybe a little. And it will be at times, but that's the point, right? To showcase our lameness. Look I'm no social princess, but I'm living proof of Murphy's law and can try to find humor in any situation, and *that's* what people identify with. That's my angle. I'd be happy if all the comments said, 'I know, right?'"

She clutches the boxed Twister to her chest as we walk back to my car.

"While other people take selfies in bikini thongs on yachts in the Mediterranean sipping thousand-dollar-a-glass champagne, I'll record a more reject reality for the less fortunate."

"Fine, but don't credit me for this madness."

She gives me a knowing grin. "This is going to be fun. You'll see."

On the drive back to campus, I glance over at her.

"So, Devin is getting married?"

"Yeah, in November. It feels like we've been planning this our whole lives. It's going to be beautiful. Hey, maybe you'll save me a headache and be my plus one."

"You sure you don't want to take someone else?"

She glances over at me. "I'm sure. Why?"

"You could be dating someone by then."

"No chance of that."

"You really think you'll last that long?"

"Oh ye of little faith. And what would it matter if I was dating? I want to take you. So, will you come?"

"Sure, if I don't have a game."

"Shit. I forgot about that. Okay, well it's the 23rd, so let me know."

"I mean, I guess I could miss one game."

I glance over to see she's grinning at me. "You don't have to do that, nice guy."

"I know."

Her smile widens.

My chest expands a little.

Fuck.

I don't feel it from her. That's the truth. I feel friendship, curiosity, but I'm not getting *the* vibes. Which may mean abandoning this friendship before it starts.

"Maybe, I'll have to see," I backpedal and see her frown.

"Okay, well, this is me," she says, hitching a thumb over her shoulder as I slow to a stop.

I lean over into her seat to see the abomination she's referring to. "What in the hell is that?"

"Mind your tongue, city boy, that there is Ole Faithful. And I swear, if you wish her any ill will, she will not start."

I scour the old two-ton truck. The color is indistinguishable between the gaping rust spots. If I had to guess, I would say once upon a year it was red. The body style can't be any younger than the seventies, and that's being generous.

"Laney, that is not safe."

"It's as old as my mother. A classic. And it passes inspection every year."

"Who do you have to bribe to get the sticker?"

She laughs. "Well, a family friend owns the shop."

"I thought as much. That thing looks like the *Jeepers Creepers* truck. Seriously, it looks like it belongs to a serial killer."

She presses her lips together and glances over her shoulder longingly at the truck. "It was my gran's."

Was. As in past tense. I'm an asshole.

"I'm an asshole. I'm sorry."

"No, it's fine," she says sheepishly. "It really is ugly as shit. I know. But I love it. It actually runs well in temps between forty and eighty degrees."

"This is serious logic you're using."

She bobs her head. "Yep."

She manages to find her keys in her purse in record speed and leans over and presses a chaste kiss to my cheek. I ignore the thud in my chest. "See you, Theo. Thanks for today."

"See you, Laney."

I wait until Ole Faithful starts on the third try and watch her drive away.

#twisterballet #newbestfriends #karateinthebasement #suckityoga #therightwaytosunsetpic #livingourrealestlife

Grannism—Don't give anyone the whole map, and only trust a few with directions.

eleven

LANEY

"H E'S GOING FOR IT," SOME GUY ANNOUNCES TO MY right as I stroll through campus. Following his line of sight, I turn to see another lovestruck sucker as he drops to his knees under the Era Tree.

"Another one bites the dust," a guy mumbles in amusement crossing his arms while grinning at the spectacle.

"Yep, he's proposing," another says.

The Era Tree is a sprawling oak with ridiculously long branches that trace the ground around a giant trunk. The ancient oak is a campus landmark and is also the setting of a TGU tradition. Legend has it, if you walk under the Era Tree alone, you'll walk alone forever, but if you walk with your college sweetheart, you're cemented together for life.

And I avoid it like the plague.

The guy grips her hand in his, and the girl nods before he stands and hauls him to her while she squeals in his arms.

"I think it's sweet," the girl next to me says shouldering her purse and clapping along with the rest of the gathered crowd.

True love exists. I'm a believer in it, but maybe just not for the women in my family.

We're too loud, independent, and opinionated.

Or maybe I'm hangry.

"Better them than me," I say before turning on my heel and slamming into a talking rock.

"Couldn't agree more." Large, muscular hands are the only thing keeping me from sprawling into the asphalt.

"Sorry," I say before looking up...into the sun. Squinting, I see thick lips, brilliant straight teeth, and amused bright-blue eyes. "Sorry," I repeat as he comes into view shielding the blinding light with his massive presence. Rusty blond hair, unbelievable build, a killer smile. My reaction is immediate. "Nope," I say, sidestepping him.

"Nope?" He asks with a chuckle. I'm another step away when I realize he hasn't unhanded me.

"That arm belongs to me," I say softly, eyes trained on my boots.

Don't look up. DO. NOT. LOOK. UP.

My eyes lift on their own accord, well technically it's my evil self-sabotaging Va-*Gina*.

Damnit, Gina!

A feeling I'm all too familiar with spreads through me as I drink him in. I may be on the wagon, but I can still appreciate the perfect male specimen.

Poison Ivy is pretty too, Gina, we're done here.

"All yours," he says, hesitantly taking his hands away.

Don't linger. Do not linger. Don't give him an opening. But they're there, the butterflies are flapping away ready to take flight...as I linger.

"Thanks for saving me a trip," I reply evenly.

"Anytime."

"Good day," I say with a ridiculous little curtsey before skittering off, determined.

Two steps. Three. Four.

And then he sounds up next to me. "Do you mind telling me what that nope was about?"

"Just an inside joke between me, and...*me*." I'm walking ridiculously fast while he's breathing easy, his long legs keeping up with me in perfect time.

"You're bruising me here, beautiful. Did that nope, mean I'm not your type?"

"Exactly."

"Ouch."

"I'm sure a...ego of your size can handle it."

"I'm not so sure, it's leading me in the direction away from class."

"Better switch lanes then, don't want to be late."

"What if you're wrong?"

"What if I'm right?"

Flustered, I bring my eyes to his. And have a *Pretty Woman* 'Big mistake, huge', moment. Thinking fast, I pause as if I feel a vibration, pull my phone from my bag, and fake take a call.

"Sorry, I gotta take this," I look to see he's not buying it, at all, but he stops his chase stuffing his hands into his jeans. His eyes roam over me, leaving me a hot mess on the sidewalk. "Shame," he says through disgustingly perfect lips before he gives me a curt nod and changes direction.

I speak to Gina on my fake call. "This round goes to me, bitch."

######

Safely inside my truck, I shoot off a text to Theo to see what he's up to. He's had practice or some obligation or another every day, and I haven't been able to catch him since we met up on Monday.

If my intuition serves me correctly, I suspect he's hiding from our project, and if that's the case, I'm screwed.

> **Laney: We have seven hundred followers.**
> **Theo: You. You have seven hundred followers.**
> **Laney: Fine. I have them. What are you doing?**
> **Theo: Working on something.**
> **Laney: Vague much?**
> **Theo: Hard to explain.**
> **Laney: Then show me.**
> **Theo: Sometime, maybe.**
> **Laney: I have to earn this privilege?**
> **Theo: Yes.**
> **Laney: Fine. Pencil me in tomorrow night.**
> **Theo: For?**
> **Laney: Something.**
> **Theo: ^^ I see what you did there.**
> **Laney: Annoying, isn't it?**

twelve

THEO

THE BONFIRE. I SHOULD HAVE KNOWN. DREAD COURSES through me as Laney circles the rows of cars looking for a spot to park her death trap. I swear the thing has a smoker's rattle. We manage to find a space a football field away from the party. Once parked, she turns on the cabin light and produces a flask from her purse.

"What's that for?"

"Icebreaker." She explains, taking a sip before passing it to me. I eye it with caution. "Don't be such a prude. I met you intoxicated."

"True." I take the flask and flinch at the burn as it goes down. "This isn't rum."

"Whiskey," she says, taking another pull. "It'll put some hair on our chests."

"Easy girl," I chide.

"I measured out only three shots. Just a little something to take the edge off."

That's when I see it, the uneasiness.

"You're nervous?"

"A little."

"You can't be serious. You're the most outspoken person I've ever met."

"Really large crowds give me anxiety."

"Is that why you don't attend many games?"

"Partly."

"Huh. You're a walking contradiction."

"It's not a big deal. I just get a little nervous." She pauses, the flask halfway to her lips. "You know I didn't get my first smartphone until I was fifteen. And I wasn't allowed to watch too much mainstream anything."

"Really?"

"My God, the catching up I had to do. I think that's why I find PR so fascinating. For years I felt out of the loop. I mean it wasn't so bad, it's not like we had dial-up or I got a ruler snapped on my hand or anything like that." She presses her brows together. "Momma and Gran, they just raised me their way. The old-fashioned way, I guess."

I don't bother to ask about her father because I know that relationship is rocky.

"Doesn't sound so bad."

"Not at all," she grins. "But in my house, Sunday is still meant for morning church, and gatherings for big meals with family and friends."

"In my house, Sunday was meant for shopping for my mom and sisters while Dad and I binge-watched TV because it was the only time it belonged to us."

"Gran used to say don't buy it, make it. That shit could get a little embarrassing." She hands me the flask. "So, you ever been to one?" She nods toward the party.

"Last time I was here, I lost my girlfriend, and she tripped and fell into someone else's bed."

"Shit, at the bonfire?"

"Yeah."

"Look," she says softly, "we can leave. It doesn't mean shit to me to be here."

"Then why are we here?"

"Social experiment?"

"Ah, the project."

"Not necessarily. Do you want to go?"

She's sincere with her offer to leave, but I look out at the roaring two-story tall fire and shake my head. "We can stay."

She eyes the bonfire and looks back to me. "Nah, I've got a better idea." Briefly scanning the parking lot, she pulls up her phone, flipping through a few notebook apps before skimming a list of pictures. Seeming satisfied, she releases the parking brake and we start a slow creep through the endless lines of cars.

"Laney?"

"Yes?"

"What are you doing?"

"We," she motions between us, "we're in this one together."

"And this is?"

"Shhhh, I'm trying to concentrate."

After a few minutes, she comes to a slow stop in front of a Volvo.

"Bingo."

"What are you doing?"

She holds up a finger and is already dialing. "Hey, Greg. I'm at the bonfire on County Road. You busy? Okay, cool, bring your truck, hell, bring three. We're about to clean up."

She ends the call and hops out with her phone in hand before shining her flashlight through the windshield of the Volvo. She comes back to the truck wearing a satisfied grin.

"Now, we wait."

"For?"

"Gotta leave something to mystery," she taunts before we again start circling the sea of cars.

"What are you hoping to find?"

"Houseman, you're getting worse than me," she scorns while carefully circling the lot and checking her phone every few seconds. Ten minutes later, Laney looks up in her rearview and throws a finger out the window at the car we've been blocking for the last ten minutes. I look back to see a tow truck glide in and hook the car up.

"You got someone towed?"

She rubs her hands together with glee. "I'd like to think we're in the business of good deeds tonight. No one leaves this thing sober. We're saving them from a worse fate."

She continues a slow perusal of the parking lot, jumping out and shining her cell phone light into windshields before jumping back in the truck and pointing them out for the tow truck shadowing us.

"Okay, I'm lost. What in the hell is going on?"

"I told you, we're doing a public service."

"Uh huh."

"Hey, a girl's gotta make a living any way she can, and I'm so broke right now I can't afford to pay attention."

"And you're making money by pointing at cars?"

"I'm a detective of sorts." She slams on the brakes just as we pass a cherry red Toyota. "Oh my God. I've been looking for this one for two months! This idiot will never learn. It's the bumper sticker that gives it away." She turns to me. "Get in the driver's seat, and when I punch it, you better punch it too. Don't lose me."

"What?"

She hops out as I yell out after her. "Laney, I can't drive this! Where in the hell are you going?"

"Don't forget the parking brake!" she shouts over the Toyota's alarm. "You have to use it, or it'll roll."

And then she's in the car, seconds later the taillights are glowing red. She shoots out in the parking lot with crazy insane reverse skills kicking rocks all over her own truck, a maniacal laugh coming out of her! "Hell, yes! Possession is nine-tenths of the law. Stay close to my tail, Houseman!"

"You're stealing a fucking car?"

"Best hurry up, this heifer keeps a roscoe in her purse!"

"What's a roscoe?"

"A gun. Last time she shot at me." She tears off, and I floor the gas to her hooptie and am thrown forward with the stall before the ancient artifact finally picks up speed, my chest up against a steering wheel that feels like it may come off any second. Laney motors ahead going warp speed as I scream like a girl when I hit my first pothole. I white-knuckle the wheel, terrified that by the time I get to her I'll be left with nothing but bald tires. Ten, excruciatingly long minutes later we make it into town, and she pulls into the parking lot of a gas station before prancing back over toward me doing a victory dance.

"Had a hotkey for that one!" She exclaims, taking back the driver's seat as I slide over.

"Laney, what the hell? You chop cars?"

She raises a finger and puts the phone on speaker.

"Polk County non-emergency."

"This is Laney Cox with Mueller's Wrecker."

"Yes, ma'am."

"I'm calling to advise you of four repossessions from County Road."

"That's the bonfire, correct?"

"Yes, ma'am."

"We've already gotten one call for a stolen vehicle."

Laney reads off the VIN numbers, makes and models of all the cars that she got towed and ends the call.

"You repo cars?"

"Yep." She tilts her head. "Well, kind of. I don't drive the trucks, but I get a finder's fee for each car I spot. By not attending the bonfire, I just made six hundred bucks."

"A hundred and fifty a car?"

"Yep. Sometimes more, if the bank is close to charging it off."

"Not bad. But you've been shot at?"

"Only by that crazy cow."

"And this is just, I don't know, *normal,* to you?" I spit sarcastically.

"Course not, but no one is shooting at us *now*. This is just business, Houseman. And no one is broker than college students. I used to feel guilty for it, but I tell you, some of the excuses are bullshit, and I've heard them all. I like to think I now have a heavy hand in teaching them a little responsibility. And it's an adrenaline rush, isn't it?"

"Not much of a fan of gunshot adrenaline."

"You get used to it."

"Pretty sure I wouldn't."

The tow truck pulls up, and a guy around our age saunters over with a grin.

"Good job, Laney."

"Greg, don't you dare give her car back."

"We'll have to drop it if she pays," he says, squinting at me sitting next to her before turning back to Laney. "Who's this?"

"Theo, and he's not a fan of our profession."

"No?" He gives me a look I'm all too familiar with. It's called 'you're a pussy,' and I immediately hate him. But even more so for the way he's feasting on Laney like a wolf licking his chops.

"Well, I'll text you what happens."

Laney nods. "At least make her sweat a little."

"For you, I will. Night." His accent is as thick as hers.

"Yeah, got to get back and tend to dem sheeps," I mutter.

"Hey, he's a good guy. And you shouldn't stereotype."

"He did the minute he saw me. He called me a pussy."

"He did not!"

"It was in the look he gave me because of your roundabout comment."

"Well, you *didn't* like it."

"I got no warning, and you know you made that shit seem shady just to mess with me because you're a pint-sized terrorist in boots. And I'll have you know I like plenty of other manly things that don't involve live ammunition. I assure you I have a *dick*." And it's bigger than Troy's. Sometimes life balances the scales for you. But right now, I sound like more of a pussy for defending myself.

Awesome.

"Alright, Mr. Cocky, I feel like you need a slice of humble pie. Care to put your man skills to the test?"

"Name the time and the place," I inwardly shake my head at myself.

"Drink the rest of this," she challenges, handing me the flask with a wicked gleam in her eye. "You're going to need it."

"We're going back?"

"Nope, but buckle up."

"You don't have any seatbelts."

"I meant it figuratively. We're going on an adventure."

"That was adventure enough."

She flashes me a devilish grin before turning off the interior light.

"Time to put your money where your mouth is, smartass."

thirteen

THEO

"WHERE ARE WE GOING AGAIN?" LANEY NAVIGATES the dark roads like she could do it blindfolded as I palm her dash waiting for impact. She snickers when she sees me braced for the worst.

"Huntin'. We're going to test your outdoor skills, Mr. I Have a *Dick*."

"That was sarcasm. I thought you loved that about me?"

"Sure I do, most of the time, but if you were mine, I'd take you down a peg or two."

We fly over a pothole and both bounce in the bench seat.

"Did you just quote *Super Troopers*?"

Her grin grows in the orange light of the speedometer, which I'm sure hasn't worked since I was sperm. "I love that you know that."

"It's a favorite of mine. What are we hunting for?"

"A rare bird."

"At night?"

"It's the only time they come out. They're nocturnal." The whiskey starts to cloud my judgment as she pulls onto a gravel road lined with trees and kills her headlights. It's when we're shrouded in complete darkness that I try to mask the fact that my balls are shriveling up. The windows are already down, and the crunch beneath the tires starts to play with my psyche while other things begin to bump in the night.

"Was that an owl? I don't think I've ever heard one in person before."

"Predatory birds stick together." I can hear the smile in her voice. "What's the matter, big city boy, you afraid?"

"Suburbs, Laney, I was raised in the *suburbs*, and I'm really not one to hunt."

I can feel her eye roll. "Okay, Mr. Cocky. We need a weapon. Open the glove box."

I do, and through the dim yellow light inside, I spot a rubber slingshot along with a box of giant BB's. "You're shitting me, right? This is the land of Republicans, and you don't have a proper gun to hunt with?"

"Where is the skill in that?" She harrumphs.

I duck, taking cover.

"What the hell are you doing, Theo? We aren't even out of the truck."

"I'm waiting for the wrath of thousands of covert Texas hunters to come out from the bush and rain hell down on us."

"It's the first of October, hunting season doesn't start for another month."

"Leave it to you to take us hunting *illegally*."

"Don't be such a wuss, Houseman. This is private property."

She steps out of her ancient truck, the door hinges creaking an ominous sound, and I follow trying to disguise my wince. If she's not freaked out in the middle of the woods, I'm sure as hell not about to show I am.

"So, what's our strategy?"

"Simple. The more noise you make, the more you attract them. Get your phone flashlight on." We both beam up, and I shine my light everywhere, especially around my feet. It does little to put me at ease.

"A bird, at night? I smell bullshit," I mutter behind her as she disappears briefly into a thick patch of trees and I keep the flashlight on my chucks to find my footing while scrambling to keep up. "This is a fool's errand. We aren't going to be able to catch anything without enough light. We, at the very least, need night vision goggles. Maybe there's an app for that."

She slaps at my hand just as I pull up my phone to check. "Put the damn phone down. There's no skill in that either. Boys and their damn toys. Just...come on."

"And what's the value in hunting this rare bird?"

"Bragging rights," she says with a sigh.

"Look, I'm not one for stuffing and mounting anything on my wall. I'm more of an abstract art type of guy."

"No kiddin'?" She stops in the center of two large Magnolia trees and turns to me.

"This is good. I'm going to kill my light. Dim yours in your pocket. I'll let you know when to pull it. Hand me the slingshot and some BBs. I'll get the first one."

I hand it over along with the ammo.

"Seriously, Laney? What possible damage can we do? It's not like you can hurt a...ouch, Jesus!" I rub the spot on my thigh that just got pinged. Her hands stay suspended in the air from where she just unleashed on me.

"That can take a bird down, easy. Now, you have to be careful. They're a bit aggressive when they feel threatened, kind of like wild turkeys, so when I give you the signal, pull out the light, and I'll pop 'em."

"So, *this* is what you do in your spare time?"

"Shut up, Houseman, and get ready." It's eerily quiet, and I can hear her footfalls in the underbrush as she steps away from me.

"Okay, I'm in position."

An owl sounds right behind me, and I jump back thankful she didn't see it.

"I don't know much about hunting, but I can't see this as being much of a vantage point."

"Don't pansy on me, Theo. This isn't my first time."

"I'm not pansying. I'm just saying. We're in the middle of the fucking woods with a rubber slingshot. And don't think for one second I won't toss you in front of me at the first sign of danger, because I'm not that guy. You *will* die first."

Her laughter bubbles up from a few feet away. "Definitely not Batman."

"What?"

"Nothing."

"Don't toss out insults. You're the one who dragged us out here. You would deserve to go down first for putting us in this position."

I'm serious. But I would miss her.

The longer we stand shrouded in the woods, the more I start to freak out. At this point, I can't even remember the direction of the truck. Mustering the ice-breaking courage from the whiskey, I manage to steady my voice.

"Whatever, let's do this."

"Aww Teddy, you afraid?"

"Now, I'm definitely letting you die first."

"Fine. Make some noise."

"What?"

"Click your tongue like you're calling a pet."

"That's ludicrous."

"It works. Noise attracts certain animals. It's the same with wild boars. You'll see."

I swallow the hairball in my throat. "Are there any around here? Wild boars?"

"Are we doing this or what?"

"This is bullshit."

She clicks her tongue repeatedly, and I reluctantly chime in with her.

"Good. Now clap your hands, but not like a regular clap, like a golf clap."

"Are you fucking serious?"

"It sounds like their young. Just do it."

"Fine." I tap the meat of my palm on my hand.

"Now, do them both."

"Why aren't you making noises?" I argue into the void, wondering if the moon has completely fucking forgotten about Texas.

"I'm not making noise, genius, because if it comes in *my* direction, I won't get a good shot off. Come on, Theo."

"Fine, but this is ridiculous."

"Stop whining."

As I stand there, my senses heighten by my loss of sight as I take note of every noise. The distant snap of a branch sounds a few yards away as the damn owl announces its presence from above me. I'm positive I'll hear that in future nightmares.

And then I hear it, a whisper of movement, a crunch in the distance. Something is approaching.

"Hear that?" Laney asks on an excited whisper.

I can hear it. It's distinct. Something is definitely out here. Another rustle in the brush a few yards away has me on high alert. "Yeah, I hear it. How do you know it's the bird?"

"Because the noise would scare most of the other ani-mals. Keep clapping and clicking." She whisper-shouts. "It's working."

Mortified, I brace myself clapping like I'm watching Tiger Woods at the fucking Masters, while I furiously click my tongue.

"Get ready with the flashlight!"

"I can't clap and get the flashlight," I sputter out.

"Right, I got it." Her light goes up, and I'm temporarily blinded, unable to see anything in front of me.

"I think I see it," she proclaims excitedly.

"I can't see shit," I clap frantically in a circle toward the sound of her voice.

I'm seconds from pissing myself when I hear, "Now, Theo, now!"

I pull my flashlight out of my pocket and scan the ground for birds, my whole-body pulsing with adrenaline.

"I don't see it, Laney!" I shout, scanning the ground left and right. "Get the flashlight off of me!" I scream like a tween as I frantically search the ground and jump back when I hear a loud strangled yelp from mere feet away. Stopping the flashlight at her boots, I bring it up to see Laney…holding a basset hound along with her cell phone…which is pointed directly at me.

"Smile, Teddy! You've been sniped!"

All the adrenaline leaves me in a whoosh as she starts to howl with laughter.

I'm not amused. "You are the devil."

"Max," she says through choked laughter, "meet the world's biggest jackass, Theo."

I charge toward her as she backs up into the tree laughing hysterically.

When I've cornered her, I can't help but flash the light over my shoulder, which only makes her laugh harder.

"Shut up, Laney. Did you hear that?"

"This is too good. Now you're paranoid."

"I'm not paranoid. I heard something."

"You heard the sound of your own fear."

I look down to the dog in her hands and swear he's smiling.

"Nice to meet you, Max, are you the undertaker when she escorts souls to hell?"

"Good boy," she coos, kissing Max on the top of his head. "He's blind as a bat, but he can smell a jackass a mile away. God, am I lucky you've never been sniped before. No one has fallen for that since Google was invented."

"I didn't exactly fall for it."

She lifts the phone in her hand. "I have video evidence that indicates otherwise."

"I'm seriously rethinking this friendship."

She hits play on her phone, and I watch as her face turns beet red in the combined beam of our flashlights.

"Yes! Look at that golf clap!"

"You suck on so many levels," I groan.

"This is so getting uploaded right now. Hashtag the last living snipe hunter."

"I no longer like you, therefore goodnight."

"Oh, come on," she taunts behind me as I fumble past a few trees. "You were getting a little too cocky."

I whirl on her, and she backs up a step wide-eyed while Max stares on at me like I am, in fact, the biggest jackass alive.

"I think I've had enough adrenaline for one night."

"Nope, you aren't leaving. Follow me."

"Follow you where? Is this where you introduce me to the brother who wears sewn skin on his face for funsies?"

"Don't be ridiculous, he's upgraded to a full nude suit."

"I'll pass."

"Theo, you don't know where you are, and *I* drove."

"I'll Uber it, then," I say, pulling up the app. "Where are we, Satan's lair?"

Her laugh slowly fades into a chuckle. "You really mad?"

I can't help my smile as she eyes me in the light.

"No, but payback is hell. It would do you good to remember that."

"I'm *really* worried," she says, setting Max on his feet.

I turn to her, shining my beam in her face. "You should be."

"Just shaking in my boots, buddy. Now, onto more important matters. *Eggrolls*. Come on, men," she barks, leading me through the trees and into a clearing where a ranch home sits behind a brightly lit front porch. Ropes of braided macramé holding plants hang from every corner around ancient wicker-furniture.

"Wait," I turn to her with an accusing stare as she bites her lip climbing the steps.

"We were in your front yard this whole time?!"

The screen door slaps behind her before she finally erupts with laughter.

#

"If you put ketchup on these, I'm going back to rough the woods."

"Don't be ridiculous," she calls from where she stands at the stove, "these taste much better dipped in honey mustard."

"You are one strange bird."

"What an amazin' choice of words."

"You are testing me," I growl, which earns me a smile. "So, what is the slingshot really for? Surely not for protection."

"I know it's not much, but it's my only option. I used to carry a taser. But I had to get rid of it."

"Had to?"

She pauses, before pulling some tin foil out of a drawer. "Due to a little trauma. I don't trust myself with one, and those around me are safer for it."

"That doesn't surprise me. What happened?"

"Nothing."

"Too quick to deny, you're *guilty*."

"Nothing serious," she wrinkles her nose, "well serious in the sense of serious. But not before it happened. It got serious, if you know what I mean."

"Nope, not at all."

"You're just going to laugh at me."

"Probably, and it's deserved, so come out with it."

She puts both hands on her hips and blows out a breath.

"I accidentally tasered a cop."

"Nooo," I say through a chuckle. "Not *you*."

She grins. "Shut up. I was getting out my license and registration, and I wanted to show I had a weapon, you know, for full disclosure and all."

"Uh huh."

"Well, I must not have watched enough episodes of *Cops* because you're not supposed to show, you're supposed to tell. And well, I was so nervous, instead of giving him proof of insurance, I gave him a shitload of volts."

"Jesus, Laney."

"When he came to, he was not happy. Thank God, he was an old friend of Gran's. I could have done some serious time for assault. I think I got away with it because he was too embarrassed to admit it happened. Whoops."

"Only you would call a felony a whoops."

"Trust me, I did not think it was funny at the time," she says scrolling through her phone. "You aren't going to believe this, but snipe huntin' already has six hundred likes."

"I thought we only had seven hundred followers."

"You mean *me*."

"Fine, you."

"Triple that now."

"What!?"

"I told you people would be drawn to it."

"Yeah, but it's only been a week, right?"

"Less than," she says with pride.

"Good job." Max nudges me at the table from where he rests at my feet, and I obey running my fingers through his short fur as I survey the kitchen which looks like it peaked somewhere in the late eighties. Laney sets an ancient egg timer and places it next to salt and pepper shakers that look eerily like the dog I'm scratching. Everything in the house is outdated, much like the furniture. Crochet blankets hang over the back of every couch. The décor is what I imagine an antique shop will look like in a few more years.

Though the house is a time warp itself, it has that cozy, lived-in feel. It's cluttered with years of pictures. Some yellowed and worn on the edges inside the frames.

"It's outdated, I know," Laney says, watching me carefully. It was Gran's; and Momma and I moved in when she got sick the first time. I was three."

She reads the question in my expression of how she passed.

"Cancer. She beat it once. She was in remission most of my life, but they caught it too late this time. She passed in February."

"I'm sorry."

She swallows and nods. "We can't bring ourselves to change anything yet."

I see brief sadness cross her features. "Sweet tea okay?"

"Sure."

She pours us each a glass as the air grows thick with silence. I'm used to the distraction of noise. It's a constant for me. The only sound in the room is the slide of her chair as she takes the seat across from me and the ticking of an old plastic clock.

"It's quiet here."

"Peaceful," she corrects.

"Where is your mom?"

"She works nights. She's an LPN at a nursing home here in Polk."

"So, you're here alone at night?"

"Suddenly you're worried?"

"I wasn't serious out there. I would have given you a running head start."

"You say that now."

We share a grin.

"I used to camp out there with Devin when we were kids. I miss it."

"Why can't you do it now?"

She shrugs. "I'm afraid it won't be as magical as it was back then. Plus, she's too busy plannin' her weddin'."

I try to hide my smile and fail.

"What?"

"Your accent. You keep forgettin' the G."

"I'm well aware my accent is thick. Some people think it's charmin'."

"Like the toilet paper?"

She shakes her head. "Ass. That little exercise did nothing for you. Seems like you could use another slice of humble pie."

"Good habits die hard."

"That's old habits."

"Potato, pot-tater."

"Har, har."

With an eye roll, she rises with the sound of the timer, puts on some crochet oven mitts, and pulls the piping hot rolls from the oven. "Finally, I could eat the ass end of a dead rhino."

And that's when I hang my head and lose it.

#newbestfriends #thelastlivingsnipehunter #lookatthatgolfclap #livingourrealestlife

Grannism—Don't go cheap on the toilet paper, just don't.

fourteen

THEO

Laney's cheerful greeting blares through my car speakers as I roll down the window for the pharmacy attendant and hand her my card.

"Theo! It's hotter than Satan's anus out here! Although I'm not sure the devil himself would buy real estate in Texas."

"Laney, you're on—"

"So, you're not going to believe this. I'm doing my own version of Ghostin' the Whip. Mother FORKER, that's hot! Good news is, I got like almost a thousand likes out of my misfortune."

"Way to make lemonade, Cox!"

"Fuckin' A, Houseman! This is real lif—oh SHIT!"

"What's wrong?"

"Radiator cap, I think I just gave myself my first tattoo… on my palm."

A little old lady pulling up next to me looking mortified leans out of her window. "You shouldn't let your kids talk like that."

I pull my rearview toward me to check my reflection. Yep, still *twenty-one*.

"I'll just pull back around," I tell the pharmacist retrieving my card while simultaneously trying to reach my phone on the floorboard to disconnect the Bluetooth. "Is it too late to add some anti-wrinkle cream?"

"Don't take it too personally, she's ninety-four," the teller says with a grin, just as Laney lets out another string of curses.

"Thanks for that. I feel much safer on the road now."

She laughs, her eyes alight with amusement as Laney's rant echoes off the walls of the drive-thru. "Better handle that."

I sigh and nod just as Laney lets out more colorful words and turn the volume down. "I don't think this is the type of woman that can be tamed."

"I believe it." The blue-haired woman says a car over. I can't help my rebuttal.

"Yeah, I told her mother we should tie her back to the radiator. But she no longer believes in corporal punishment."

"What's that?" Blue hair leans in straining to hear more of the offensive voice coming through my car speakers.

"I said I'll make sure Daddy spanks her bare ass *real good* when he gets home." I give her a slow wink and drive off.

That might've been wrong, but it felt so right.

"Theo!" Laney shouts. "Are you even listenin' to me?"

I park under a tree and grab my phone, taking it off speaker.

"Not much of a choice, ma'am. Me and the good folks of Rite Aid heard you loud and clear."

"What?!"

"You were on speaker. I was refilling my inhaler. It's okay. It only took me thirty minutes to get to the window."

"I'm sorry."

"Perfectly fine, I have nothing better to do and all the gas in the world. So, your version of Ghostin' the Whip? I'm thinking Ole Faithful isn't being so faithful."

"It's ten degrees too hot for her to be agreeable today."

"You need to let go of that thing and bury it."

"Lookie here, sir, this baby has been alive for almost forty years and will run until the end of time as long as I can find the right parts."

"It's ancient. When you fill out a form at a motel, do you put vehicle, Type: Dinosaur, Color: Rust?"

Silence. I went too far. I've offended her.

"Yes," she says quietly.

"What?"

"That's *exactly* what I put."

"You're kiddin'," I drawl out with a grin.

"Nope. This is amazin'. You, good sir, could turn out to be my sentence finisher."

"Where are you? I'll come get you."

"Guess."

"Taco Bell."

"As I live and breathe!"

"Laney, that's just predictable at this point."

"Dorito. Taco. Shells."

"I'll be there in ten."

"You're a true-blue hero, Houseman."

"No, I just have a working vehicle. You should get on my level."

"I can't hear you," she taunts dryly. "I'm chewing. See you soon."

#brokeandbrokedown #myversionofghostinthewhip
#whylortwhy #livingmyrealestlife

Grannism—Work hard but make hard days'
work with whiskey.

LANEY

Theo: How's it going?
Laney: Working.
Theo: Coffee Shop?
Laney: No, Bingo.
Theo: You run bingo?
Laney: This should impress you. It's one of only three jobs I haven't been fired from.
Theo: Color me impressed.
Laney: For a whopping $50 a week. I get to yell out the alphabet to the fine senior folk of Polk. Sad part is I scare most of them who nap between letters. Yep, the letter O just scared Mrs. Morgan into wetting her Depends. It's a rough job, but it pays for my gas.
Theo: I won't keep you.
Laney: I'm good. What's up?
Theo: There's a hero party tonight.
Laney: ?
Theo: It's like a pre-Halloween party where you dress as your personal hero. I wasn't going to go, but I thought maybe if you had nothing better to do, we could go together.
Laney: Let's do it. We can shake the dust off from

being the only two people who didn't attend the bonfire. I know just what to wear!

Theo: I'm too afraid to ask. Pick you up at nine?

Laney: You dressing up as a cowboy?

Theo: Dream on.

Laney: You could totally pull it off.

Theo: Sorry to disappoint, but no cowboy exists in me.

Laney: Fine. See you then.

Ten minutes after nine, I hear a knock on my door and open it, leaning against the frame in a sultry pose. "Well, Helluurrrr."

Theo immediately bursts out laughing when he takes in my curly gray wig, oversized glasses, layered pearls, flowered muumuu, athletic socks, and sliders.

"Good evening, Mrs. Doubtfire."

"Oh my God," I chuff in aggravation. "I'm so disappointed in you, Houseman."

It's then I fully drink him in and tonight...Houseman looks hot, like h-a-w-t hot. He's dressed in a black T-shirt, a tweed jacket that's flipped up at the collar, a kilt, and his Converse high tops. All his hair is gelled up and sticking out in all directions, the rest frames his face. He scrapes his palm down his smooth jaw, and that's when it strikes me. His beard is gone.

"Do I look weird without it?"

"Not at all. Who are you supposed to be anyway?"

"Angus Mohr, well a member of Angus Mohr. They're a Scottish-Irish rock band. I couldn't think of anything else, and I had this in my closet, so I made it work."

"You just so happened to have a kilt lying around?"

He lifts his chin. "Most *real* men do."

"That's my explanation?"

"That's the one you get."

"You get more mysterious by the minute, Houseman, but

I'm feeling it." I give him another thorough once-over. "You've got some pretty hot legs."

His mouth lifts into a lopsided grin. "Yeah?"

"Yeah," I nod honestly, studying his thick-toned calves while trying to shake off the daze of seeing him in this state. He helps me slide on an old ratty robe before we step outside into the chilly night.

"I'll give you another chance to guess," I say under the light of the porch, pulling a loaded black squirt gun from my purse and holding it sideways to his temple in a kill shot. Tilting my head, I widen crazy eyes. "Say one more wort, fool. One. More. Wort, and I'm going back to jail."

He chuckles. "No clue."

"Tha Lort is testing me. Madea, man, Madea!"

"Oh yeah." He nods. "I get it now."

I roll my eyes. "You're trying to bullshit a bullshitter."

"Fine, you look *nothing* like Madea. First of all, you're white with female bone structure. No one is going to get it."

I swallow and try again. "Helllurrrr."

"Yeah, sorry, no one will guess."

"You underestimate me."

"You don't think this is a little politically incorrect?" he asks as I shut my door and lock it.

"I can have a cross-dressing, gender-bending, hero of color if I want to. And she goes by *my* moral compass, which is pleasant until *pissed*."

He chuckles. "If you say so."

"Just drive the car, Houseman."

Theo turns the ignition and bagpipes blare from the speakers.

"You call this noise music?" I shriek, covering my ears.

"Spoken like a true old lady!" Grinning, he turns it up, and I groan.

"You need to expand your tastes, Laney."

"I have King George. I assure you I'm in good hands."

"King George?"

"Good God, man, do you know nothing of country? George Strait."

"Uh huh. Well, listen to this one, you should appreciate it."

He shuffles the music, hits the gas, and we're off. After a few seconds of the song, I look over at him and shrug.

"Not horrible, I guess."

"That's because I'm betting it's familiar. Wait for it." He lifts a finger.

"Oh, he's singing Johnny Cash!"

I start rocking out to the Irish version of "Ring of Fire" nodding my head enthusiastically with the tempo which makes my wig bob ridiculously fast on top of my head. Theo glances over at me and bursts out laughing.

"What?"

Smirking, he shakes his head, sizing up my costume. "You're crazy."

"Just a word to the wise. To any woman, crazy can be the best of compliments or the worst of insults. Be careful how you deliver that word to a woman."

"Thanks for the advice."

"Anytime, my friend."

I'm not sure why, but the mix of humor and curiosity in his eyes makes my heart skip a beat. I love that look. It's endearing and blankets me in warmth. It's the kind of look that tells the recipient they think you're worth getting to know. To me, this look is always the first sign that something's brewing.

Do I want something brewing with Theo?

He's the first guy I've befriended in a very long line of penis mishaps. The friendship is already important to me, and I don't want to ruin it. While he's not my typical type, I find myself strangely drawn to him the more time we spend together.

"What?" He asks, sensing my stare as he navigates us away from my drive.

"Just getting used to you beardless."

"Shit, I knew it was too much."

"Not at all, I like it *a lot*. But why'd you shave it?"

"Starting a new one for Movember."

"Ah. So, this is kinda like aerating the dirt."

He chuckles. "Guess so."

"Well, I like it either way. Not that my opinion matters."

"I could use all the help I can get."

"Ah. Trying to get lucky tonight?"

"Always." He gives me a slow wink. His confession doesn't sit well, but if he's making statements like that, then maybe he's not interested in more than friendship with me.

"Well, if you do get lucky, don't let me get in your way."

He draws his brows. "What do you mean?"

"I mean, I'll call an Uber to get home if need be. Don't let me slow you down, okay?"

"Yeah, sure," he says, glancing at the GPS on the dash guiding us to the party.

We're silent the rest of the way which Theo fills with a playlist of the strangest music I've ever heard. Russian and French rap, more Irish rock, and a side of EMO. Ears ringing when we pull up, I retrieve my flask from my purse and start to tip it back just as Theo puts a hand on the bottle to stop me.

"You don't need it."

"I mean, it's a party. We're not going to be sober in half an hour anyway. You know?"

"I do. But you need to know you don't have to medicate. You're tougher than you think."

He's so sincere, I can't help but to try and believe him.

"Just my icebreaker, but yeah, fine." I screw the cap on and pull a tobacco rolled cigarette from my purse as he lifts a brow.

"It's not a real joint. It's just a prop."

"And it does not help your cause at all. Now you'll look like Mrs. Doubtfire smoking a joint."

An hour later, we're both feeling a bit warm and fuzzy as we circle the party avoiding clouds of weed. This shindig is being hosted by not one, but two large neighboring houses that have joined backyards. Several fire pits warm us all while scantily-dressed fairies walk around passing out shots. It's clear this party's been orchestrated by a group of campus professionals. Theo and I are both impressed.

I study the fire pit we're standing at as we warm our hands. "I'm totally going to do this at home."

"What?"

"Look." I kick at the bag. "All they did to build the pit was to soak the concrete bags in the package, stack them in this cool pattern, and paint over them. Boom. Fire pit. And it looks legit."

Theo inspects the bags. "Pretty smart."

"Bet they got the idea off Pinterest. I'm going to build one for me and Momma. We love a good fire."

"I'll help you."

"I can handle it."

He frowns and starts to speak when his name is called from a few feet away.

"Houseman!" A guy approaches in a similar kilt toting his girlfriend behind him. She's a cute blonde who's dressed in old school running shorts, a Sun Drop T-shirt, and red headband.

"Oh my God, I love it! Sun Drop girl!" The guy lifts his hands and starts beatboxing Snoop Dogg's "Drop It Like It's Hot" as she starts to awkwardly white girl break-it down.

"That's awesome," I declare through my laughter as she executes a horrible version of the worm. "I wish I'd thought of it."

"Thanks," she says with a grin.

"Okay, Houseman, I'm calling bullshit on *two* guys who just so happen to have kilts lying around the house."

"Gotta keep the mystery alive," Theo says just as the girl goes to speak up. "Zach, Lindsey, this is Laney."

"Helllluuurrr!" I say energetically looking at them both with hope for recognition.

"Mrs. Doubtfire!" They say in unison as Theo looks over at me with raised 'I told you so' brows and I drop my head in defeat.

"Not Mrs. Doubtfire?" Zach says with a chuckle. "Then, who?"

"Don't you dare tell them," I threaten Theo. "Sorry, but you're gonna have to guess."

They both shake their heads.

"No idea."

"Not a clue."

"It will come to you," I assure them.

They both shrug, well, Lindsey more like shudders rubbing her arms against the cool night air.

Zach pulls her close to him. "Cold, baby?"

"A little, I should have thought the shorts through."

"Why don't you and I go grab a beer and then huddle by the fire," I suggest to Lindsey. "You can warm up, and Zach here can play wingman for a bit."

Theo turns to me with palpable concern. "You don't have to do that."

"Hush, I'm in need of some woman talk anyway. I'm going to try and unravel some of your mystery. You go on and try to find some Irish luck."

I grab Lindsey and start to walk away, peeking over my shoulder to see Zach talking while Theo keeps his eyes trained on me. I wave him away and mouth. 'Go.'

"Y'all aren't together?" Lindsey asks when we're a safe distance away.

"We're just friends. And I've been monopolizing his time lately, so I feel guilty. What's with the kilts?"

"Zach's in a band, and they used them last St. Patty's day."

"Theo's in a band, band?"

"He subs for the other guys sometimes."

She rubs her hands together as we near a fire. "How long have you two known each other?"

"Just a few weeks," I say.

"You sure there's nothing there?"

"We have, like, nothing in common."

"That can be fun."

"I love hanging out with him, but I'm kind of on the wagon with men."

"I hear you girl, until Zach, I was in the no penis zone too."

"Game changer, huh?"

"Most definitely. Three years and counting."

"Wow. Good for you."

Lindsey shivers again, and I pull off my robe. She accepts it gratefully.

"This was a stupid idea," she says shivering as she wraps it around her. "I figured the beer buzz would kill the cold. But at this point, I'm pretty sure I could saw wood with my nipples. It was eighty degrees yesterday!"

I pull the flask from the pocket of the robe. "Gotta love

Texas. Work on this to warm you up for now. I'll be right back with beer."

Scanning the expansive yard, I manage to find a keg line and take my place surveying the heroes surrounding me. When we all step forward, Austin Powers looks back at me, perusing my costume with a question in his eyes.

"Helluuuurr," I say, nailing it.

"Ah, Mrs. Doubtfire."

"No, man. That's Helluuuuu. I said Helluuuuurrr."

"Uh, *okay* baby. Sounded the same."

"Yeah, well, your accent *sucks*."

A faint chuckle rumbles behind me as I step up in line when it's my turn. "Two please," I squeak as a guy in a Trump mask starts pouring while I shake my ass a little to the music pumping from the house.

The same throaty chuckle sounds again when I dip my hips a little in celebration and grab the offered two Solo cups full of foam. Goosebumps rise on my neck as I look over my shoulder and behind me stands…Batman, in the most realistic party costume imaginable. He looks like he stepped straight off the set of the movie. And front and center of that bat mask shines sparkling blue eyes. Beneath the perfect rubber nose, thick lips.

"Nope," I say, sidestepping him.

"Nope?" He repeats, eyes widening. "Hey, I *know* you."

"No, you don't," I say, scrambling for my senses.

He stops me with a hand on my arm. "And now I know you remember me."

"Wrong again. Haven't been spelunking lately."

"I've been thinking about you."

"You should stop that."

He chuckles. "Who are you here with?"

"A date."

"Tired of him yet?"

"It's a she for the moment." *FUCK YOU ALL TO HELL, GINA!*

"Even better."

I lift my nose in an attempt to keep my glasses from sliding off as he lifts a gloved finger to help me, slowly pushing them back in place. In thanks, I give him the hairy eyeball. "Of course, you would say *that*."

"I just meant, I'm glad it's not a guy."

"Well, I'm here with one of those too."

Take that, Gina!

"At least let me get your number."

I scour his costume, it's incredible. No man has ever looked better in thick gray tights. The bulge between those two muscular thighs is enough to make my mouth water. The Lort is testing me in a big, big, bat way.

I look up to the sky. "Why? I've been so good. I've been going to church. I only showed up tipsy that one time."

A deep chuckle sounds out, drawing my attention back to my nemesis.

"Maybe it's His intention we get together."

"Don't use the Lort as an excuse for your agenda."

"I would love to take you out."

"Yeah," I say, lifting a beer and draining half of it, eyebrow cocked before I let out a harsh exhale. "And show me a good time?"

"Exactly."

"Best fifteen minutes of my life?"

"Ah," he says, his bat cape catching in the wind as he extends to his full height, chest out, voice gravelly when he speaks. "I have a much better hang time than that, I promise.

But I was thinking of something more along the lines of dinner and a movie. A proper date."

Gina bursts to the front of the line, waving a white flag.

"You don't want to buy me dinner."

"Well, I can see by your costume you're more into old man river or some shit, but maybe I can try and remedy that."

"I've dated quite a few of you, and I promise you I'm not *bat*-ting a thousand. Pun intended."

"Cute. But I really would like to take you out."

I summon my inner Madea. "Look, *boy*, the only number you're about to need is Nine. One*t*. One*t*. You got dat? I know it's hard to comprehend."

He chuckles. "Are you Madea?"

Why Lort? Why must he be the only one to get it?

He leans in, the smell of his cologne magnifying my loss of brain cells.

Danger. Danger. Danger.

"That wig and those glasses can't disguise how beautiful you are."

I jerk back. "Flattery will get me pregnant. I'm seventy years old. Do you really want that? I'm well past the men-da-pause."

He throws his head back with a laugh. "Come on, beautiful, just give me your name."

"Ma to the damn d-e-a. Madearrrr and I don't date batmens no mo, you heard me?"

He towers over me, his masculinity blinding. It's all I can do to keep from clutching my pearls when he speaks again, his voice low. "Silky dark hair, legs for days, shiny perfect kissable lips, I remember you well, Ms. Nope."

"That's right, it's Ms. Nope, as in no-pe-nis." Thick lips and a blinding smile render me speechless as he shakes his Bat head. "Now, run off to ya cave and leave an old woman alone."

"Just one date?"

"Lort no, I've outgrown you! Now I really mus-be going."

"You're breaking my heart."

"There you are," Lindsey says scouring Batman from head to foot, her eyes widening a little when they meet mine. "And I can see what's keeping you." I thrust the beer her way to shut her up, and it sloshes over my hand before she takes it.

"Mr. Dark Knight was just on his way to fight some injustices."

"The only injustice here is you not giving me a chance to take you out."

I've reached my limit. "Take your cave dwelling firm ass on!"

He lets out a long breath and leans in again as I stand on shaky legs. "I'm not giving up. I'm going to find you."

"Good luck with that, I'm no longer on your radar."

"Just a matter of time," he says through Batman lips that have Lindsey swooning next to me.

I grip Lindsey by the arm and drag her dickmatized ass away as I give him parting words over my shoulder. "Yeah, well if you see my porch light on, it's not the signal, it's my new *bat* zapper. Fair warning."

He shakes his head through a throaty and ridiculously sexy laugh as I chug what's left in my cup.

"Good God, I love Zach, but that was one hot ass Batman."

"Trust me, that was a neon 'stay the hell away' sign as far as I'm concerned."

"I doubt he's hard-pressed to find company looking like that, but why in the world would you turn him down?"

I drain the rest of my beer. "Because tonight, I'm the one with super-human strength. And I told you I'm on the wagon."

"Whew," she says, fanning her face, "good for you, but can you imagine the role play with that one?"

"My va-*gina* has, my friend," I say, turning back in his direction to see he's still watching me. A slow grin spreads over his mouth when I'm busted displaying clear remorse.

"Your who?"

"No one, Lort, girl, help me get out of chere."

She giggles, grabbing me by the arm to lead me away and then stops turning back to me, her face lightening up with recognition. "Oh, I get it now, you're Betty White!"

#

When we find our boys, I slow my walk when I see Theo talking to a brunette who seems comfortable with him as Lindsey sidles up with Zach and greets him with a kiss.

"That robe is doing weird shit to me," Zach murmurs into her hair, and she laughs. The girl chatting Theo up places a hand on his chest as I stand awkwardly to the side of him. After a few uncomfortable minutes, I move to pace the party but am stopped by his hand tugging on my muumuu, pulling me back toward him. Dark brown eyes briefly meet mine.

He's asking me to stay. So, I do.

We both leave the party solo a while later, shivering before he cranks up the heat in the cabin. The drive home is filled with an odd silence which, of course, I'm forced to break.

"So, who was that girl?"

"One of the girls I've made breakfast for."

"Huh?"

"When my roommates have a sleepover, I usually end up making the girls breakfast."

"Why?"

"I don't know. I guess I feel bad for them."

"They aren't victims, you know?"

"I know, but I can't help but think they deserve better."

"They do, but they have to figure it out for themselves. And she was looking at you like she wanted a repeat, but *not* with your roommate."

"That's not my style," he says passively.

"I know."

"I just remember how hard my sisters took it when they got their hearts smashed. I don't want to be the guy who does that to any woman, you know?"

"You really are a good egg, Theo. Stay that way."

"I'll try."

More silence.

"Well, you'll be proud to know I was tempted tonight by the devil himself and passed with flying colors."

"Oh yeah?" he says, keeping his eyes on the road.

"Yes. And I Kung Fu'd that shit like a boss."

"Proud of you," he says, pulling up to my house.

"Okay, what gives?"

He wrinkles his nose. "Ghost pains. I guess."

"Your ex?"

"Kind of."

"Explain, or I'm not getting out of this Honda."

"Nora and I used to hang out with Zach and Lindsey a lot."

"Those two are hard to watch if you bone alone."

He tilts his head back on his headrest and his chest pumps with a chuckle.

"That's better. So, what exactly is a ghost pain? You miss her?"

"No, I don't miss her like that," his voice is low, and I can see he's somewhere in his past. "I guess a ghost pain is remembering the future you once thought you'd have." He clears his throat. "It's nothing. I'm an idiot."

I draw his face toward me with my palm on his cheek. "You, my friend, are a lot of things, and a smart ass at times, but *not* an idiot. And I hope like hell for ghost pains one day. It'll mean I've loved someone hard and finally done some good living." Slowly I lean in and press a kiss to his cheek.

"Night, Theo."

"Night, Laney."

#heroparty #notmrsdoubtfire #matothedamndea #newbestfriends #heworeaskirt #butlookatthoselegs #livingourrealestlife

sixteen

Theo: How are you feeling?

Laney: Like I want to peel my skin off. Mom is making me wear oven mitts when she's home. How in the hell did I contract chicken pox at twenty-one?

Theo: It could be worse. It could've come in as shingles. Those are supposed to be a lot more painful.

Laney: How do you know?

Theo: I looked it up.

Laney: She finally left for work, and I can't stop scratching. I'll give you everything in my savings to come and get at my back with a rake.

Theo: No can do. What did you do today?

Laney: Glued a great pyramid of Doritos for worship.

Laney sent an image

Theo: That's pretty impressive.

Laney: Had to do something with my hands. And it's gotten two thousand likes.

Theo: That many?

Laney: Do you ever check the damned page? We have almost nine thousand followers.

Theo: WTF!

Laney: Yep. Ever since the Ghostin' the Whip post we've gained momentum.

Pause...

Theo: I think I see why.
Laney: Why?
Theo: I'm just going to table this discussion for now.
Laney: Whatever. (eye roll emoji) I know I have abundant cleavage.
Theo: What are you doing right now?
Laney: Binge watching this old reality show called Rock of Love.
Theo: What's it about?
Laney: This old lead singer from an eighties hair band called Poison and the twenty women competing for his, ahem, heart. Ironically, I've been trying to figure out all day if he's wearing a wig.
Theo: Why don't you just Google and find out?
Laney: Because it's a train wreck and far more entertaining to guess.
Theo: How long are you contagious?
Laney: A few more days. Have you had chicken pox yet?
Theo: My mom hasn't texted back yet to let me know. Sorry. I have a game coming up, and I don't want to chance it.
Laney: Shit, I guess this cheese will have to itch alone.
Theo: And on Halloween (sad emoji)
Laney: I know. SUCKS! I can't watch scary movies alone in this house, I'll be terrified, and Max will have nightmares. No candy corn for me either. #livingmysuckiestlife

Theo: Sorry. But if it makes you feel better, I'll watch with you.
Laney: You don't have to.
Theo: QT. What episode?
Laney: Start on one. I'll re-watch.

Five minutes later…

Theo: Definitely a wig.
Laney: I know. Poor guy. Can you imagine being known as the leader of a hair band and losing all your hair? Ouch life, ouch.

Ten minutes later…

Theo: These women are idiots.
Laney: Some of them, yes. Some were doing it to further their careers.
Theo: As what?
Laney: TV personalities. Plus, this is the result of pure marketing genius. Watch how they spin nothing into something. How they pause for effect. I might have a midlife rocker to PR for one day. This is good research.
Theo: You want me to believe we're watching this shit to better your education?
Laney: Work with me.

Twenty minutes later…

Theo: I feel less intelligent for watching this.
Laney: But you can't look away, admit it! It's the spin they put on things I tell you. And Brett is the perfect

ringleader. He plays the peacekeeper, but he's the antagonist.

Theo: Why, oh why are they crying over him? They've only known him for a few days, and he's in drag.

Laney: I think he's sort of cute.

Theo: Check your temp.

Laney: I'm serious, he's got pretty eyes.

Theo: He's wearing eyeliner. I demand we find something else to watch.

Laney: It's called guyliner. Fine, you pick something.

Theo: Ancient Aliens.

Laney: Oh, hell no, you criticize me for my show, but have you seen the hair on some of those ancient astronaut theorists?

Theo: At least some of it's logical.

Laney: It's mostly bullshit.

Theo: Fine, onto episode two.

Laney: I knew it, you're hooked!

Theo: QT Episode two

Thirty minutes later...

Theo: Jesus, they aren't even captioning the French girl correctly. They're spelling it the way she's talking. Z car. Really?

Laney: Only you would be worried about that, instead of commenting on her huge French tits.

Theo: I highly doubt they are French.

Laney: Not your type?

Theo: My dick shrank when I saw her come out nipples blazing. No Class.

Laney: What's your type? Let me guess, Daphne from

Scooby Doo?

Theo: Why do I talk to you?

Laney: Because I'm entertaining.

Theo: Ha. ^^^ it's the first G you've ever used. I still read it as entertainin'.

Laney: You're an ass.

Theo: I swear I heard you say that.

Laney: That's cause I'm behind you.

Pause...

Laney: Made you look.

Theo: Wouldn't put it past you.

Laney: I look horrible. I will spare you.

Theo: Bet it's not that bad.

Laney sent a photo

Theo: I'm not going to lie. It's bad. What are those pink splotches?

Laney: Supposed to help the itch. It's not.

Theo: Poor baby.

Laney: Bet that's not your type.

Pause...

Laney: I was just messing with you.

Theo: I think you're beautiful.

Pause...

Theo: You there?

Laney: Yeah. I was wiping my tears away. You hit me when I was vulnerable. I feel so bad, and I guess that just got me a little emotional. This really hurts. Like bad, like oww.

Theo: I'm sorry you're hurting.

Laney: Just a few more days, right?

Theo: Right.

Theo: You are, you know. Truly beautiful. I mean that.

Laney: Stop, you're going to make me cry and itch.

Theo: Sorry.

Laney: No, you're awesome. Really, thank you. I needed to hear that.

Theo: Anytime. So, more Rock of Love?

Laney: You don't have to.

Theo: I want to.

Laney: You're the best ever. Episode three?

Theo: On it.

Laney: Happy Halloween, Houseman. (pumpkin emoji)

Theo: Happy Halloween, Laney. (candy corn emoji)

Laney: Aww, you got me candy corn.

#chickenpoxingit #itchin #freddiekruegeraintgotshitonme
#snackstax #doritosarelife #notreatsforme
#thishouseisaprison #livingmyrealestlife

Grannism—They say a kiss is worth a thousand words, I say hand-holdin' is where it's at.

seventeen

LANEY

TWO DAYS LATER, I'M SITTING IN BED BRUSHING MY HAIR AFTER my second shower when my phone lights up with Theo requesting FaceTime.

Screw it. He's already seen the damage.

I swipe and answer. "Hey, how was the game?" I ask to the face of a guy I don't know. "Oh my God," I drop my phone in my lap and cover my face with both hands. "Who are you?"

"Rest easy, doll, we've been warned."

I peek through my fingers down at the screen. "Uh huh. Hi. Who are you? And where's Theo?"

"I'm Pete," he grins, and I can't help but notice he's adorable even with a crooked front tooth, messy brown hair, and light blue eyes. He nods over his shoulder. "He's back here. He asked me to call you."

"Oh? What for?"

Mischief shines in his eyes. "I'm in charge of the get well card."

Confused, I lean in. "The what?"

In the background, I hear. "Dude, get off my nuts, you're standing too close."

"It's a bus, asshole, everyone's too close."

"Are we doing this or what?"

"You better not be recording this shit, Pete."

Theo's voice sounds up next. "Would you guys shut the hell up?"

"Sit down back there!" I hear, who I assume is the bus driver, call out.

"Damn, Schmitty's already bitching. Hurry up!"

Pete smiles crookedly as D12's "My Band" starts to play, and a huddled group of Rangers comes into view with Theo standing front and center. The only other person I recognize is Zach, and I wave to him enthusiastically as they begin their routine. I'm already laughing when they start rapping animatedly, piled on top of each other, some in the aisle of the bus and some hanging over the back of the seats.

"This is epic!" I shout, knowing they can't hear me. The phone pans on Theo who does a sly shoulder brush, rapping along with Eminem verbatim before they all take turns with their verses, stealing the camera and pushing each other out of the way for attention. It's hilarious and warms my heart. I'm grinning from ear to ear, watching as they clamor for the camera before Pete turns it on himself to mouth his own verse. It's well-orchestrated, and I'm highly impressed. When the song is over, the guys pop up on screen one by one with well wishes.

"Feel better, Laney!"

"Get well, Laney!"

"She's hot, even with the dots."

Pete turns the phone on himself.

"So, when you're feeling better, we can—"

Theo growls, snatching the phone away. "I'll take it from here, asshole."

He comes into view, rolling his eyes before delivering a megawatt smile.

"Hey you, how you feeling?"

"That was incredible!"

His grin widens, warming me from the inside. "Thought you'd appreciate it."

I hear the driver then threaten to throw them off the bus as a voice calls out. "Aw, eat ya sammich, Schmitty!"

Theo and I both crack up.

"Seriously, that was epic. When did you put that together?"

"Eh, when you spend a shitload of hours on a bus both ways, you get creative. That's an oldie but a goodie."

"Well, it was YouTube-worthy, I swear, I loved it, thank you," warmth spreading in my chest as I study him. His band jacket unbuttoned, he's wearing a white V-neck beneath revealing a little of his neck and chest. His damp hair curls up at the ends around his ears, and a headband peeks out beneath the soaked mane swept across his forehead. It looks a little more like he just performed at a rock concert rather than half-time. It's sexy, and I find my cheeks warming as I study his lips and the look in his eye.

"Glad you liked it, that could've been embarrassing."

"For who? I thought you weren't the type to get embarrassed."

"This, I take seriously. It was our debut."

"They seem like a fun bunch."

"Totally."

"Y'all hang out much other than in the band?"

"I hang with Zach when I have time. The rest I can do without until we're ass deep in green pleather."

"Heard that, asshole."

"Meant for you to," Theo retorts with a shrug.

"So," I greedily drink him in. "With you, what you see is what you get, huh?"

"Pretty much."

We're grinning at each other like idiots. And it strikes hard then, I like what I see. I like it *very* much.

eighteen

LANEY

"**H**AVEN'T SEEN MUCH OF YOU LATELY," DEVIN SAYS, giving me a sly side eye. We're on our way for her final dress fitting, and a champagne lunch her soon-to-be mother-in-law has arranged.

"Sorry, I've been busy with school and—"

"Theo."

"I like him, okay? He's a lot of fun. He's smart and funny, and we go to the parties and stuff together, so we don't have to fly solo. He's kind of a loner, like me and just about the best guy I've ever met."

"But nothing is going on?"

"No." She eyes me, and I turn to face her in the front seat of her monster truck.

"Look, I am attracted to him, okay? I'll admit it. It crept up on me slow, and now I'm fully aware of it."

"That's because it's more than looks attracting you at this point."

"But he *is* good looking."

"I'm not disagreeing," she says, slowing at a stop light. "He's got a certain something."

"But, and I mean but, I've *never* had a guy friend like this. Ever. We talk about everything. And I mean everything. We're brutally honest with each other."

"That's good."

"It is."

I look out the window and sigh. "I don't know if he's attracted to me. He told me I was beautiful the other day, but it was when I had the pox. But he texted it in a way I felt like he meant it. But it's not like he lingers at my door when he leaves me or anything."

"And you want him to?"

"What if he does?"

"Answer the question, Laney." She parks in front of the bridal shop and turns to me.

"I might?"

"Don't torch your friendship over a might."

"Exactly."

"So, this friendship you have with him is genuine."

"It is. Yes."

"Sounds a lot like what Chase and I have. Friendships like that are the basis of a good and lasting relationship."

"I'm aware."

"But you've never had it, so it's only fair I point it out."

"Right."

"But until you know for sure, keep Gina out of it."

"I will."

"How long has it been now?"

"Almost a month and a half, penis free."

"Impressive."

"Don't you mock me," I say, shutting the truck door and leaning over her hood to scorn her. "I'll have you know I've faced off with temptation twice, not only that, but by the same fine-ass man and came out victorious. I'm getting so good at this I feel it might be my duty to write a 'how-to' handbook for those like me."

Just as I finish my sentence Chase pulls up in his Jeep, his cabin loaded with bulging, sweating masculinity. It's all I can do to keep my mouth closed when they hop out, muscles rippling with the aftermath of their morning workout.

Devin tilts her head, weighing my expression with a grin. "That's right, you haven't met the groomsmen yet."

Swallowing hard, I meet the eyes of tall, dark, and, ridiculously fucking handsome before ripping them away, straightening myself upright and averting my eyes.

"Yeah, I wouldn't dip your pen in ink just yet," Devin says snidely right before her fiancé sweeps her into his arms and I make it safely to the other side of the shop door.

nineteen

THEO

Laney: Good morning. You should be so proud of me.
Theo: Should I?
Laney: Yep, I got tested once again yesterday and passed with flying colors. I think I'll buy myself a taco later to celebrate the nurturing of my celibacy.
Theo: Proud of you.

I ignore the twinge of jealousy that threatens. Aside from my confession on Halloween, I've kept anything other than my platonic feelings out of the relationship. But those *other* feelings are getting harder to ignore. It was the drive home from the hero party when I started to feel them. When she asked me what was wrong, I'd blundered the truth a little. The truth was, I was worried I might be making the same mistake with Laney as I did with Nora. I'd been way too laid back with Nora, afraid to use any assertiveness for fear she wouldn't like that side of me. With Laney, I'm still totally unsure if I should make a move. And if I did, what would her reaction be?

It bothered me that she wanted me to feel free to hook up with other girls, and that she wouldn't stand in my way if I did. The budding truth is that I want her to care. It's that simple. I spent some of the drive weighing if the friendship was worth keeping if these feelings continue to grow one-sided. But at times, I catch her looking at me in a way that suggests more, and it gives me hope.

My growing attraction is proving to be more than I can handle in the Teddy zone. And each time she looks at me, I refuse the pull. Even if at times I feel like she wants me to kiss her, I'm just not sure that it's 'try the nice guy' curiosity on her part. I could play her guinea pig, but at what cost to me? I'm not that guy anymore. I owe it to myself not to second guess if a girl wants me or not.

Not only that, it's the relationship part that scares the hell out of me. Between Laney's track record, and my disposition on relationships we don't exactly mesh. She's told me herself, several times, she has a gypsy heart. And that, in and of itself, is a recipe for disaster. I need to take that statement at face value, and if so, what could we possibly start together?

Laney: Come get a coffee before class. On me. (coffee emoji)

Theo: Sounds good.

Like every day since the party, I push those thoughts away. Until I'm sure, I'm not fucking up our friendship on an inkling. The ball is just going to have to keep bouncing where it is. But it might be time to make her aware it's there. Faint steps sound down the stairs of the house that I know don't belong to either roommate. "Good Morning," I greet as I pull some dripping bacon from the pan. "Have a seat if you want, you're just in time. Nothing fancy, just eggs and bacon. I hope that's okay?"

"Theo?"

Every muscle in my body clenches in recognition of that voice.

I turn to see her gawking from the entrance of the kitchen, wide eyes raking over me as she stands covered in nothing but Troy's jersey.

"Lightly scrambled, right?"

Mouth parted, she looks in the direction she came. "I-I—"

"Don't run off. What's it been, a year? We should catch up," I say, pushing the eggs around the pan doing everything in my power to keep my shit together.

"What are you...uh..."

"Doing here? I live here," I answer evenly, plating her breakfast and placing it on the table. "We're fresh out of linen," I say, tearing off a paper towel and pulling a plastic fork from the drawer. "You know how it is. Lot of traffic coming *in* and *out*."

"I'll just g—"

I pull out the metal chair, and it scrapes noisily on the floor.

"Have a seat. Don't want you missing the most important meal of the day after *that* workout."

"You have to believe I had no idea."

"Take a seat, Nora."

Her eyes search mine for empathy she'll never find, her lips quivering before she slowly sinks down into the seat. I painstakingly take my time pushing her uncomfortably close to the table.

"There you are. Juice?"

She nods as I pour her the last of Troy's juice.

"H-how have you been?"

"Peachy." I slam the empty carton on the table and glare down at her. "You?"

"I've been—"

"Good to hear," I snap, "Make sure to sign the guestbook on your way out."

"Theo, please believe me. I had no idea. I would never hurt you like this."

"Hurt me?" I harrumph, pointing to my chest. "No. You no longer have the ability to hurt me. This isn't hurt, Nora, it's disgust. Eat up."

"I'm not hungry." She's on the verge of tears, and I couldn't care less.

From behind, I lean down, placing my hands on the table on either side of her and lean low to whisper in her ear. "This is the part where I typically give my usual pep talk. You know, to comfort those with conscience enough to regret being *used*. But don't worry, Nora, I'm well aware you don't have a conscience. And there's no way I could possibly think less of you than I already do. But I can promise you this, you're still very much the *same* girl you were when you walked through that door last night."

She bursts into tears and oddly, I'm not satisfied.

"What the hell is going on?" Troy asks as he enters the kitchen and glances down at Nora before lifting accusing eyes to mine.

"Oh good, you can keep her company. I have a full day."

"What happened?" Troy asks, leaning down to try and console her, his posture intimate, which only further infuriates me. I spent years knowing her, memorizing her, worshiping her, loving her, and he knows her in a way I never will. It's dick jealousy, pure and simple, and it should surprise me that I can still feel that when it comes to her. I'm acting like a caveman when I'm the one who gave her the walking papers. And for good damned reason.

Still, the serrated knife that's just been daggered into my back is unforgiving.

Troy looks between us utterly clueless. I should take some comfort in the fact they're both bystanders of fucked up circumstance due to their own brand of self-destructive and narcissistic behavior, but I'm just angry. Angry at myself for caring.

"Kudos on this one, she's a rarity. Truly, one of a kind. She has her picture-perfect future mapped out. But, be careful, she has a pair of sharp scissors and will cut you out without warning."

"What the fuck, man?" Troy says, bowing up to me in ridiculous defense.

"I'd give you more of a rundown on the girl you just fucked," I say, spitting the word out with intent, "but time is precious, and I've wasted enough on her."

Gathering my shit from the hall, I hear their exchanged whispers before I slam the front door and make my way toward my Honda. Fuming, I toss my case and backpack into the backseat when Troy approaches.

"Jesus, man. I had no idea."

Slamming the door, I cross my arms. "Of fucking course, you didn't."

"I don't know what to say." He runs a hand down his face. "I fucked up."

"Did you even talk to her?" I clench and unclench my fists. "Do you ever really talk to *any* of them?" His silence is deafening. "If you would have spent more than five fucking minutes luring her into your bed, you might have been able to connect the dots. Instead, you've fucked my ex!" I'm seething, and I hate myself for it.

"Tell me what to do to make this right."

"You can't do anything." I snap, dangerously tempted to take a shot towards a fight I can't possibly win. She's no longer worth it, but I can't help pointing out the time I thought she was. "That girl meant everything to me, for *years*, and you fuck her and treat her like she's disposable. Can't you see how wrong that is?"

Eyes cast down; he shakes his head. "Tell me what to do."

"How about you grow the fuck up a little?"

"It was a mistake."

"No, hell no," I say as he brings guilty eyes up to mine. "You don't get to claim that. That was intentional. She was *my* mistake. To you, she was just last night."

Slamming my driver door closed, I turn the ignition as Nora comes into view on the porch. Her porcelain complexion splotched with evidence of her tears. I can't help myself, I drink her in. Long dark blonde hair, dark blue eyes. With the stab of recognition, somehow, I know this is how it would have felt had I caught her red-handed, but then it would have been a million times worse. Most of my anger stems from the time that's passed and the fact that even though I told her differently, she still has the ability to singe me. Because today she just burned me bad. And why? Because there's no poetic justice for suckers like me.

Grannism—Everyone should do something bat shit crazy
once in a while, it's good for the soul.

.

twenty

LANEY

THEO STANDS AT THE BACK OF THE LINE, HIS EYES CAST DOWN on his black high-top chucks. He looks adorable today in dark jeans, a V-neck, and a checkered sweater vest. I love the way he dresses—prep meets rock and roll—and his style is all his own. He's trimmed his beard a little, and it's closer to his face. His ear length brown hair curled slightly at the ends framing his jaw.

Though he's dressed to the nines, his posture is deflated. It's when I take a second look, and he doesn't try to catch my eyes while I scribble an order, that I know something is wrong.

I nudge my co-worker, Carrie, who's just finished layering the perfect dick on top of a cappuccino. Carrie is not a fan of our mostly male customer base either. "I'm taking ten. It's important."

She nods, stepping in front of me to take the next order as I walk down the line and approach Theo while he rubs a clenched fist along his forehead. I pull his hand away, searching his face.

"Hey, you. What's going on?"

"I made breakfast this morning." He swallows before bringing tumultuous eyes to mine, "for Nora."

"Jesus, Theo," I whisper. "Come on." I pull at his hand,

encasing it with my own as he tightens our grip and squeezes. He needs me. I try to ignore the zing in my chest at the realization as I walk him to the back of the coffee house. We stand at the open back door, and he pulls his hand away from mine and starts pacing.

"What happened?"

"What happened? Troy fucked her. In *my* house, feet away from me. And I'm jealous. Isn't that pathetic?"

"No. Anyone would be pissed."

"It disgusts me," he manages through a clenched jaw. "How can I feel *anything* after all this time. After what she did?"

"I think we're wired to want what we can't have. It's not wrong to feel the way you do. You were cheated on and just got your nose rubbed in it."

"Why, why him? Why guys like him? Tell me what's so appealing about that kind of guy. Look, I'm not saying all gene lottery winners are hollow inside. But tell me why, when it's abundantly clear what some are after, do women temporarily decide to loosen their morals for twenty meaningless minutes?"

I swallow. "I'm not the spokeswoman."

"No, but you're a subscriber to that same type of asshole."

"I promise you, once the buzz wears off and the feelings, or lack of kick in, it can feel pretty shitty."

Accusing eyes meet mine. "Yet you go back for more."

"Whoa, down boy, used to," I remind him, "and stop pointing that sword at me. I'm not the enemy."

"I want to hate her. I *do* hate her. I hate that I got all territorial and jealous."

"Theo, you're still a man, and he pissed all over the house. I get it. It makes perfect sense."

"How can it make sense to you? You've never felt this."

"Hey," I close the distance. "Stop beating the help."

"Sorry," he says, shoving his hands in his jeans. He leans on the frame of the back door and looks up to me with desperate eyes. His hurt circulates through the air between us. "I mean it. I'm sorry."

"It's fine."

"God, I'm never going back there."

"Yes, you are," I say softly. "This too, shall pass. And you look...you look," I avert my eyes, "you look really good, Theo. There's no way she's not regretting it right now."

"Troy is over six foot with an eight pack, and I've got mabs."

"Mabs?"

He gives me a reluctant grin. "Maybe abs?"

I burst into laughter, and he shakes his head with a groan.

"I can't ever seem to get a damn leg up with women. *Ever.*"

"Well, I'm in the same boat. And do me a favor, don't ever introduce me to that asshole."

"Wasn't planning on it, but why?"

"The first reason is obvious, he's my kryptonite. But the *real* reason is because I will rip his balls from his body."

His lips turn up.

"It's cute you think I'm kidding."

"I have no doubt you would."

"Oh, I will. It's the version of Crazy Laney you *never* want to meet."

"You're a good friend, Laney." His voice is soft, face crestfallen due to what I'm sure is a burning image of his ex-girlfriend post roommate romp.

"I'm so sorry. But I assure you, that particular brand of poison never tastes as sweet as the first sip. After that, it's just nasty aftertaste. Abs definitely don't make the man."

I palm his cheek. "And I might've been a little trigger

shy in revealing this to you, Theo, but you aren't anything to sneeze at. Like at all."

His eyes connect with mine fully, and there's a sort of recognition in them I've never seen before.

"There's been times I've wanted to tell you," nerves fire off as he studies me carefully. "It's just never really been fittin' to admit it, b-because we're friends."

Something heavy lingers in the air, and I pull my hand away. I'm not allowed to touch him again until I know for sure if I want more than friendship. But don't I know? I'm jealous right now that he's jealous about his ex. Isn't that sign enough?

Hey, Gina, now would be the time to speak up.

But it's not my nether region that's pulsing faster by the second, it's the organ in my chest that's starting to make the most noise.

"Anyway, I've got just the thing for today." Opening my locker, I pull out the metal container that my buddy, Fraz, gave me in case of emergency and open it, before approaching Theo. "Trust me?"

"Not even remotely." He eyes the gummy. "What is it?"

"It's a pot gummy, you know, an edible." I waggle my brows.

"I don't do pot."

"No one says 'do' pot. You smoke it. Or in our case, *eat* it. And we'll do it together."

"What are you doing with that in your purse?"

"Saving it for days when my new best friend has a meltdown. That day has come, my friend."

He gives me a wary glance. "I have class in an hour."

"Then class will be a blast. It's supposed to be super mild. I think."

"You think?"

"I mean we aren't smoking it, so it can't be as harsh, right?"

"I don't know. I've never done it."

"Me neither. I'm doing it with you."

"I don't think this is the answer."

"Neither is obsessing about your ex, and I'm not in the mood for a hangover. Live a little, Houseman," I say, tearing the disc in half and popping it into my mouth. "Down the hatch," I instruct holding the other half up to him. "Just a little buzz to take away the blues."

"Right," he takes half of the gummy, chewing it while cringing before he swallows. "I can't believe I just did that."

"Ex-hate will make you do stupid shit, and now we're both going down the rabbit hole. What class should I pick you up from?"

"Music Composition. Sam Houston building. 203."

"Okay, I'll be waiting outside the door when you get out. Go, it shouldn't hit you until you get to school."

"That was stupid," he says, shaking his head and readjusting his backpack.

"I got it from an old high school friend a couple of months ago. I trust him. This will be great, you'll see." I raise up on my toes and wrap my arms around him. He hugs me back while murmuring a low, "Thank you."

Backing away, I kiss his jaw, loving the sensation of his beard tickling my lips. What I see in his eyes, lights a fire in me. His gaze travels to my lips, and I sense the hesitation to pull away and grow more curious about the fire brewing in my chest. I want to be kissed by him, but *not* when he's in the midst of mourning his past with another woman. I nudge his shoulder.

"Go. I'll see you in a bit."

Forty-five minutes later...

"Devin. Devin? Devin! Can you hear me? I feel like I've been in this bathroom for hours."

"Yes, yes, I can hear you, stop yelling, moron. What's up?"

I press my cell closer to my ear and whisper. "What in the hell did Fraz put in this gummy?"

"Oh my God, you took it?"

"No, I just called to tell you I didn't. Things are totally normal, and I haven't locked myself in the bathroom at school. This is what *high* feels like?"

"I wouldn't know, I'm not high. Why did you have to do this on inventory day? I can't even come watch you freak out."

"I got off my shift and came to school to grab Theo like I promised. But once I started walking down the hall, my legs turned into noodles, and I felt like I got shot in the neck with a tranquilizer dart. Everything is getting...slower. I've been sitting on this toilet hiding ever since, and I swear this song has been playing forever."

"Girl, don't drive."

"I can't even walk."

"How much did you take?"

"Half that disc."

"You were only supposed to take an EIGHTH! Those edibles are strong!"

"Oh no," I lift my hands up in front of me. "I think my hand's webbing. Is this normal? I hope Theo is okay."

"He took it too?!"

"Yes."

"All those times I asked you to get high with me and you wouldn't but for *him,* you will? And Theo doesn't seem the type to do something like this. What were you thinking?"

"Stop making me out to be the culprit."

"Aren't you?"

"Yes. But for good reason. I had to pull out the big guns. Emergency high. His roommate screwed his ex last night. Wretched bitch. I just didn't want him thinking about her all day. He was so sad."

"You sound jealous."

"I'm pissed *for him*. I care about him a lot."

"Uh huh."

"I swear to God if you start singing Christmas Carols right now."

"I won't."

"Good, can you please tell me how to get out of the bathroom?"

"Jesus. Maybe Dad could cover for me so I can rescue you two."

"I've got this. We'll Uber it home."

"Swear to the Lort?"

"Aww, you Madea'd me. You must really love me."

"Of course I love you, you idiot. You need to leave school now. Get Theo and get the hell out of there before it hits harder."

"On it. Wait, it's going to hit harder?"

"I don't know, just go get him."

"Just have to figure out who makes this toilet. It feels like Jell-O on my ass."

"Seriously?"

"It's comfortable."

"Laney, go get him. If he's in as bad of shape as you, this could be disastrous."

"Oh," I snort, yanking at the toilet paper. "That's right. He's got a rep as a Grand Band Man."

"And he's on *scholarship*, remember? I'm pretty sure getting stoned at school is frowned upon."

That sobers me. "I gotta save him!"

"You think?"

"I think this song's on repeat."

"It's been like fifteen seconds."

"I don't believe you," I mutter as I glance around the bathroom stall. "You have got to try out this toilet."

"Laney, FOCUS! Get Theo and get out of there!"

"Right. I'm on it. Devin?"

"Yes, girl?"

"Why don't we eat more Jell-O together?"

twenty-one

THEO

M Y LEGS WON'T MOVE NO MATTER HOW MUCH I WILL THEM
to. I feel like I've been sitting here for years.
Everything is vibrating.

I'm going to die.

Pulling out my phone, I text Laney.

Theo: I nees to leave. I don't tink tis is mellow.hi. Can come now?

Laney: I'm working on the Jell-O.

Theo: ?

Laney: How long is this song!

Theo: IDknow. I cat ducking feel my fat.

Theo: Fet

Theo: Fet!

Laney: I coming to slave you.

"Hey man," someone says to my left, and I jump back in my seat and clutch my phone to my chest.

"What do you want?" I grunt, lifting a shoulder and lean away from him.

Three rows of students turn back to look at me as the guy widens his eyes. "Wasn't talking to you, bro, chill out."

I concentrate on opening my eyes as wide as his to appear more normal and hear a giggle from beside me.

"Hey, are you okay?"

"I have something in my feet."

"Oh shit, he's probably on Molly," the girl whispers. She's not pretty like Laney.

"I'm not," I whisper. "Not on *that*."

"He's trippin'."

"Please don't say that to people," I whimper. Just then, the door to the classroom bursts open, and everyone, including my instructor, looks toward the open door at Laney as she lands a plane. She's looking right at me mouthing in slow motion, and I lean into my desk straining to hear her.

"Dude, I think she's here for you."

Laney speaks up, taking a few steps into class. "Excuse me, sir, I need an urgent word with one of your t-t-udents, students."

"You're interrupting my lecture, young lady."

She nods in perfect understanding. "I polizise. He's having an allergic reaction to his medication and needs this," She pulls out an EpiPen. She probably bought it in case I have a reaction around her because she's my best friend in the whole world. And I don't want to have sex with her all the time.

"Go right on ahead."

Laney waves me down to her.

"Medication, my *ass*," someone snorts from below.

"Oh man," the guy next to me says. "I would give my left nut to be on your level right now. And with her too, *damn*."

I shake my head. "That's not what's happening. I'm not going to let my feet not move."

"Okay," he says with a chuckle as Laney looks at me and waves her hands slowly.

She's so beautiful it makes my chest hurt. I rub it with my fist and hold it up to her so she can see before pulling myself to stand. Uneasy on my feet, I slowly make my way down the steps thanking each one in sincere gratitude. "I appreciate you." Laughter erupts to my right just as Laney grabs my arm when I reach the last one.

"He probably won't be back," Laney says. "Sorry about that."

Outside the class, she grabs my face with both hands and pulls me down eye level with her. Honey eyes bore into mine while her lips shine like diamonds.

"I may never return to them," I tell her feeling a lump form in my throat.

"Return to what?"

"My feet."

"Hang in there, okay?"

"I love your hands on my face."

"Listen to me, Houseman. We ate too much. We are Snoop Dogg at the Chronic Olympics high. We have an Uber coming in five minutes. I need you to find your feet."

"I dunno that's plauisbble."

# # # # #

"Dave in the white Taurus, do you believe in Doritos?" Laney asks from beside me in the back seat as I study the lines dancing on my jeans.

"I believe in Doritos," I tell her.

She grabs my hand. "I know you believe. I want to know if *Dave* believes."

"Why? He's not your boyfriend."

"He's a person."

"He looks like Carrot Top without hair."

"That's not nice, Houseman. Dave, I think we should stop for tacos."

"We do not need tacos. I need feet."

"Jesus, are you two drunk? It's 10:30 a.m."

"We're doing weed," Laney snorts softly before her lips quiver. "Forgive us."

Dave smiles at her in the rearview, and I want to tell him not to smile at her like *that*, but my tongue is swelling. "Imma need that apic pen."

"You don't need it. I promise."

"I'm thinking you two don't do much weed."

"First timers!" Laney proclaims. "Does this window go down?"

"Sure," Dave says. "Do you mind changing your destination for tacos?"

"No," I say, shaking my head. "No tacos. Everyone knows what's happening to us."

"What's happening to us?" Laney asks, pushing the button over and over. I stop her hand before I run my fingers through her hair.

She moans. "That feels so good."

"Thank you. I want to do it sometimes a lot."

"You can do it all the time," Laney says, leaning down to put her head in my lap.

"You're going to make me cry," I rub my chest.

She puts a hand on my face from below, looking up at me with earnest eyes. "Don't cry, Theo."

"I hate to break this up, you two, but we're still here."

"Sorry?"

"We arrived five minutes ago."

Laney slowly raises to sit and looks out the window. "Look alive, Houseman. We made it."

"My eyes feel so slippery." I blink them over and over.

"Come on," Laney says, pulling at my arm. "We have to get out."

Dave opens the door, and I wince from the sun reflecting off his head. "Do you two need help inside?"

"I just need to feel," I admit, emotion clogging my throat.

"It's going to be okay, man," Dave says.

He's so close when he speaks, I jerk away from him.

Laney grabs my hand, pulling me from the car. "I've got you, Theo. Bye, Dave."

"You two be careful."

"We're positive," Laney tells him, throwing my arm over her shoulder.

"You think he knows I can't feel my feet?"

"He's aware. You stay put." She says, depositing me on her porch. "I think I have some eggrolls."

"*Oh*, I want them *so bad*. Will you bring them to me?"

"For you, I will."

"Thanks, Laney."

twenty-two

THEO

THE SUN WAKES ME PEEKING THROUGH A CLOUD UNDER THE overcast sky. I rouse with a wad of hair in my mouth, covered in a sleeping Laney. The warmth streams through the teepee window at the top of our fortress. Fuzzy memories come back to me in waves. Laney had pulled out half of her gear from the shed next to her house insisting we camp out, so we didn't disturb her sleeping mother who had a shift in a matter of hours. Stoned out of our minds, it took us a small eternity to pitch the tattered tent amongst the thick of the trees in her front yard. Safe in our cocoon, we unleashed laughter that lasted for hours. And I'm positive she made the pizza delivery guy shit his pants when she jumped out into the drive waving her hands like a lunatic to intercept the delivery from reaching the front door. I can't help my chuckle when I remember the look on his face.

My stomach is sore from all the laughing we did.

What started out as the worst morning imaginable, easily turned into one of the best days of my life. Because of her.

She shifts, her thick locks tickling my nose as she slumbers sprawled on my chest. The air inside the tent warms as she burrows further into me, gripping my bicep and holding me to her with a thigh stretched across my stomach. I need to take a leak, but I fight like hell not to disturb the peace. Instead, I stare down at her, memorizing what I can—flawless brown skin, a freckled nose, dark lashes, and full, bee-stung lips.

I'll never fucking learn.

Even with the red flag of Nora tossed in my face only this morning, I can't stop imagining what it would be like to truly be with Laney.

My attachment is much too evident at this point as I study her, and that's all I seem to be doing lately when I'm not thinking about her. I don't want to contemplate our differences. Not with the way she fits so perfectly on top of me. No matter how hard I've tried to stop it, I've fallen under her spell. She makes me want, and often.

She's entirely too much woman to ignore.

Pressing a kiss to the top of her head, I inhale her signature scent of mint and citrus. I love the smell and allow myself to indulge while I have this chance. Holding her to me, I slide my thumbs against her skin in a caress. We're both fully dressed, but with my thoughts, I feel exposed, despite still being in our cocoon.

I'm completely myself with her, and she with me. I know this. I don't question our connection or the authenticity of our friendship. It's not chemistry we lack, it's the readiness on her part that I need to feel. And after that exchange in the coffee shop, everything shifted, at least for me.

I no longer want to be adorable to Laney.

The clarity has my heart aching and my eyes wide open.

I can no longer be Laney's friend.

My dick is rock hard by the time she moves, her soft groan only fueling my desire.

Sleeping bags lay piled beneath us in our makeshift

fortress. I'm more comfortable than I've ever been in my life, even with a raging hard-on. I'm positive we fell asleep mid-sentence with smiles on our faces.

Laney stirs, and I brush the hair away from her face while she lifts her chin, bringing light brown eyes to mine.

"Hey."

"Hey."

We're close, so close I can see the faint green circle around her irises and the flecks of amber gold within. She studies me just as carefully, and I relax in the feel of her resting so contently on top of me.

"I feel like a lazy cat."

"Don't move," I mumble, running my fingers through her hair.

"Feels so good," My dick jerks at the sound of her raspy voice and my pulse picks up. "Are you cold?"

"No," there's clear heat to my voice that I try to disguise as sleep. "I'm good."

Her eyes pool before she averts them, her lashes flitting over her cheeks as she surveys my chest. She's turned on too. I can hear it in her voice. It's then I feel *it*, from her. "Epic nap."

"Best sleep I've had in a long time."

We share a shy smile as she palms my chest, covering my heart.

"You feelin' okay, right *here*?"

"Perfect."

"Really?"

"Yeah, haven't thought about it at all since the coffee shop."

Her eyes light, and it's then, I know. "Good."

Just as I'm about to grip her face, she giggles into my

neck. "We took like four times the amount we were supposed to. *My bad.*"

"Another whoops?"

"Yeah," she laughs. "Sorry, but it wasn't so awful, was it?"

"No," I thread my fingers through the silky strands at her back. "It never is with you." I gently nudge her. "Hey, when did you buy an EpiPen?"

Smiling, she pulls away from me to sit and starts sifting through her purse, producing a slender white container. "It's not an EpiPen. It's one of those discreet tampon holder thing-amajiggies. Looks like an EpiPen, doesn't it?"

I grin. "Clever."

Fearful eyes search mine. "I'm really sorry. You could have gotten into big trouble."

"A reaction to meds was the perfect excuse. Only you would use enough ingenuity to come to my rescue and save me with a tampon."

"Tampon holder. And that's true. I *am* a genius."

I roll my eyes. "I wouldn't go that far."

Her blinding smile has the ache returning in my chest. "Well, today was the best day, ever."

"I agree."

I sit up, pulling my vest down to try and cover the bulge in my pants. "Thanks for saving me, *again.*"

"Anytime," she says, glancing over her shoulder to look back at me. "I mean that."

It takes every amount of reserve strength I have not to pull her to me and kiss her. Instead, she lifts her phone to show me our latest post, and I crack up at the picture and the hashtags.

"It's the perfect picture to describe today."

I look over to see her staring at me. "Yeah. It is."

#outlaws #gummietuesday
#nexttimefollowdirections #campinginthefrontyard
#bestdayever #whoops #whoneedsfeet
#thefaceoftwopeoplewhoshouldvebeenarrested
#uberdaveisasaint #believeindoritos #bestfriendssolidified
#livingourrealestlife

twenty-three

THEO

"WHERE ARE YOU GOING ALL DRESSED UP?" TROY asks as I pull on my jacket.

"Rehearsal dinner," I mutter. I've been avoiding him all week, and he's let me. He tried to come down to the basement to talk, but I'd shut him out.

I can be a dick when I want to be.

Troy sits on the couch tossing a football up as I do a last-minute perusal.

"Who's getting married?"

"A friend of a friend. What's it to you?"

A loud, exasperated groan leaves him, and I turn in his direction.

"Jesus. How many times do I have to say I'm sorry?"

"You don't. I'm over it." And it surprises me how much I mean it.

"You serious?"

"I mean I don't want to hug it out with you, but yeah, I'm completely over her. I've got something much better going on."

"That so?"

"It's so. Just do me a favor and start vetting before you bring anyone else here. Not that I have any more exes. But let me make one thing clear, I don't want yours, and I don't want you ever taking a second look at mine."

"Got it. I'm not going to...see her again." It's all I can do not to roll my eyes. He stands and pulls out a few bills from his wallet. "For what I owe you."

I take the money as a sign of good faith and spot the duffle packed at his feet. "Where are you going?"

He shrugs. "A few guys are headed to Shreveport this weekend. I'm going to check it out. Lance left a note on the fridge that he's out until Tuesday, so the house is all yours."

"Nice."

A horn sounds outside, and Troy pulls his duffle from the floor. "Later."

"Later, man."

He pauses at the front door. "We good?"

"Yeah, we're good."

#######

I pull up to the circular drive, in wait for the valet and text Laney. The country club sits on the edge of a massive golf course. The other side is a mix of butterfly ponds. Even in late fall, the landscape is on point, and I can see why Devin picked it to host her wedding.

Theo: I'm here, waiting in line for the valet.

Laney: Thank God. If I have to listen to this idiot best man tell me about his new Camaro one more minute. (eye roll emoji) I think I saw a tear in his eye when I told him I wasn't a fan. Boys and their stupid toys.

Theo: But is he pretty?

Laney: Yes. And I'm not interested. Now come save me.

Theo: On my way. And you most definitely are a shitty judge of character.

Laney: Not this again. I told you, Brett chose her because she was younger. I didn't say they belonged together.

Theo: I knew halfway in she was wrong for him.

Laney: I've created a monster. You're addicted to reality TV.

Theo: You're the one who started it.

Laney: Take it down a peg or two, Houseman.

Since the day in the tent, we've become inseparable, well, as much as our schedules will allow. Laney is still managing to swing three and a half jobs and keep up with classes, while I utilize my weekends on the bus studying my ass off in an effort to make sure I can spend every spare minute with her. It's hit or miss, but we make it work. More than once, I've seen that 'kiss me' look in her eye since that day, but we've rarely been alone, and it's never been the right time. And in a way, I'm still waiting for permission. Old habits die hard, but I'm to the point where I'm just as determined as my object of affection to break them.

Theo: Just gave up my keys.

"You clean up nice, Houseman."

Smiling, I look up to see Laney staring at me from beside the double door entrance, her phone in hand, looking breathtaking in a form-fitting black dress, the material hugging her curves. Her hair hangs in loose waves around her shoulders. Her eye makeup is a little darker, her lips too. The neckline dips low, showcasing the beautiful curves of her breasts. My mouth goes dry as I imagine the things I would do with my tongue in the center of that universe.

"You look so beautiful," I join her where she waits for me. Her breath hitches. "I know you meant that. I *felt* it."

"Good."

Lifting on her toes, she slowly leans in pressing her lips against my bearded cheek, and it takes everything in me not to turn my head.

"Thanks for coming."

"Thanks for having me."

twenty-four

LANEY

THEO SIPS HIS DRINK BEFORE TOSSING HIS HEAD BACK WITH A laugh while Chase moves his hands animatedly. I can't hear a word they're saying, and I can't tear my eyes off him. He looks so damned gorgeous in a mint green button-down and slacks that fit him perfectly. His long bangs are swept away from his forehead, and the rest of his unruly hair is tucked behind his ears. His smile is blinding, keeping me incapable of seeing much of anything else. He looks...happy. Even in a room full of strangers, he exudes the type of confidence I'm drawn to. A confidence I envy as I do my best not to nip at the drinks surrounding me. I'm nervous. This is my biggest side job yet, and the happiness of my best friend solely relies on me executing it without a hitch.

Right now, I wouldn't mind taking a sip from the drink in Theo's hand. But not from the glass, from the lips attached to it. I'm turned on just imagining what his lips could do in the midst of that transfer. A little pride runs through me when I see his drink of choice tonight is whiskey.

I've influenced him a little, just as he has me. I find myself opening more and more to his musical tastes, and every once in a while, he lets me DJ with something more of my choosing.

We're meshing, and we've come eerily close to having the

routine of a couple. To any outsider, we look like one, the only part that's missing at this point is the part I can't stop imagining. Gina no longer stays silent when I'm around him, in fact, she won't shut the hell up. But her voice takes a back seat to the feelings that engulf me when Theo's around. Right now, the pull feels magnetic, and my legs proved useless when he got out of his car. Over the last two months, I've felt like I've been peeling layer after layer of this man away and there is still so much to discover.

After a few brief introductions, I had no choice but to leave him and tend to Devin, but it seems he's charmed everyone he's met tonight. And I can see why so clearly, it's becoming painful. How did I not see it before?

I have hours of maid of honor duties ahead, and all I really want is to spend time with him.

He takes another sip of his drink and runs a hand down his newly-trimmed beard as I slam into a cater waiter, distracted.

"Sorry," I mutter too embarrassed to meet my victim's eyes and quickly resume my pace around the party.

I'm not much of a beard girl, but on him, it just works. And it works well because as of late, it's sent my imagination into overdrive. I can't help but imagine the feel of it brushing along the top of my thighs.

As if he can hear me, Theo's eyes lift, his dark gaze searching the party finding me watching him before a slow smile curves his lips.

Devin's voice jolts me back to the ground I hadn't realized I was floating above. "Laney! We can't use the send-off sachets. It's too dangerous for birds to eat. I'm going to have to redo them all! How did I not know this?"

"I'll handle it," I tell her ripping my eyes from my plus one and pulling another drink from her hand. "Stop trying to drink yourself stupid. We agreed this would be a gentle buzz night, remember?"

"We've still got the programs to fold!"

"My mom is doing it after her shift. She'll bring them tomorrow. And like I told you a thousand times, no one has programs at a wedding."

"Well, *my* mother wants them!" Devin shrieks, looking gorgeous in her white dress, her hair twisted up in the perfect 'southern princess' updo. The only thing taking away from her look is the sight of terror in her eyes.

"Hang in there, okay? I'm your girl. I have a few hours tonight to work on the flowers. And then we're all set."

"Did you get the out of towners the welcome packet—"

"Done, they all got them when they checked in."

"Oh, thank God," she drawls out in exaggeration.

"Devin, it's *all* done. This will be exactly like you wanted it. And if we forget something, it wasn't important enough to remember. See that man over there?" I nod past her shoulder where Chase is looking on at her like he's seeing her for the first time. She follows my line of sight and nods, wiping a tear from her face.

"He's the only thing you're missing right now, and it looks like he could use a little one on one with his fiancée."

Devin turns to me with watery eyes. "God, I'm turning into *that* bride, aren't I?"

"No, you just want it to be perfect, but it's only 'cause you love him so much. Take a break, get him alone for a few minutes and do questionable and naughty things to him and I'll meet you back in the suite. I've got this. If I didn't, I would speak up."

She turns back to me. "Sarah isn't here yet."

"I just texted her. She couldn't get out of work in time for rehearsal, but as soon as she gets here, I'm runnin' the whole thing through with her."

Devin's lips quiver. "You're the best."

"Go on," I say as we both collectively ogle the men staring back at us.

"Okay," she says, letting out a shaky breath. "But I feel it's necessary to point out your date is looking at you like he wants to do questionable things to you *publicly*."

Theo's got one hand in his black slacks, the other cupping his drained whiskey glass. His eyes hungrily sweep me from head to foot even as I watch him do it, and he doesn't bother to look away. Our eyes hold for a moment before Chase blocks our view of him.

"Did you just see that?" I whisper.

"Girl, I *felt* that."

Chills erupt over my skin as Devin turns to me with surprise in her eyes.

"Is it me or does the Band Man look hot as *hell* tonight."

"It's not just you. And it's not just tonight." I grip her hands in mine as if I'm about to share the secret of life. "Devin," I swallow, "he's *always* been hot."

"Did something happen between y'all?"

"No." *Yes*. I'm just not sure when it happened for him.

"You mean not yet."

As much as I want to confide to one best friend about the other, now is not the time.

"We can discuss this later, after your honeymoon. Your groom is getting antsy, and I think your mom just cornered him."

She sighs. "Not again."

"What's that all about?"

"Who knows? She's full of piss and vinegar lately. That's why I'm so glad I have your mom as backup."

"Better go save him before she changes his mind about marrying into this."

"Good thinking."

"I am the best."

She hugs me, and all the tension leaves her shoulders.

"I love you."

"You too, Devil."

"See you back at the suite."

twenty-five

THEO

R APT, I WATCH AS LANEY CIRCLES AROUND DEVIN, PULLING A drink out of her hand every few minutes, while talking to the staff. She's taking her job seriously and has barely had time to enjoy the party. Every couple of minutes she searches for me and mouths *'I'm sorry'* to which my reply is the same. A smile and a wink. I'm having a decent time even though I'm in a room full of strangers. Devin's groom, Chase, chatted me up during most of dinner. Even without the new camaraderie with the groom, I've been to enough of my dad's company functions to know how to schmooze. I'm comfortable enough in my element but know Laney's fighting not to sip a drink at this point.

She's nervous behind her smile but running the show like a boss. She looks incredible in her dress, and I'm having a horrible time keeping my eyes off her. Several times tonight, I've imagined lifting that hem and doing wicked things with my mouth. I want to taste her, I want it so much, I've drunk myself into a buzz that has me thinking about all the dirty things I would do to her given the permission.

Though she's playing it cool, I can see the tension in her shoulders. The more I sip, the more I know if I spent five minutes between those gorgeous legs of hers, I could ease that stress. Whiskey is good for my libido.

She saunters over to me just as I receive a fresh drink, takes it from me, and drains half.

"Sorry, I had to have it. I went a record-breaking three hours without a drop. And wow, that tasted way too good."

"I never meant to police you, I just wanted you to prove to yourself that you didn't need it."

"Hey, I need the training. How in the hell am I going to venture out in strange cities, *alone*, if I can't handle a few hundred people around me? I'm glad you push me to do good things for myself. Don't stop, okay?"

"Promise."

"Besides, the drink was for my aching feet. I hate heels."

"Well, you look damn good in them."

Curious eyes lift to mine. "You flirtin' with me, Houseman?"

"I might be."

She worries her lip as I imagine her moan. "See, good whiskey can make you brave."

"I can put this down and show you brave."

"Oh yeah?"

She gazes up at me with need that has me momentarily speechless, so I nod, wishing that I could lean in and just fucking kiss her. But we aren't alone. At all.

"You okay? Need any help?"

"You're sweet to offer, but I can handle it."

"I can see that. You may have missed your calling."

"You think?" She smiles with pride. "I did the table settins' for the dinner. You like them?"

"Very elegant." I didn't notice them, but in my defense, I have a penis, and right now it's pointed straight at her and has been the whole night.

"Well, I've got the hall flowers and five bridal bouquets to finish after this. I'll be here all night. So, you can go when you're ready. I'm sorry. After the wedding, I should be able to give you the attention you deserve."

She's flirting. I don't point it out, because she's nervous and I'm not sure if it's this new shift with us, or the wedding.

I set my drink down on the bar. "I'll help."

"No, no," she frowns. "No way, you being here is plenty. I'm sorry I've been running around and haven't gotten to talk to you much."

"Let me rephrase. Laney, I *want* to help."

Amber eyes search mine. "Really?"

"Yeah, why not?"

"I don't know. Wouldn't you rather be at home working on, whatever you work on all the time and refuse to tell me about?"

I chuckle. "No, I'd rather be helping you."

She lifts to her toes and presses a kiss to my cheek.

"You keep doing that," I say, my voice coated in whiskey and arousal.

"You keep letting me."

I lean down and kiss her cheek before slowly pulling away.

Her eyes widen before she smiles. "What was that for?"

"Existing."

Her breath stutters as I stare down at her with intent. I'm not going to last much longer and from the look in her eyes, she won't either. This has to happen. We owe it to each other to test this chemistry. Not only that, I feel for her. I feel a hell of a lot more than I'm comfortable with for never having kissed her.

"Laney," a short brunette calls, rolling through the door of the party with a suitcase in hand, eyes darting around in panic.

"That's Sarah, one of the bridesmaids. She's runnin' late." Laney looks back to me apologetically. "I have to run through the ceremony with her. It shouldn't take long. Will you wait?"

I grip one of her hands and slide my thumb along the top of it. Her lips part. "You know I will."

She grabs my drink from the bar and finishes it as I lean in and whisper. "You've got this."

When I pull away her eyes close, goosebumps covering her chest. In this moment I would move heaven and Earth to have her alone. Cursing the timing, she murmurs a, "Thank you," to me before she walks away.

#######

Laney: I'm so sorry, it took longer than I expected. They should be serving dessert. When you're done, I'll be in reception, it's just down the hall.
Theo: Got it. Want anything?
Laney: No. I won't fit in my dress tomorrow. It's already too tight.
Theo: Strawberry shortcake?
Laney: Damn you, Houseman. Yes, please.
Theo: On it.
Laney: You are the bees-knees.

Laney's dessert in one hand and my fourth cocktail in the other, I pad down the quiet half of the country club as the wedding guests sound noisily at the entrance, buzzing after the night's festivities while waiting on their cars. Soft country music drifts from the room down the hall. Soundlessly, I open the door and spot Laney at a large eight-top on the other side of the massive room. Heels kicked to the side, she sways—barefoot— back and forth to the music, smelling the half dozen roses in her hand. Holding the door with my foot so I don't alert her to my presence, I lean against it watching as she dances around, cutting stem after stem of fully bloomed pink roses and laying them on a table covered in crystal vases. She sings along to the song, her long hair moving in the opposite direction of the sway of her hips. I'm totally drunk on the sight of her this way. And it has nothing to do with the whiskey warming my insides. Guitar music fills the air as she spins in a melodic circle before tossing a few roses into a vase. She lifts a pitcher of water, pouring it onto the freshly cut stems and spots me, her eyes lighting up.

"You were watching me?"

"Yes," I say unapologetically, moving toward her because there's no way in hell I can't.

"This one has got me feelin' all kind of romantic," she says as I approach. "Alabama."

"What?"

"The song, it's Alabama. *Old school* country."

"Ah."

She wrinkles her nose. "Do you like it?"

"I like that you like it."

She sighs, lifting the pitcher and dividing the water into the vases. "I'll never convert you."

"No, you won't, but I'll listen to it if it makes you happy."

She pauses her pour, her eyes lifting to mine. "What a sweet thing to say."

"Speaking of sweets," I smile, lifting her dessert. "Take a load off and eat this. It's incredible."

"I know. I'm the one who made sure it was on the menu." She darts her eyes around the hall. "I've still got so much to do."

"Laney, I'll stay until it's done." I set her dessert and my drink down on the table and gesture for her to sit.

She stutters on nervously. "I just, I was gonna get the bridesmaids to help a little, but Devin is a hot mess express and well—"

"Laney, I'll stay."

"I can handle it, I just—"

"Ask me for help, Laney."

She looks up at me pensively. "What?"

"Ask. Me. For. *Help.*"

She blows out a harsh breath through lush lips. "Will you help me?"

"Yes, now," I pull out the chair in front of her, "sit."

"Gah," she says, ogling her dessert. "This looks so good."

I tug her into the chair and cut into the dessert, bringing the fork to her mouth. She takes the offered bite, and as soon as it hits her tongue, her eyes close. "Exactly," I murmur, leaning in. I catch the goosebumps that spread on her skin as I scoot her chair closer to the table.

"T-thank you."

Moving to the other side of the table, I sit behind the waiting pile of sachets. "So, I'm taking it we're replacing the insides of these with this?" I raise an insulated bag full of filler.

"Exactly, but the ribbon is hard to—" she gapes at me as I untie the ribbon without ruining its integrity. "How in the hell did you figure that out?"

"I helped with one of my sister's friends when they got married. I was stuck doing the bitch work."

"It's not *bitch* work."

"You know what I mean. It's tedious work for a *guy,* and you know how my sisters love to torture me."

I quickly swap out the sachets as she forks in her dessert in record time.

"You eat like you're in the military," I chuckle. Her cheeks heat, and I guffaw. "You're embarrassed? I've seen you eat seven tacos in five minutes."

"Way to make me feel like a pig, Houseman."

"I love the way you eat, it's adorable."

"Well, I promised Max we'd cut back," she says around a mouthful, "*two* months ago."

"You're perfect," I declare, carefully fastening another ribbon around the sachets that will no doubt be discarded into the trash this time tomorrow. "It's such a waste. All this work and no one will really remember it."

When she doesn't answer, I look up to see her staring at me.

She clears her throat. "I disagree. I remember the details, and I think that's what makes these things special."

"If you say so," I say, waving a sachet in her direction.

"I *like* busy work." She stands and begins to clear thorns and leaves from a few roses in record time using simple kitchen shears.

"Where did you learn to do that?"

"Job number eight. It was my favorite. I wasn't fired from that one, either. They closed down, went bankrupt. I don't know why I didn't try to find a job as a florist anywhere else, I loved it. A hell of a lot more than repo."

"So, go back to it."

"I might," she says thoughtfully. "I really do love it. Look," she measures the flower length against the vase. "See, you have to measure the stem against the container, so it hangs slightly over the lip and then cut them longer moving inward. That's what helps the presentation. Too much off and you don't have enough stem to work with. It's the cut that makes all the difference. Most people don't know that."

"Fascinatin'."

"Smart ass."

"You love it."

"I do," she says softly. "I really do."

Our eyes meet, and I see that same blush creep up her neck.

"Some people think flowers are a waste of money, but I think they are a real gift. They have these short life spans where they brighten up everything around them."

"What's your favorite?"

She hesitates. "Ah, can't decide. Don't you smile at me!"

I raise my palms in surrender. "It's just not surprising."

"I know. What can I say? It's my one true weakness."

"Speaking of indecision, the next time you feel like texting me to ask me to Target, or Walmart, or anywhere money for product is exchanged, the answer is no. *Forever*."

She waves a rose in my direction. "I saw the tears in your eyes last time we were in electronics. But I suspect it was because they were playing *Finding Nemo*." She sniffs a flower to try and hide her smile.

I point an accusing finger her way. "I have allergies."

"I know. Okay. Okay, I know how bad it is shopping with me," she grumbles.

"Don't get upset, I was mostly kidding. Well no, I mean the part about not going shopping with you ever again. I really mean that."

"Shut up," she says in false aggravation. "Let's get to work, Houseman."

"I'm all yours." I watch her carefully and love the way my statement blankets her.

Three hours later, I'm cracking my neck as she finishes the details on each table, fidgeting with her arrangements before wiping off any fallen debris from the crisp white linens. I stand in the center of the dance floor and check out her work.

"It's perfect."

"Really?" She asks, looking around wistfully.

"Yeah, really. Come here."

She walks toward my offered hand and grabs it when she reaches me, and I pull her to me in declaration, kicking any amount of respectable friend-zone space to the fucking curb.

"See," I slide my arm around her back, lifting our entwined hands into position before I begin swaying to a smooth, feminine cover of "Wicked Game". "This will be their view."

"It's awesome," she murmurs.

"It really is."

"I'm…"

"What?" I whisper, loving the feel of her in my arms.

"I'm proud." There's a smile in her voice. "For a second there, I was worried I wouldn't pull it off."

"You did. This looks pro."

"Wow," she says giddily. "I hope they think so too."

"They will."

She turns to stare up at me. "Thank you. I would have been here twice as long without your help."

"My pleasure, Ms. Cox."

"You aren't a bad dancer."

"I'm an excellent dancer."

She grins up at me. "And so modest."

"That too."

"You could use another slice of humble pie."

"Got my fork ready, where's it at?"

I see it then, her intent. She's giving me the window, and I'm about to jump through it with both feet.

"Laney!" A voice calls from the entrance of the hall, and we both glare in the direction of the interruption.

"Devin snuck some shooters into her purse somehow. She's in her dress, drunk, on the balcony, singing "Bohemian Rhapsody" at the top of her lungs."

Laney looks to me perplexed.

"Go," I say, hanging my head. "I'll see you tomorrow."

I still haven't let go of her, and she hasn't moved either.

"It's okay if you—"

"Go. It's Devin. I was quite fond of her until a minute ago. See you tomorrow."

She smiles. "Okay."

Reluctantly I pull my arm away from around her and step away, kissing the back of her hand.

"Night, Laney."

"Night, Theo."

#lastnightasasinglelady #shesgoingoutwithabang #dontdrinkandIdo #policeweresummoned #handcuffswerestolen #donttrythisathome #mybestfriendswedding #livingmyrealestlife

Grannism—If he's paying attention to the right things, you'll rarely ever have to give directions.

twenty-six

THEO

"**B**Y THE POWER VESTED IN ME BY THE GREAT STATE OF Texas, I now pronounce you man and wife. Chase, you may kiss your bride."

"Ahhhh," Laney shouts out enthusiastically when they kiss, which earns her a few laughs, mine included. Laney tosses her flowers up in the air, and the rest of the bridesmaids follow just as the photographer clicks the shutter. Her infectious excitement for her best friend is both audible and palpable.

I'm so fucked.

The minute she stepped into view down the aisle in her pink tulle dress and shiny new boots, the feeling in my chest overwhelmed me. And then she'd searched the sea of faces until she found mine, her smile beaming brighter as she winked at me. It was when she reached the rest of the waiting bridal party that I noticed the best man ogling her with clear intent. Immediately, I wanted to wipe the smug smirk off his lips with the way he was objectifying her.

I could hardly blame him, she was radiant; her hair in soft curls, half up, half down, pink gems and diamonds glittering around her neck, resting on her flawless olive skin. And those lips, dear God, those shiny pink lips. But it was the light in her amber eyes when she spotted me that kept the lump in my throat through the entire ceremony.

The need to go to her, to claim her, is blinding me. I've always considered myself a level-headed guy, but as of this moment, I can't fathom a good enough reason not to go to her with all the confessions waiting on my tongue.

Swallowing, I do my best to keep idle when she starts her retreat down the aisle. When she gets to where I stand, she stops, holding her arm out, *for me* and I gravitate towards her, and wrap her arm around mine, making the rest of the trip down with her. When we're past the threshold of the double doors, she turns to me, lifting on her heels, eyes piercing mine before kissing my cheek. I'm just about to speak when she bolts, running to tackle Chase and Devin into a group hug.

"I love you guys so much!" She squeals as they hug her tightly before backing away. And then she's back to business and barking orders. "Go, you have about ten minutes before the photographer finds you." She grabs Devin's bouquet and turns to the bridesmaids. "Okay ladies, line up and look alive. It's picture time."

I stand to the side as they all file out and Laney looks back to me, jerking her head toward the open door. "You coming?"

"I'll wait here."

She frowns. "Sure?"

"Of course. Go."

"K. See you in a bit."

That 'bit' turns into an hour or more as the reception goes from a classy cocktail hour to a free-for-all. Everyone in attendance seems to have brought their all-nighter 'A' game. The whole of the party is buzzing, overly affectionate and dancing like they're in a night club. It's easily the best wedding I've ever been to.

I've only seen Laney a few times, and each time our eyes connect, it's lightning to the chest, a crackle of energy passing between us that I will no longer ignore. She looks so fucking beautiful that I'm constantly searching for her, only able to steal glimpses of everything I want, and just as quickly she's gone. When the space is too much to take, I crane my neck searching the raging party for any sign of her. Relief comes when the DJ starts the wail of a siren to introduce the groomsmen. They all bound in from the double doors, lining up at the side of the groom who stands waiting on the floor. Grinning, because I know what's coming from watching countless years of videos, I lift my camera to the entrance when Fergie's "London Bridge" starts to ring out, the heavy bass thrumming throughout the ballroom.

"This should be good," Mark—a close friend of the groom's family—that I've been chatting with says, just as his hater date chimes in. "This is *so* overdone." The double doors open, and I see Devin with her bridesmaids in V formation behind her. I'm nervous for all of them, until they collectively take their first few steps, causing every jaw in the room to drop.

Devin owns the floor, mouthing the dirty lyrics to her groom, her eyes only for him, her dress lifted slightly as she shakes her ass, making her way toward him. She looks stunning, and I can only imagine how he's feeling watching her.

"Ladies and Gentlemen, Mrs. Chase Hart!"

The crowd goes apeshit as Laney comes into better view behind her, and they all dance in sync like they've been doing it for years. She looks sexy as hell manipulating her body left and right, jutting her boots out to carry her sway. My heart painfully pounds in my chest as I watch them all dance like it's their fucking job.

"Okay, I'll admit, this is good," Hatorade says next to me.

"Yeah, it is," I whisper, unable to rip my eyes off the sexy wet dream in boots. The only girl in the world as far as I'm concerned.

"Ladies and gentlemen, the maid of honor, Elaine Renee Cox!"

I grin because I know she hates her full name, but it doesn't seem to bother her as she shimmies in step with the rest of the bridal party as their names are called out one by one.

When Devin finally makes it to Chase, he's waiting with open arms, and she dives into them. He devours her mouth, leading the rest of the room to cheers while something inside me snaps and I make a beeline for the maid of honor.

Laney sees me just before I reach her, and I grab her hand, leading her toward the exit.

"Oh my God, my dress is tucked in my panties, isn't it? I thought I felt too much air down there," she says, fumbling behind to keep up with me.

Unable to manage a word, I drag her through the endless crowd of buzzing Texans.

"Theo, where are we going, what's wrong?"

Outside the reception, in the hall, I pin her against the wall, grip her chin, and hear her breath catch just before I crush my mouth to hers. It's a bold statement, and I'm making it in front of the drunker half of the wedding with zero fucks to give. As far as I'm concerned, the minute our lips touch nothing can touch us.

Capturing her surprise and using it, I slide my tongue against hers, and she opens, letting me have full access while she fists the top of my jacket, to pull me in. Relief covers me briefly, and I kiss her my confession. I kiss her long and hard to show her everything I've been hiding, everything I'm feeling. I kiss her so deeply, I'm unsure if I'll ever be able to tear myself away. She clings to me, going limp as I plunge my tongue in again, and again, my heart soaring, my head surprisingly calm as I grow unbearably hard. She rips at my hair, kissing me back with equal fervor as I hoist up her leg a little grinding into her to show her just how much I want her.

When I finally pull away, I brave a look down at her and see wide-eyed wonder.

"I won't apologize for doing that."

"No apology necessary," she says, her voice raspy, filled with lust.

"I should have done that a long time ago."

"I wanted you to, really." She darts a nervous glance over my shoulder. "I'm glad you did it when you did."

I bend my head so we're eye level, my gaze intent on hers. "I'm sensing a but—"

"My mom, she's uh, standing like four feet away." I drop my head to her shoulder and can't help my chuckle.

"Fuck." Turning my head to buy time due to the tent in my pants, I see an older replica of Laney clutching her chest like she's expecting her heart to fail any second. Grabbing Laney's hand with one of my own, I adjust my angry cock with the other a split second before I turn to meet her mother's gaze, her brows reaching her hairline. She's probably never seen her daughter get kissed like that. And I'm praying to God that her eyes remain on my face.

"Mom," Laney's voice squeaks as we approach. "This is Theo Houseman."

She narrows her eyes on her daughter. "Just the friend, huh?"

"It's, uh," her eyes focus on me the second I interrupt, "Nice to finally meet you, Mrs. Cox."

"You just massaged my daughter's tonsils with your

tongue, Mr. Houseman, and you're wearing her lip gloss. Call me, Deidra."

I wipe the shine from my lips. "Yes, ma'am."

"So," she says, shaking her head as if to get the illicit image of us out. "Do you kiss all your friends this way?"

"No, ma'am."

"I see." She trains her gaze on her daughter. "Laney's had nothing but good things to say about you."

"I'm really fond of her, as well."

"That's evident."

"Momma!"

"Sorry, ma'am, in her defense, that kiss was on me."

"I'm pretty sure you weren't kissing yourself."

"Mom, I'm about four seconds from leapfrogging you out that door," Laney's face turns a shade of red I've never seen.

A silent stand-off ensues. The force is strong with these two.

"Just chill out on the PDA until I make it home, please," she says brushing past us to grab some champagne and opening the hall door. "Nice to meet you, Theo."

"You too, ma'—Deidra."

She eyes us both with expectation. "I'll expect you at dinner next week."

"Looking forward to it," I say, just as the door drags closed behind her and Laney and I burst into laughter.

#herbestfriendswedding #getdowngirlgoheadgetdown #justmarried #cantlookaway #thisgirlisfire #livingourrealestlife

Grannism—Don't smoke, but if you do,
make sure the sex is worthy of it.

twenty-seven

LANEY

I'M POSITIVE IF I HAD MY CHOICE OF DREAMS TO PLAY OUT, IT would be the one I'm currently living in. Theo has his arms wrapped around me, and we're on the dance floor mere minutes after Devin and Chase left for their honeymoon. My arms around his neck, I remain powerless to the look in his eyes. All I want is to feel his lips again. But we've been buying time since he'd kissed me in the hall, trying to keep it PG for my mother's sake while never straying too far from the other. We'd kept a respectable distance in the last few hours until minutes ago when Theo wordlessly plucked me away from a conversation with the bridesmaids and led me to the dance floor to finally grant me my two-step. And I must admit, he wasn't bad at it. The music changes to slow and sultry as we dance entranced, no longer able to avoid the pull.

"Small talk seems stupid right now," I whisper heatedly.

"It's not us."

"No, it's not," I say as his thumb caresses my back.

"Are you nervous?" He asks, warm brown eyes penetrating mine.

I run my fingers through the damp hair on the nape of his neck. "No. Maybe a little. This just got heavy, didn't it?"

He bites his lower lip briefly and nods. "Yes."

"What are we doing?"

"I don't know. Do you want to stop?"

"Take me," I say without hesitation.

His brows lift. "Take you?"

"Take me, right now, to wherever you're planning on sleeping tonight."

The ride home has been silent, the air between us thick with gunpowder so heavy I can taste it. The longer he drives, the more my hunger builds. Fingers threaded, we exchange longing glances before I finally give into temptation and guide his hand to the hem of my dress. He takes his cue, sliding it up my legs as I sit back in the seat, my chest rising and falling in need. Studying his profile, he seems infuriatingly calm while my heart bangs against my chest in anticipation. But I have no doubt he's thinking along the same lines when he brakes at a stoplight and leans over, reaching for me. I meet him halfway, our lips locking, his tongue thrusting, devouring, as he slides a warm palm up my thigh and brushes his fingers along the side of my panties. "Lift your dress," he orders gruffly into my mouth, and I obey pulling the tulle away to give him better access.

Moaning into his mouth, I grip his hair and kiss him eagerly. Fingers exploring, he slides them beneath the elastic of my underwear to find me embarrassingly soaked.

He breaks our kiss, when the light turns green and slams on the gas, rocketing us down the empty road leading to his neighborhood. He pulls his fingers away, brushing his knuckles along my center before roughly moving them to the side and dipping a thick digit inside me. My back bows from the seat as I gasp out his name, gripping his hand, urging him for more as a groan leaves his throat.

"Theo," I whimper, spreading wider as we fly down the street.

He adds another finger, cupping the entirety of my sex, leaning forward in his seat to drive them deeper.

"Theo, hurry," I murmur, lost in his touch.

He steers with one hand while driving me out of my mind with the other. The friction of his palm causing me to start quaking next to him. I feel so out of control I grind against his hand. My orgasm close.

He slows his fingers and shakes his head. "Not yet."

"Theo!"

"Fuck," he groans, taking another turn and parking at the curb.

We collide over his console with weeks of pent-up sexual tension playing out through our tangled tongues. We're both so out of control that I can't tell who's moaning what. Hands grappling, I cover his thick, stone cock in his pants and he jerks at the contact.

"We're only a minute away," he says as I bite his bottom lip.

"I can't wait."

"Laney—"

"Please, Theo, touch me."

"Damn," he says, slipping his hand under my dress before moving my panties to the side and pushing his fingers into me. I damn near scream in his mouth in welcome.

Shaking in his hold, he plunges his tongue as he twists his fingers, running them along my G, back and forth until I detonate when he strokes my clit with this thumb. Crushing his mouth to mine, he captures the first of my orgasm on his tongue and then breaks our kiss to watch me come apart, my breath leaving in short gasps. He grips my chin and savors every second while his fingers milk every ounce of pleasure from me. Covered in sweat, I sink back into my seat spent as he pulls his soaked fingers from my panties and runs one of them along his bottom lip before licking it clean. It's so damn sexy, I can't resist pulling him in for another kiss. He delivers, thrusting slowly, intensely, all the while re-stoking my fire.

Lifting the hand he just pleasured me with, I kiss his palm repeatedly, and then turn it over and press and hold my lips to the back of it. He pulls it away to cup my cheek, reading my thoughts as I sit stunned in my seat. "Hold on, Laney," he murmurs before kissing me chastely on the mouth and adjusting back in his seat to drive.

I gaze at him in a stupor as he takes the two streets to get to his house. Thankfully the driveway is empty, and I'm grateful for the privacy.

He exits the car and comes to my side, offering me his hand. Stepping out into the cool air, I lean into him, my forehead against his shoulder. We both know what's about to happen, and some part of me still fears the after, no matter how incredible the moment feels. I want more, but I would rather go without than lose him. It's fear that has me shaking in his arms. I've never felt so much in my life at once. Passion, lust, fear, ache, need, hope.

He again reads my thoughts, his voice gruff with want. "We don't have to. I would never ask—"

"Theo," I say on a plea, pulling him tightly to me. He kisses my temple before he leads me through the front door and up his stairs.

twenty-eight

LANEY

THE DOOR CLOSES BEHIND ME, AND I STAND IN THE MIDDLE of his bedroom at the foot of his bed. I'm so turned on there's no way to play it off like he doesn't have this paralyzing effect on me. No man has ever looked at me the way he did after he kissed me. Silent behind me, I move to face him but am stopped by a gentle hand pushing the hair away from my neck just before his lips descend. Moaning, I sink into his hold as he gently trails his soft kiss and tongue covering every inch of my neck from one side to the other. He takes his time as I rub my thighs together, the throb between becoming unbearable.

"Theo," I murmur as he continues to lick and suck, the pressure slowly increasing until I'm swept up in his worship, my legs useless beneath me. "I-it's too quiet, and I have a feeling I'm about to get loud."

"We're alone."

"I know…but still."

His chest hits me from behind as he exhales a chuckle that causes an eruption of goosebumps across my chest and down my arms. "Hold on. Don't move."

"No chance of that," I whisper, my voice unrecognizable. I can still feel his touch, *everywhere*.

In seconds light music fills the air, and he's back, his grip tighter, as he resumes his seduction. He's playing me perfectly as he gently pulls at my skin with his teeth before he soothes his soft bite with the eager laving of his tongue. I'm so wet I would be embarrassed if I couldn't feel the hard bulge at my back. He brushes his stiff length along the small of it, and I moan in response as he bites the side of my neck, gripping my hair and gently pulling to open me further.

"I've been wanting to kiss this neck for so long," his words come out in a hungry rush as he lifts my dress, cupping me while pressing his cock in harder, "this is always hard, just from wanting you." He slips a finger inside my panties and slides the pad of it along my clit, twisting my neck back to claim my mouth. Tongues dancing, he expertly toys with my center, rubbing me with the perfect amount of pressure so that I'm whimpering in his mouth. And then he's on his knees, taking off my boots, one by one before sliding warm hands up my thighs. His lips are everywhere, on my calves, the skin on the back of my knees before trailing to the tops of my thighs, and then I feel his breath between my legs a second before he places a tongue-filled kiss to my clit. My knees go weak as he works beneath my dress, licking me over my panties with mastered precision, my heart thundering as another orgasm builds.

"Theo."

He moves my panties to the side a breath before I feel the long swipe of his tongue.

"Theo!"

"Just a taste," he murmurs, his tongue flicking out again as I try to remain balanced on shaky legs. And then he's at my back, encasing me, my stuttered breaths coming fast. After the slow descent of my zipper, my dress pools at my feet and I'm bare—save my underwear—as he turns me to face him, his mouth again on mine, his hunger evident with every thrust of his tongue.

That's when I fold in his arms until he sweeps me up in his embrace and deposits me in the center of his bed. I feel completely coveted, worshiped, and it's addicting. Instinctively, my hands go up, tangle in his hair and I pull him to me kissing him with undeniable need.

When he pulls away, he stares down at me with a question.

"Yes, yes, God, yes," I cry out, lifting to help him shed his jacket and tie before I start to work his shirt buttons one by one before we collectively discard it to the floor. I trail my fingers along the hard wall of his chest, stroking the small smattering of hair in the center before covering his arms in my touch. Though lean, he's well-defined, subtle curves of muscle accentuate his biceps. Studying him is an easy chore, his long wavy hair, dark eyes, a slightly wide Roman nose, sensual full lips. He rests on his feet, hovering above me in his bed.

"You are so beautiful."

He traces my nipple with his finger and then leans in to capture it with his mouth.

"So perfect," he murmurs, his eyes alight with lust as he lifts them to mine.

"Theo, I want you inside. I want you everywhere."

His eyes darken with his command. "Say it again, Laney."

"I want you, Theo, so much."

He reaches over to his bedside drawer and pulls out a condom as I unbutton his slacks and free him from his briefs. Mouth watering, I stare down at his cock and stroke the tip of him with my thumb. His eyes close, and I rise up to kiss his chest, his neck and pull him back to my mouth. He tastes me thoroughly before pulling away and stilling my hand.

"I want this to last."

I nod as he unwraps me, slowly peeling my underwear away, while stormy eyes pierce mine. It's all I can do to keep from pushing him back on the bed and filling myself with him.

He spreads my legs, his eyes roaming appreciatively along my body, soaking me in. "I've thought about this, about you like this, so many times." He strokes my skin, my sides with his fingers. Surprising me, he lifts me by the neck and brings me to his mouth, kissing the life out of me before gently laying me back against his pillow. He rises then and admires me from where he stands toeing off his shoes and socks before revealing himself entirely, shedding his boxers along with his pants before they collectively fall to the floor.

He's beautiful, and the look that he's giving me is slowly taking my breath away as it intensifies, until I'm suffocating in his rapt attention. I'd give up air to keep this feeling. I'd give anything to keep it.

Once he's rolled on the condom, I reach for him from where I lay, dying for his lips, his mouth, his kiss, his intoxicating touch. Fully naked, he separates my knees, his warm hands exploring as he keeps his gaze locked on mine. "We do this, there's no going back."

I don't have time to respond when he slides both hands from my calves to my center before he dips and nudges my clit with his nose.

"Oh my God," I say, grabbing the pillow next to me to bite into it. Licking me furiously, he reaches up and jerks it from my grip. Speaking between licks.

"I." Lick. "Want." Lick. "To." Lick. "Hear." Lick, lick, nudge. "You."

I'm so close to crying at the feel of his mouth. It's so effortless on his part, like a vibration as he laps me up with such precision, I erupt in moans, thighs squeezing his head as I rip at his hair. He continues to suck until I'm a pool of pants and tears. Once satisfied, he resumes his intoxicating exploration of my body cupping my breasts before laving each nipple, trailing his kiss up to my neck before he settles between my thighs and claims my mouth.

"I want you so much," he murmurs. My whole body responds with the arch of my back, and I greedily suck his tongue before he envelops a peaked nipple into his mouth.

"I'm so ready, please," I whisper hoarsely. "Now, Theo, *please*."

He lifts onto a forearm before positioning himself at my entrance, his eyes catching fire, his mouth parting as he slowly begins to press in. I couldn't look away if I wanted to, the twist of his features is too beautiful. He's both long and thick, and I can feel every inch of him as he slowly thrusts in, his eyes pooling to a liquid black. It's then I realize he's shaking.

He's just as nervous as I am.

He thrusts into me, stealing every ounce of breath from my body.

"Oh shit," he grits out before glancing down to weigh my expression.

"Just move," I gasp out. "Just move. We can do it again. We can stay here forever. Theo, move."

And he does. He buries himself to the hilt pressing his forehead to mine.

Nothing in my life has ever felt better, and I whisper as much as he tries to steady himself.

"Move," I urge, locking my legs around him. Rearing back, he presses in harder, and we both cry out to the other.

I bite into his shoulder just as he grunts out, "Jesus, Laney."

He eases out and back in, as I stretch around him until he's fully seated. And then we're moving, I meet his thrusts, our skin slapping while we exchange hungry kisses and moans. Our mouths seal together as the hunger catches up with the both of us. Chests colliding, we combust into a fit of need. Grappling with the unbelievable feel of him, I can't control my breaths, my moans, I can't control anything, so I let go and feel everything.

"I can't," he pants into my mouth, "hold off."

"Come," I urge him as we collide over and over until we can no longer take, but give in.

He comes long and loud, his features pulling, his mouth beautifully parted, eyes filled with wonder before he collapses on top of me.

Legs wrapped around him, I pluck at his hair with one hand and rub the expanse of his back with the other. I've never felt so close to anyone as I do in this moment.

"That was perfect," I murmur. "But you already know that. We get an A plus for chemistry, Houseman."

I can feel his smile against my chest. "Am I crushing you?" He asks, trying to move off me. I lock him to me with my legs. "Stay."

Content, I feel his every exhale, the slow of his shake, his pounding heart, and the fuzzy warmth spreading through my limbs. We lie there breathless and sated for a few minutes before I speak up.

"What an idiot," I murmur into his hair.

"Who?"

"Nora. She's the dumbest woman on Earth and thank the Lort for that."

He pulls away chuckling despite my protest and stares down at me. "It wouldn't have been this good with her."

"No?" I ask with a smile as he gazes down at me with surety.

"No, that was all *us*," he says, covering me with warm hands in both caress and worship. "So soft," he says before pressing a kiss between my breasts.

A melody fills the room as I stroke his skin, and the pads of his fingers brush along the sides of my body.

"I like this song. What is it?"

"John Lennon. 'Oh My Love.'"

We sink into the lull as he gently strokes every part of me with explorative fingers.

"It's pretty."

"It is. These are Yoko days."

"Oh?"

"Yeah. Most people think she was the anti-Christ, but you know the song, "Imagine" that he's most remembered for?"

"Yeah, I know it."

"Well, he got the idea for it from one of her poetry books."

"Really?"

"Yep. She inspired him. No one really understood them, but it didn't matter, and they didn't give a shit either, because they understood each other."

"Kind of like us."

He lifts his head along with the side of his mouth. "Yeah, a little like us." He leans in pressing a kiss to my lips. "I'm going to clean up." I mourn the temporary loss of his weight, but admire his naked ass as he walks to his bathroom. I hear the telltale sign of the disposal of the condom and water run before he slips back in bed and pulls me to him, so my leg is hooked across his stomach. My head rests on his chest as he pushes the hair away from my face with lazy fingers. He stares down at me wordless, and I tilt my head to look up at him.

"Well, things certainly took a drastic change today."

"Mmm."

"Mmm?"

"Mm-hmm."

"Not much for words after sex, huh?"

"That appears to be the case. But in about two minutes, we're going to have sex again. QT," he says, pressing his fingers to my lips. "Save your strength."

I giggle into his chest. "No complaints here. Guessing now's your chance to make up for lost time?"

"Only with you," he assures.

"I won't complain about that, either."

Understanding passes between us before he slowly leans in to take my lips. At the last minute, I turn my head, denying him, which earns me a scowl.

Biting my lip, I grip his growing erection in my hand and quirk a brow. "Not where I want to kiss you, Houseman." I lick my lips and widen my eyes. "My turn."

He groans, filling my hand with the impulsive thrust of his hips as I push away from his chest, blazing tongue-filled kisses down his body, my hair trailing behind me. He grips my locks in his hand, moving them out of the way to stare down at me with wonder.

I pump him in my hand, and his eyes hood. The silky skin of his dick over the rock-hard muscle has the pulse returning between my legs as I envelop him in my mouth. His body jerks at the feel of it while he traces my face in a loving caress with his hands. Licking his delicious girth with my tongue, I cup his sack as he hisses through his teeth.

He lets out a harsh breath, his eyes soaking up the intimate act as his hands continue to lovingly stroke my face. I take my time, licking and sucking him, taking special care to press my thumb below his sack, which makes him jump in surprise before something like a growl leaves his lips. The more I suck, the more attention he lavishes with his hands, and I love how he makes me feel worshiped while I'm the one with the job to do.

With one last pull, I release him from my locked jaw with a pop and lift my attention to where he lays above to weigh his reaction. I'm met with a small smile, lust-filled curious eyes and the gentle stroke of his knuckles on my cheek before he traces my bottom lip with his thumb.

"That felt so good."

Massaging his thighs, I dart my tongue out to lick him from root to tip and watch his eyes flare.

"I'll never get that picture out of my head."

Pumping him with my hand, I massage his leg before drawing him back fully into my mouth. I haven't a plan past wanting to keep that look on his face for as long as possible.

"Laney," he rasps out, slowing my movement with gentle hands. "I want you again, is that okay?"

All I can do is nod. He reaches over and grabs another condom from the strip on his nightstand, and I take it from him, slowly rolling it on. We both watch his cock pulse inside the latex, ready, before I rise above him and position myself. He grips my hips, exhaling harshly, features twisting beautifully while I sink down on top of him.

Emotions running rampant with the look of awe on his face, I shut my eyes just as he whispers my name. If he sees what I feel in them, I'm done for.

He traces my nipple with his finger before cupping my face. "Laney."

Bracing myself for impact, I slowly open them and my whole body shudders. He's with me, utterly and completely lost in our connection.

Filled to the brink, I lean toward him to ease some of the discomfort, and my hair falls into his face. He watches my every movement, rapt, eager, the lust-drunk look in his eyes my new drug.

I can't get enough of his reaction to me, and I pray it never changes.

"You feel so damn good," he murmurs thrusting up and holding my hips so I'm on the verge. I've had good sex, dirty sex, but I've never had *this* kind of sex. My emotions are everywhere, foreign and addicting.

Panicking, I ride him faster, my heart grappling with my new reality. Gripping the back of my neck, Theo pulls me an inch from his lips, forcing me back into this moment with him. "Trust yourself," he whispers hoarsely, "trust *me*."

He seals our mouths, capturing my relief, and I get lost.

twenty-nine

THEO

W E MADE LOVE, AS CHEESY AS IT SOUNDS, BUT THERE isn't another word for it, not at all. It wasn't sex, and it was far too intimate to be fucking. Well, maybe the third or fourth time could be considered fucking. Those were more porn than promise, but neither of us had any objections. I'd fumbled through the first time lighting her up and thanked God endless years of foreplay without payoff had actually done me a shitload of good. Laney's moans had directed the rest. And some of the direction had come from her sweet, yet filthy mouth which I'd kissed a thousand times last night. And it's a night I'll remember for the rest of my life.

"Morning," she says softly from the entrance of the kitchen.

I turn to see her looking around the house for other signs of life.

"We're alone until tonight."

"Yeah?" She asks sheepishly.

"Yeah, have a seat, I'm making French toast."

"Smells so good."

Her cheeks go hot, a crimson blush settling over her skin as she makes her way toward me.

"We were both sober last night," I say, pulling her to me

when she gets close enough, running a finger along her cheek. "So, what's with the blush?"

"I don't know."

I lean down and take her lips, and she kisses me back with urgent fervor. Feeling her unease, I kiss her thoroughly before I pull away and catch her eyes. "Stop it."

"Stop what?"

"This doesn't have to be weird."

"*You're* making it weird."

"You're uncomfortable. I don't want that."

She looks up at me with anxious eyes. "Then you shouldn't have left me in bed wondering if you were freaking out."

"Shit, I'm sorry. I wanted to fix you breakfast. And clearly, *I'm* not freaking out."

She nods toward the platter of toast. "You made an entire bread bag of French toast for *two* people."

"Watch me eat half."

"You're sure that's all?" She asks, her eyes darting around.

"Laney," I turn off the burner, leaning against the cabinet and pull her to stand between my legs. "I will never, *ever* regret it. Ever."

"K."

"I wanted it to happen. Have wanted it to happen for a while now."

"Me too," she says, finally meeting my eyes.

"I want to do it again," I tell her honestly and her face lights up with a grin. "*Often.*"

"Me too."

"Good. That's settled. Now, powdered sugar on top or no?"

"Yes, and then some," she says tucking a napkin in *my* T-shirt before sitting down with a raised fork. "Let's do this."

######

LANEY

Theo guides me down to his basement, which is pitch dark. "Is this where you introduce me to your roommates who like to bind and torture for funsies?"

"Cute." He flips on the light when we hit the landing, and my jaw drops. "Holy shit!"

The basement spans the width of the entire house, and there are thousands of dollars in instruments organized throughout.

"Okay, what in the hell is this? Are you storing the band's equipment?"

"No." He shakes his head with a grin.

"So, you're in a band too?"

"Nope."

"Fess up, sir. Who do these belong to?" I walk through the room full of brass, several different drum sets, including a pair of bongos and every string instrument imaginable.

"You're always asking what instrument I play." He shrugs.

"You play *all* of these?"

"Not yet. I'm up to eight. Prince played thirteen. I'm determined to beat him."

"This is insane."

"I'm a music major," he crosses his arms. "Why does this surprise you?"

I stop at the short piano in the far corner of the room and press a key. "I guess because you didn't tell me *any* of this." I narrow my eyes. "Why?"

"Because this is personal to me. I don't play much for an

audience unless I really know what I'm doing. And this is where I work."

"This is your job?"

"I run an app-based business selling ditties, you know, jingles for commercials and other promotional stuff."

"You what?"

"Yeah, it's pretty easy, really. I either compose my own or take an old track and mix it up with something new."

"So, you're a musical prodigy?"

"I wouldn't go that far. I spend a lot of time on this. I was playing piano as a toddler. I mean I'm pretty good at most instruments, but I like to consider myself more of a musical architect. I plan on doing scores for movies and more advertising stuff when I graduate and can give it the time."

"Do you sell a lot of ditties?"

He chuckles, and I scowl.

"Enough with the accent bullshit, answer me. You've been living a double life."

He sucks his lip into his mouth, and it's so sexy I forgive him.

"Honda is one of my best customers. I could probably get you a discount."

"I refuse to indulge in that conversation. Now fess up. Do you sell a lot of your *songs*?"

"I do okay. I just sold an entire library."

"You're serious?"

"Yeah. It's paid for most of these." He gestures to the room full of instruments. I giggle and point to one standing next to the wall. "You're going to learn to play the harp?"

"Yeah." He gives me a sheepish grin. "That's why I don't let my roommates down here, I'll get my man card revoked."

"They are morons and this, this is...highly impressive, sir.

Seriously, this is a much better plan than my multiple lines of income."

He chuckles. "And I don't get shot at."

"That was *once,*" I glance around still shocked by his revelation. "So, which do you play in the Grand Band?"

"Not telling."

"Oh, come on! You know I could probably find out online."

"But you won't."

Surveying the makeshift office next to his piano I see a desktop, a laptop and a bunch of other computer equipment.

"What's all this?"

"This is where I mix it up."

"I'm going to need a demonstration."

His eyes light up. "I might have cooked something up for you."

"Really?" I rub my hands together before I climb up onto his piano crossing my legs. His eyes flare as he studies me sprawled half-naked in his PBS T-shirt and panties.

He takes a seat at the bench gently moving my crossed legs to rest on the edge of the piano but not before pressing a gentle kiss to my ankle. It's when his fingers start to move expertly along the keys that my jaw drops. The more he plays, the more my breath picks up, and my thoughts drift back to last night. He had completely and utterly wrecked me with the way he'd taken me, and I was already dying for more.

Did I know this man at all?

In the two months we've been friends I realize just how much of a mystery he still is. If last night was any sign of what I had to look forward to, I'm all too eager to learn more. I'm already a puddle of want just inches from his skilled fingers. I study him closely; taking in the thick black of his lashes, the almond shape of his eyes, the sleek lines of his scruff-covered jaw, the talented full lips that had me moaning his name for hours, his poise on the bench, and the confidence with which he plays. It's all too alluring, and I'm practically salivating as I gaze on at him.

"Something is telling me your current thoughts are not wholesome in nature," he says before looking up at me confirming his suspicions.

"This is actually very sexy, Houseman. You could've cured your abstinence much sooner by using this tactic. It's one hell of an aphrodisiac. Hell, you could have had coeds everywhere throwing their panties at your feet."

"I don't want *them*," he says, leaning in, his gaze unwavering, penetrating, to make his point. He continues to play as I let his sentiment warm me, slightly overwhelmed by the secret he kept. He's not just good, he's incredible.

"I swear, Houseman, you surprise me at every turn."

His fingers dance along the keys effortlessly before he pulls them away. "This isn't what I wanted to play for you."

"Well, come on then, show me what you've got."

He leans in past my legs, opening the laptop perched on a small black desk next to the piano and clicks on the pad a few times before turning back to the keys. "Three, two, one," the computer speaks aloud, and I jump back and grin down at him. "What's that?"

"I'm showing you," he chides, his face twisting adorably, "patience." The subtle appearance of a smile covers his mouth before his eyes drift down to the keys as he starts to manipulate them into something familiar.

"That's Alabama!" I yelp out before cupping my mouth, my eyes growing wide. He ignores my outburst, keeping perfect time as he plays along to the recording of "The Touch".

'Oh my God' I mouth, a shy smile on his lips when he registers the surprise on my face.

He winks and my throat swells. It's not just the piano, it's the drums, the heavy guitar, the bass, he's mastered and recorded every instrument, every part of the song, to play it, for *me*.

"But you just heard this two nights ago," I whisper, unable to hide the emotion in my voice, "how did you…" I falter, the threatening sting behind my eyes getting the best of me.

I stare down at him, anxious to get close, to get back to him, to his lips, his kiss. I'm a puddle of desire, hell-bent on getting the rest of his attention, longing to put *that* look back in his eyes.

Unable to stay idle, I slink down into his lap, interrupting his fingers. He temporarily allows it before resuming with me wrapped around him. With my face buried in his neck, I realize it must have taken him every spare minute away from me before the wedding to get this done. "It's beautiful," I murmur into his throat, straddling him on the bench hugging him tightly to me.

You're beautiful, I want to whisper so badly, but I'm suddenly afraid of what I feel. How did I not see this? How could I have not seen this incredible man for what he is? In a matter of life-altering hours, Theo has just become the most irresistible man I've ever known. If I'm completely honest, I've been falling for him, in pieces, since the night we met. And for the first time since we started the relationship, I'm unsure if I'm worthy of such a gift. The gift of knowing him, of seeing him this way, of being on this side of his affection.

I might've fallen slowly, but I just landed impossibly deep.

My eyes burn, a little because of the fear, but more because of this gesture, because of who he is and what he now means to me.

I no longer, nor do I ever want to be just Theo Houseman's friend.

I kiss his throat over and over and pull away to mouth the words of the song to him. He watches me, rapt, his fingers never straying from the piano.

We're polar opposites in some ways. I'm too country, and he's a whole lot of everything else. We shouldn't fit, but we do, and our fit is nothing short of spectacular.

There's no wool in the world thick enough to make me blind to that.

He continues his serenade, drawing out my desire as I clutch him to me. When he plays the last of the notes, I let him see just how much he's affected me. He pushes the hair away from my face as a grateful tear trails down my cheek.

"Jesus, Houseman," I whisper, slowly dipping in to kiss his nose, his brow, his temple, his cheek, before he turns his head and claims my mouth and we both are swept away. His eyes light up when he closes our kiss with a satisfied smile.

"Again," I moan against his lips.

He obliges, angling my face and drawing me back in to deepen our kiss.

Frenzied, I kiss him back.

Addicted.

Needy.

Starving for more.

He stands with me attached to him to hoist me up the stairs, but we only make it halfway.

Grannism—Don't trust cat people. They want low maintenance relationships.

thirty

Theo: Damn you woman, you changed every fucking radio and XM station in my car to country! I spent half my drive fixing it.
Laney: Prove it.
Theo: I am so going to redden your beautiful ass when I see you.
Laney: Have to prove I did it to dole out the punishment.
Theo: Says you.
Laney: See ^^ I've already got you talking like me. It's only a matter of time.
Theo: I think someone is acting naughty to get a little attention.
Laney: Prove it.
Theo: I hate Thanksgiving.
Laney: I miss you, too. It's a good thing we got together when we did. The public is starting to SHIP us.
Theo: Yeah?
Laney: They're pretty much demanding it. Do you ever check the page?
Theo: No. I'll do better.
Laney: The wedding video went viral thanks to you.
Theo: Crushing it. Proud of you.
Laney: US. It wouldn't be the same without you.

Pause…

Theo: You're only an hour and a half away. I can come home early.
Laney: You can't, your parents' anniversary party is this weekend. And your sisters keep threatening to come down. Give them a good dose of you so they won't threaten you anymore.
Theo: You can come here.
Laney: Can't leave Momma alone. It's our first real holiday without Gran. We're going to Black Friday in a few hours.
Theo: I just shed a tear for your mother. Like a real one.

Theo sent a photo.

Laney: Stop. I just totally got sad.
Theo: Adulting can suck it.
Laney: I miss you, too.
Theo: Happy Thanksgiving, Laney
Laney: Happy Thanksgiving, Houseman. (blows kiss emoji)

#turkeyday #stuffed #facetimeselfie #livingourrealestlife
#imalittlebitcountryhesawholelotrockandroll

thirty-one

THEO

YELL NIGHT. ANOTHER GRAND TRADITION. THE BAND'S required to show up to the pre-game pep rally and I must admit with my new nighttime distraction, I'm finding it harder and harder not to skip out. I have a thousand other things I'd rather be doing than playing for half a stadium full of die-hard Ranger fans. Like spelling the alphabet between Laney's legs while she begs for mercy. While Troy and the rest of his team stand on the field facing the bleachers next to the ring leaders, I sit with Zach and the rest of the band at the top row of our section, belting out old chants in between playing fight songs to gear up for one of the last games of the season.

The Rangers had a good run but missed a shot at a championship due to their last few losses. And as much as I hate to admit it, I'm happy about it because it means I get to spend more time with Laney, rather than the next few weeks practicing day and night for a college bowl half-time show.

When I had texted her earlier, she told me she was shopping tonight for a red Toyota, and so I hadn't asked her to come. I know she needs the money, and I could never guilt her for paying her own way just to fulfill the tradition of a midnight kiss. I'm not at all comfortable with the dangerous part of her job, but I know if I try to say anything at this point, it will pose the question of what rights I have, or if I have any say at all. I'm not about to stick my head under that guillotine, yet. We're way too new. Still, I hate it. My first instinct has always been to protect her, even though she'd refuse it.

Though her schedule is insane, she's attended most of the home games to support me, with or without Devin, which I know is a big step for her. More often than not, we skip the parties or crowds of any kind to spend all of our time together, alone.

No part of me feels like I've been missing out on anything. Except for tonight, when the lights go out.

The top of the hour is fast approaching, as I face facts that this will be yet another Yell night that I don't have any-one to kiss when the clock strikes midnight. The time when we're granted with a full minute to put our relationship status on public display. Some part of me is dying to claim her, but I know better than to back her into that corner, not when dealing with a gypsy heart.

This is one Grand tradition that can make a lone Ranger feel like a bag of dicks, which has always been the case for me. Nora never bothered to come to a single Yell night, her Friday nights with her girls far too important to miss than a show of devotion for me.

But the truth of the matter is, I'm not alone. And I don't need to take part in this tradition to know it. I've got a pint-sized terrorist in boots who is constantly reminding me we're in, whatever it is we have going, *together*.

Zach blows warm breath in his hands as we freeze our balls off in wait for another cue to play.

"Lindsey here tonight?"

"She came last time. I told her it was too cold and to stay home."

We both stand and shout our part as the Yell leaders start another chant before resuming our seats.

"Laney isn't here?"

"She had to work."

"How's that going, man?"

"Good, really good."

"Getting serious?"

"We don't talk about it."

"You mean you haven't asked."

"I'm not about to screw with something that's not broken."

"Well I don't know if you've noticed, but prying eyes have been on us since we sat down."

"What?"

"Check it out, nine o'clock." I look to our left to see two sets of curious eyes watching us from the stands below. "Laney is making you look good, man, if it doesn't work out with her, just know you have options."

One of the girls gives me a wave, and I nod, giving a polite smile before averting my eyes.

"See what I mean?"

"Not interested."

He jabs me with an elbow. "So, it is serious."

"It's new. We're doing it our way. I'm not going to fuck it up by acting needy. Besides, she doesn't work like that. She would rather choke before admitting she needs anyone."

"I hear you. Lindsey was a little dick bitter when we got together. It took time to get her out of it."

"I didn't mean it in a bad way. I'll tell you this much, she's nothing like Nora. I don't have to wonder if this thing is important to her because she looks out for me. She listens to me and my music, asks me about my day, and gives a damn about my moods."

"Nothing like Nora."

"Right," I nod. "She works so incredibly hard, all the time, around the clock, in school, at home. She makes time for me even though she's constantly running, but she makes it look easy even when I know she's stressed out. I respect her. She doesn't take advantage of me the way Nora did. It's different with her."

"Good for you, man."

We both stand and yell when prompted and then raise our instruments to play the fourth of our five-song set.

Back in our seats, Zach turns to me.

"You have plans for after?"

Just as I'm about to answer, the lights go out and I'm seized from behind with an arm around my neck. The smell of citrus and mint fills my nose as a husky voice whispers in my ear. "Houseman, in the stands with the *saxophone*. Mystery solved."

Turning in her hold, I ignore the catcalls filling the stadium as soft lips find mine, and she sinks into me when I eagerly meet her kiss, swiping my tongue along her lower lip just as she opens for me. Greedy, I push the dangling sax on my chest to the side before pulling her flush against me. Seizing her in my hands, I thrust my tongue into her mouth, kissing her thoroughly, the sensation of her moan vibrating against my tongue.

We're still locked in the kiss when the lights come back on, and she pulls away, her eyes darting around in surprise. I follow her gaze to see a startling amount of cell phones poised in our direction, taking pictures. "I suppose the cat's fully out of the bag now."

"I don't give a damn," I say, stepping over the row of seats separating us, so we're alone in the aisle above. I pull her to me and full-on kiss her again. When I close the kiss, she draws my freezing hands from her face to warm them between her own gloved hands. She spots Zach over my shoulder and greets him. "Hey Zach."

"Hey Laney," He greets back with a shit-eating grin before turning back toward the band to give us some privacy.

Laney looks up at me through dark lashes.

"That was my first kiss on Yell night, Houseman, and I wanted it to be with you."

"It was mine, too."

"Really?" A pride-filled smile beams from her as she rubs my hands between hers. She looks beautiful bundled up in a pink North Face jacket and beanie. Her glossy, dark-brown locks twisted in long twin braids and resting on her shoulders, her cheeks rosy from the cold. "You take good care of me," I tell her as she warms my hands.

"Do I?"

"Yeah, you do, and I'm coming up with ways to thank you for it right now."

Were in the midst of over-the-top PDA but no one is paying attention to us due to the bullhorn announcement of the all-stars for the year.

"I think I may know a way you can thank me," she murmurs. "Mom is working tonight." Her voice drops to a husky whisper. "Want to meet me in the chemistry lab in an hour?"

"Fuck yes," I whisper back, "be naked."

"No issues there." She leans in again, her eyes pooling. "The lab tech told me today that if you want, we're safe to play with gloves *off*," she grins sheepishly, "that is if you want."

My dick jerks inside my jeans as she weighs my reaction.

I lift one of her braids in my hand, rubbing her silky strands between my fingers. "Oh, I *want*. And don't take these out."

"Why?"

I lean in close. "Because the minute I get to the lab, I'm

going to reenact the fantasy I'm dreaming up right now to show my appreciation for that kiss."

Her mouth parts and I lean in and gently suck her bottom lip before pulling away with nothing but intent in my eyes. "I'll give you one guess where my next kiss will be."

"Theo," she sputters out, her forehead pressed against mine, breaths coming out in cloudy puffs from her swollen lips.

"That's enough, Mr. Houseman," my band director says bursting our bubble from where he stands at the bottom of our section.

"Young lady, I don't know how you got in here, but this is reserved for band members *only.*"

"Sorry about that, sir." She turns to me giggling. "*Whoops.*"

"Go on," I say not giving a shit about the attention we've drawn, or the lecture I'm sure to get, but drawing on the affection of the girl who's standing in front of me. "I'm right behind you."

It's then she says three words that strike me right in the chest. "It's a date."

thirty-two

THEO

"U P, BUGLE BOY," KEVIN SPOUTS KICKING THE END OF my bed. "It's D-day."

"Kevin, for the last time, I don't play the fucking bugle. Get the hell out of my bedroom."

"Punishment starts in an hour. You signed up. We leave in twenty. Dress for mud."

I reach for whatever is on my dresser and throw it at him and hear a satisfying "ugh" come out of him when I nail him with my Magic Eight Ball.

"You pussing out?"

"Yes," I say simply. And then think better of it and rise to sit on the edge of the bed. "I'm up."

Kevin gives me a lopsided grin. "I'm almost proud of you, precious."

"Get out before I make you spell precious."

"Don't piss me off, you're going to need me. Clock's ticking. Put your panties on."

The thirsty look in his eyes instills a small amount of fear. "Out."

He shuts the door behind him as I prepare myself for battle. I'm smaller than ninety-nine percent of the guys doing camp today. When I signed up weeks ago, I was mildly buzzed and feeling invincible partly due to the girl, okay mostly due to the girl. Some part of me knows I did it to try and prove something to the masculine part of myself; while the more sober, more intelligent part of me knows it's suicide to try and fight my way through a mile-long booby trap with dozens of bloodthirsty athletes.

Once dressed, and after putting any lingering Napoleon complex aside, I put my game face on and head downstairs where a few guys wait, draining Red Bull. Troy greets me with a fresh can.

"Amp up, you'll need it."

"That shit is poison."

"Drink it," he says with a hint of warning. "Drink fucking two and stay close to me."

"I'm good," I insist taking the offered can and popping it. He jerks his chin. "Totally different kind of field today."

"I'm up for it."

He grins. "Let's do it then."

Slight unease coats me as I hop into Troy's truck along with a few of the other guys before he peels out. It's when I see the obstacle course come into view from the side of the highway and dozens of muddied men twice my size gasping for air at the finish line that I sink in my seat. I'm terrified but do my best not to alert the fear-smelling, steroid-infused bees chattering around me with excitement.

Troy reads my posture and chuckles before cranking up the music as Kevin puts a reassuring paw on my shoulder. "We've got you, man."

I do the only thing I can, I nod and pray.

######

At the starting line, I survey the course, my mind racing with potential tactics. A short sprint, followed by a climb over a nine-foot wall, then a crawl through the mud beneath barbed wire. Beyond that, it's child's play—hills, ropes, and tires.

Ted Nugent's "Stranglehold" starts blaring through several large speakers around the course just as I decide my best bet is to flank Troy, and so I shift in line next to him. I scan the eager crowd of blood-thirsty testosterone to my left and know, without a doubt—I'm. About. To. Fucking. Die.

Steady guitar thrums into my ears, picking up speed and something in me shifts to beast mode as I study the hellacious trek paved out for us. I'm probably high off the Red Bull, but I feel like pounding my chest and yelling a war cry as my fingers itch at my sides. I think of the girl who just last night looked at me like I was the sun revolving the Earth.

I've fucking got this.

I lift my chin in defiance, batting any doubts away.

It's when the bullhorn sounds and activity spikes on either side of me that I charge, tackling the sprint like a motherfucking boss celebrating my triumph of being one of the first to make it to the wall, well ahead of the hulk parade. The pride-filled grin I sport is smashed off my face when I catch the first elbow.

"Jesus man, that was epic. I've never seen a guy fly so far, so fast, and still get the worst fucking time," Kevin laughs uncontrollably as I down my sixth beer in five minutes. Troy shakes his head laughing every time he glances my way, unable to get a word out, but I see a new respect in his eyes when he looks at me. At the finish line, and for the first time in my life, I'm at the King's table. I can't say that I hate it. I wasn't an outcast in school, I just was the one everyone waved to while walking down the hall before they reached someone more important. Aside from my high school best friend, Nora was the first one to stop for me. She was the first person to take the time to get to know me. I'd latched onto that interest. It made me bolder.

But Laney's attention makes me feel invincible.

Maybe I subjected myself to this massacre partly for her. But in all my years, I'd never taken the chance, never pushed myself like this and always just assumed I wasn't capable of the athleticism or the stunt I pulled today. And the truth is abundantly clear, I'm nowhere near fucking capable. Despite that, I can't regret it. To an outsider, I got pulverized, but every minute of the hell was a personal victory for me. It must show because the guys are crowded around me.

"Jesus dude, you need a medic," Troy says, looking me over.

"I'm good," I say finishing my beer and reaching for the collective duffle we brought before searching it for my phone. "Do me a favor and take a picture."

"Crowd in, assholes," Troy says as the guys gather around, dwarfing me. Muddy and bloody, I flex my arms in front of me Hulk-style. Troy takes a few pictures while trying not to piss himself laughing.

I scroll through a few shots and pick the most humiliating of the three before uploading it.

"You're seriously posting that?"

"Favor for a friend."

"A friend, huh? She worth it?"

"You have no idea."

"Well, she looks good on you."

I grin through bloody gums. "Yeah, she does."

He nudges me with a beefy elbow, and I keep my groan inward. "Life gets a lot sweeter when you're getting some on the regular."

"Please don't go thinking we have anything in common."

Troy scowls. "You always going to rag on me?"

I nod. "Probably."

"What's her name?"

"Laney."

"When am I going to get to meet her?"

"How about fucking never?"

He holds his hands up defensively.

"Bygones, man."

"Yeah, let's drop it."

He claps me on the back, and it's all I can do to keep him from seeing the tears brewing in my eyes.

"Do me a favor, dude, don't touch me."

He chuckles as Kevin delivers two fresh beers. "To Bugle Boy and his first Tuff Man!"

And last.

But I don't bother to correct him.

The guys collectively raise their glasses, and I join them despite the ridiculous pet name because, for a brief second, it feels good to be king.

#tuffman2019 #invincible #hulkedout #ownedthatshit #therockhasnothingonme #livingmyrealestlife

Grannism—If someone truly cares for you,
you won't ever have to wonder about it.

thirty-three

LANEY

POURING MORE SHAMPOO INTO MY HAND, I BERATE MY HOUND. "You want to tell me how in the hell you got sap all over you?"

Max yelps as I grip him tightly to me while the hose runs at our feet. "You aren't a young buck anymore. What in the world were you thinking?"

Max grunts as I give him his third shampoo. I swear I hear his snide laugh at my efforts. I'm rinsing him when I hear the crunch of tires and a car door close.

"Theo?"

"Yeah, it's me."

"Over here!" I yell from the side of the house. Max starts to struggle against me, pining for Theo's attention as he approaches.

"Hold on, you little shit, at least let me dry you off." I manage to get him partially toweled off and release him when I look up to see Theo covered in mud...and blood. I physically flinch at the sight of him.

"Oh my God!"

He raises butchered arms up, "I'm alright. Don't you worry." His hair is coated in mud, a blue headband sits lopsided above his brows like it got knocked down and he never bothered to fix it. His eyes are glassy, and his grin crooked.

"Are you drunk?"

He lifts his pointer and thumb close together. "Lil bit."

"I've been texting you all day."

"I've been doing guy stuff."

"Guy stuff, huh?"

He flashes a proud grin. "I did Tuff Man."

"What!" Covering my mouth with my hand, I can't help my smile. "And you call me crazy."

"About you."

He saunters up to me in full drunken swagger. "I'll have you know I did my worst, and it's been well documented and publicly posted all for *you*. I've been a very good boy and have come to claim my reward."

"Have you now?" I ask, shaking my head.

He bites a swollen lip, his eyes roaming me appreciatively before he bobs his head. "I guess a kiss will do."

He leans in, and I step away.

"Mind if I scrub you off a little first?"

"What's a matter?" He turns his head and lifts his chin, his hands fisted on his hips. "Can't handle all this *manliness*?"

I laugh through my reply. "Too much for me, baby."

He shrugs and holds out his arms with a sigh. "If you must."

"Keys, phone?"

"Phone, inhaler, I got dropped off." He says, handing me his phone and then puffing his inhaler before tossing it into the grass. Slipping the phone into my pocket, I survey the damage. His eyes are swollen to slits, there's a cut above his right brow, and his chin is purpling.

"Stand back, Houseman, this is going to be cold." I put my finger on the mouth of the hose to create a pressure spray and manage to get most of the mud off him. He's got scratches everywhere as I gently wipe away most of the grime covering his lower half.

"What is with the men in my life today? First Max decides to hump a sap-covered tree, and you show up looking half dead."

"I got stung by a bee, too, I think," Theo supplies in a slur. "That's why my eyes are swollen."

"Did that bee pin you down and kick the shit out of you too?"

He chuckles, but I see his wince.

"Yeah, well, *tough man*, Max decided to play commando today too, so you get the same treatment. Take off your shirt."

It's when I see twice as much mud caked on his torso that I realize my work is far from over.

"What in the hell made you think this was a good idea?"

"I got talked into it."

"This little Indian summer must have put idiot in the air."

"I can't even argue with that right now."

"Good thing, you would lose. Come on, I smell like a wet dog, but you're going to have to deal with it." Theo follows me inside as I gather half the contents of my medicine cabinet before I lay down a towel on my bed. "Strip to your boxers." He complies, gracing me with a smirk. I wet a washcloth and take a seat on the mattress next to him before gently cleaning the cut over his eye.

"What happened here?"

"Elbow."

"And here," I say tapping the purple on his jaw before wiping over the small cut on his lip.

"Another elbow?"

"And your arms?"

"Barbed wire."

"Jesus."

"Lort," he says through swollen lips in perfect Madea, and I grin shaking my head. "You're something else, Houseman."

"You're *everything* else." He's so sincere with his sentiment, it damn near brings tears to my eyes. Clearing my throat, I rub some Neosporin on the cut and press the cooling cloth beneath his eyes as they trace my face and dip down to my chest before doing a slow climb to meet mine. "Did you take something for the sting?"

"Yes, Mom."

It's then I meet his gaze and see amusement. "Don't you 'yes, Mom,' me. What in the hell are you trying to prove anyway hanging with a bunch of dumb ass jocks and get—"

Gripping my wrists to stop my fuss, he takes my lips in a kiss that dizzies me. With each swipe of his tongue, I melt into him, the fight leaving me.

"Mmmm," I murmur into his mouth as he draws me into him, fully tasting me before he pulls back with a grin.

"You keep kissing me like that," I say stupefied.

"You keep letting me," he says, his voice hoarse.

"You want a pain killer?"

"I've got one, I'm staring at her."

"Smooth. But that was a bullshit stunt. Seriously," I say dabbing his lip. "Why would you do that?"

"Aren't I allowed to do a penis thing once in a while?"

"Definitely a *dick* move."

"You're so clever," he leans in for another kiss, and I turn my head.

"Seriously, what's gotten into you?"

He shrugs. "I *was* basically raised by a bunch of women. I never really got dirty. I wanted to see what it's like to roll around in the mud."

"And?"

"And I got my ass kicked. And I don't like mud. But in a way, I feel like I got into my first fight. It felt good...kind of."

"Yeah well, you won't be singing that tune when the beer wears off," I say dotting the cuts on his arms with witch hazel. "Men. You guys claim women are a mystery, but it's because you idiots run on impulse."

"Sometimes impulse is good," he says huskily with clear insinuation.

"You're ridiculous," I sigh as I try and fail to brush more dirt away from his hairline until I'm forced to give up. "We both need a shower, badly."

The side of his mouth hitches. "Then we better get to it before the rigor mortis sets in."

"How romantic. I'm the proud owner of two insane beasts."

Shaking my head, I lead him into my bathroom. He doesn't move when I begin to strip and has no shame at all as he crosses his arms at the door while carefully following my every movement.

"You comin' in with your clothes?" I ask, pushing down my cutoffs.

"Nope."

Unhooking my bra, I smile in his direction and let it fall away. His eyes flare as I finger the sides of my panties.

"What are you doing, Houseman?"

It's the first time I've been consciously aware of being completely naked in front of a man in years, and I love it. It's his stare, the way he appreciates me, compliments me without uttering a single word. His curiosity is sexy as hell as is his need-ful expression.

"Theo?"

In front of him now, I look up at him through my lashes. He unhooks his arms and slowly, so slowly, slides warm hands down my sides before gripping my ass. It's all I can do to keep from moaning.

Eyes full of amber fire, his lips part as I hang on a breath. "You're so…"

"So?"

He leans in and nips the shell of my ear. "Beautiful, crazy, unusual, perfect…alive."

"All I heard was crazy."

"Of course you did," he says before biting down on my shoulder and pulling me against his erection. "Did I say it the right way?"

"You're drunk."

"So, take advantage of me," he murmurs, manipulating me into a puddle in his arms. He turns me to face the mirror and captures both my hands behind my back, holding them tight. He bites my neck again and again as my clit pulses between my thighs.

"Theo?" I barely recognize my own voice. I'm so turned on, in tune with his reaction to me, to the way my body responds to him. He pushes his boxer shorts down with one sweeping movement, and I can feel his girth at the top of my back. We're just standing there, staring, admiring. He pins me to the counter with his thighs, intent on his seduction as I moan in response and then he's inside me in one swift thrust. I scream out in welcome as he holds me close to his chest, never breaking the contact as he rides me, our eyes locked.

"Oh God."

He bites his lip, sinking in again, and again, taking his time, as he uses the hand he's not binding me to him with to massage my breasts, weighing them in his hands, brushing deft thumbs over my nipples. Groaning, he slides a hand down my chest, past my waist until his fingers meet his cock sliding along my center in time with his thrusts. I go feral, thrashing in his hold, but he only presses me lower, so that I'm bent and taking more of him. He pistons, losing some of his control when he fully fills me and both our mouths part. And then I'm set free as he drives. Braced against the counter my nipples grazing the cold surface as he thrusts like a madman and we both start calling out to the other with praise and affection.

"Yes," he murmurs, "this is what I've been looking for," he grunts out as he presses tongue-filled kisses on my back. "For you, Laney," he growls as he rears back and thrusts in *hard*.

"Theo!" I cry out hoarsely as he rubs my center with his middle finger stroking me expertly while my legs begin to shake. He cups my mouth and draws me back to him as I detonate, my whole body shaking with the weight of my orgasm as he slows his pace, his fingers working methodically at my clit and making it last a small eternity.

Tears of euphoric orgasm streak my cheeks while I go slack against him. He caresses me everywhere, keeping us connected as he murmurs to me.

"I love watching that." Fingers tangle in my hair, and he pulls at the fistful he has and sinks his teeth in my flesh just before he pulses inside of me with his release, his face twisted in a sexy grimace. When he comes down, I turn in his arms and capture his lips. Surprised by what's behind my kiss, he matches it, kissing me back just as aggressively. I rip my lips away and look up at him with narrowed eyes.

"Look, I'm going to have to call bullshit."

He frowns. "On what?"

I start the shower and test the temperature of the water before we both step into the tub under the spray.

"Seriously, Theo?" I say wetting my hair and turning to give him access to the shower head. "You want to tell me where you learned all that?"

His lips part in a smug smirk. "When you spend five years of your life trapped in foreplay, you get good at it. I paid attention."

I lift a brow.

He shrugs and clears his throat. "And I quote, 'clitoris, learn how to find it and then worship it, because it may save you some relationship miles.'"

"You really scare me sometimes."

He gives me a sly grin as his wavy hair gets drenched by the faucet.

######

THEO

"Should I feel guilty for the things I've done to you in your child-hood bed?"

She looks up at me, our legs tangled on her damp sheets. "Yes, you should totally feel guilty. I was rocked to sleep in this room. And you're a filthy, drunken lover."

"You love it," I say, running my finger through her thick locks.

"Shocked the shit out of me."

"Why?"

"I don't know. I should know by now nothing is what it seems with you."

I try and fail to hide my prideful grin.

She rolls her eyes. "Don't go gettin' a big head."

"Don't go cuttin' this hair," I murmur to her temple playing with the locks laying on my chest. "I love it."

"You do, huh?"

"Yes, it's beautiful."

"Then, I won't."

"Good."

"We should probably get dressed. My mom gets off in an hour or so."

Neither of us move, so I pull her tighter to me. I love the feel of her against me. I'm getting used to it.

"So, who did you daydream about when you were in here?"

"Tim McGraw."

"Of course."

"Don't hate. I used to put a cowboy hat on Ken and plan our weddin'. He was going to ride up on a horse. We were going to have those picnic pattern paper plates. Classy, I know. But he was my first crush."

"Who was your second?"

She shrugs. "I kind of got over the boy craze after him. My dad visited and brought me an old briefcase filled with letterhead and office supplies. So, I ditched my Tim dream and decided I was going to be a professional. I still have the briefcase."

"When is the last time you saw him?"

"Tim? In concert when I was five."

"Not Tim," I say, pressing my chin against the top of her head.

"That was the last time. I think my mom ran him off for good after that. It was probably a relief for him. He never fought her on it."

"I don't understand. When's the last time you talked to him?"

When she doesn't move, I nudge her. "Laney?"

"That was the last time."

"Wait, you don't talk to him at all? You told me you didn't talk much."

She rests her chin on my chest, guilty light brown eyes trained on my Adam's apple. "It's not a big deal. I'm sorry I wasn't truthful, it's just not something I freely go around admitting to people, you know?"

"You can tell me anything."

"I know. I'm sorry."

"No, I'm sorry."

"For what?" She moves to sit, her hair cascading over her dusty pink nipples. "Do you have any idea how lucky I am to have been raised by two headstrong women? Seriously I don't wrestle with it." She taps her temple.

"But you're talking about it."

"Only because it came up. It's not something I dwell on, like ever. Gotta let people be who they are. Jimmy Cox did not want to be my father. If it was forced, it would have made us both miserable anyway."

"You're right."

"Aren't I always?"

"Hell no. No. Not at all." She grins and stands, and I admire her from my place on her bed. "I'll bet your clothes are dry." Hazel eyes trail down to my dick as it swells in wordless appreciation.

"Get up, maestro, you don't want to make another bad impression on my mom. Even though what you've got going on there is *mighty* impressive."

I move to stand and feel every muscle in my body scream in protest along with the beginning of an epic headache.

She pulls a long T-shirt over her head and grins. "Feeling good now, tough guy?"

"Even my earlobes hurt."

"Poor baby." She slaps my bare ass. "Come on. Let's get you dressed and full of grease."

"Laney," I whisper. When she turns for the door, I pull her back to my chest. Arms wrapped around her, I simply hold her, and she lets me. No words are spoken. No declarations are made. We don't need them. At least that's what I tell myself.

Grannism—Don't go trying to find the pretty in ugly people. That's like saving your sunshine for shit. Even in better light, it's still a glowing turd.

thirty-four

LANEY

EELING MELANCHOLY, I LET THE BACK DOOR CLOSE AND SIT on our porch bundled up in my favorite fuzzy blanket with Max at my heels. My phone buzzes in my lap, and I beam when I see Theo would like to FaceTime.

I answer with a smile, but I can't see him at all because it's pitch dark.

"Hey, I can't see you."

"This FaceTime is more so I can see you."

"Oh?"

"Yeah. What's wrong?"

"Nothing."

"Laney."

"You're getting to know me scary well."

"Scary bad?"

"No. Of course not. Devin well."

"That's good."

"It's awesome," I say with a shaky voice. "You're awesome."

"Tell me what's wrong."

"It's just Gran. She's not here." I don't realize how much I'm hurting until I say the words and I'm misty-eyed. "This is my first Christmas without her and I just...I miss her so much."

"I wish I was there to grab your hand right now and pull you to me."

His words warm my heart.

"Me too. Why are you whispering?"

"I'm in my closet."

"The three stooges messing with you?"

"I told them I was going to call you and they all had conniptions wanting to meet you. It took me an hour to slip away undetected."

I laugh, and it feels good.

"Tell me about her."

"I'm afraid I'll cry."

"So, what? She was with you for twenty-one of your twenty-two years. You're allowed to be upset."

She was painfully absent on my birthday last week too. Luckily, I had a Grand Band Man who picked me up after his last game day and took me through the drive-thru just before midnight to let me eat my weight in Dorito shell tacos. Right after, he'd presented me with a bow covered box of Famous Amos cookies. I insisted it was enough and that he cancel any other plans he'd made. He'd briefly fought me on it, but finally relented.

"I really wish I could see your face."

"I can see yours. Hi, Max."

"How did you know he was with me?"

"He's the other man you're sleeping with. I just assumed."

"He's at my feet whining now because he misses you," I say honestly.

"I miss you too. Come on, tell me about her."

"Well, she was strong, like unbelievably strong, and strong-willed, funny."

"You just described yourself."

"Yeah, well she knew her place in the world."

"You will too."

I nod, unable to hold my tears.

"She's the third hero, isn't she?" He asks, knowing the answer.

"Yes," My voice cracks and I turn my head away from the camera.

"It's okay to cry in front of me. I hate the sight of it, but holding it in isn't good for you."

"I just," my chin wobbles uncontrollably. "I've been trying to hold it together all day for Mom, you know? But today was bad. It felt so empty here without her. Christmas Eve was our thing. Mom said she was going to nap a while ago, but I know she went to cry."

"I think it's awesome you had a relationship like that with her. I don't know that many people that close with a grandparent."

"She was a spitfire, so special."

"Again, you're just like her."

Tears shimmer in my eyes as I smile at him. "I really want to see your face."

"I—"

The invasion of light cracks on screen and my wish is granted for a split second before a shriek fills the air.

"I found him!"

"I swear to God, Courtney, if you don't get the hell out of here, I'm going to tell Mark about the time you got pulled over for indecent exposure."

"You will not."

"Test me."

I sit idle as he glares back at her, my smile growing.

"I just want to meet her!" Courtney coos in the background

as my view is obstructed by the brawl over his phone. "He's got her on FaceTime," Courtney yells as the struggle ensues.

In the next few seconds, I hear the sound of footfalls, and an 'oomph' come out of Theo and more threats.

"I'm going to hurt you, Court. Stop it."

"We are awesome! There is no need to be ashamed of us."

"Ironically, I am."

"Courtney, get him out of that headlock, he's on the phone!"

"Turn the camera around so we can wave," another voice says as I get dizzy from watching the struggle. And then he's moving his face, coming on screen, his hair disheveled when he finally brings it up to his face. "I'll call you back later. Sorry—"

"Let me say hi," I protest as he glances behind him and picks up his pace. In the next second, I get a good panoramic view of the ceiling. "Baby, I'll call you back."

"Oh, he's calling her baby!"

"Oh my God, Teddy! That's so sweet!"

"I knew people called you Teddy!" I declare loudly.

"Yes, girl," one of them pipes up and I see arms again flying as a beautiful girl with Teddy's eyes comes into view. "And don't let him tell you different. Hi!"

"Hi," I parrot with a smile.

"Wow, you aren't what I expected, but in a good way."

I can hear Teddy cursing. "I swear to God, we are about to fight like men."

"Just let us talk to her!" She screams back over her shoulder.

"I'm sorry, Laney!" Theo says, his voice cracking with fear.

"It's fine, Teddy!" I yell into the phone with a laugh.

"So, *you're* the one my brother has been talking non-stop to Mom about when he thought we weren't listening."

"I hope so."

"Well, I'm Jamie, his favorite."

"Not anymore!" I hear him yell in the background and another "oomph."

Another voice sounds out. "She was your favorite? Really, Teddy? That hurts."

"I'm so going to get you for this. Hang up, Laney. Just hang up!"

Another head pops up on the screen. "Hi. I'm Brenna."

"Hi."

"So did Teddy tell you 'bout us?"

"Sure did," I say through a laugh.

A third head pops up. "Did he tell you how protective we are?"

"I have the best of intentions, I assure you, Courtney."

She gives me a pride-filled grin. "In the flesh."

"Well, rest assured, your brother is in good hands and schooling me on a lot more than I would like to admit."

Jamie speaks up. "He's special, isn't he?"

"Very."

"Yeah, as in helmet wearing special," Courtney says, rolling her eyes.

Brenna's eyes light up. "You should come for New Year's! You can sleep in my room."

"Oh, I uh, well I have to stay here with my mom."

Jamie thumps her ear. "That's an invitation Teddy should extend."

"Where is he anyway?" I ask.

Jamie and Brenna look back to Courtney who shrugs. "We probably have about ten seconds left."

I shake my head with a laugh.

"You know, Courtney, you and Theo look a lot alike."

"That's funny you mention that," Jamie says, "because we have this pillow."

A loud boom sounds as Brenna lifts something into view just before the phone is knocked out of her hand, and I'm again staring at the ceiling.

"Jesus Christ, no!" Theo says with a voice full of panic. "You guys are so dead!"

Brenna's face pops into view in front of where the phone sits on the floor. "I'll steal your number from his phone and text you. We'll set something up. Lunch and shopping?"

"Sounds good."

Taunting laughter follows as Theo retrieves his phone and comes into view, looking perplexed.

"What did they do to you?"

"Locked me in the closet," he's breathless, and I can't stop laughing.

"Not funny."

"Sorry, poor baby."

"I'd have been *much* better off with brothers."

"Ouch, Teddy!" I hear from somewhere in the house.

"Go straight back to hell, *Satan!*" Theo shrieks.

"Alright guys, kids, it's Christmas."

"Really, Dad?" Theo says panting. "Now you're going to butt in?"

"God, I love your family already."

"You can have them." He shakes his head solemnly. "I should have called you from the car. You don't have to go shopping with them."

"I want to. Sounds fun. They seem awesome."

"Give it a year or twenty." He walks to his bedroom, and I

demand he give me a tour. He does a slow sweep of his room. It's clean, and it's obvious the house is nice. There are vacuum indents in the carpet.

"Big. Comfy."

"I like your bedroom better," he says suggestively. "Or my other room."

He lays back on his bed, the phone hovering above his face.

"I love this view."

"Yeah?" He says before playfully biting his lip. "What's good about it?"

I lift a brow.

"Funny, I like it just the opposite."

"You weren't saying that the other night."

"Should I shut my door so we can discuss this in more detail?"

"Nah, my mom is in earshot."

"You sure you're okay?"

"Yeah, I'm good now. Watching the sideshow with your sisters got me out of my headspace."

"Sure?"

"Yeah, I'm sure. Hurry home…" I feel the blush creep up my face. "I mean back."

"Home," he says. "I don't live here anymore."

"Right."

"Don't be embarrassed."

"I'm not."

"I'm ready to come home, to *you*."

"Okay."

"Merry Christmas, Laney."

"Merry Christmas, Houseman."

thirty-five

THEO

L YING ON MY BED, IN MY NEW NAVY DRESS PANTS, COLLARED shirt, and tie, I bounce my stress ball off the ceiling. I've never been so restless in my life. While I love my family, they are nowhere near as entertaining as the feisty brunette who's taking up a majority of my thoughts, my time. Things moved fast after we got physical, and I had to convince myself on the drive giving us space would give me perspective. But at this point, it's all I can do to keep from packing my car and making an excuse to head home. Nora crosses my thoughts, and I shake the image away of her tear-soaked confession.

"It just happened."

It's the only thing keeping me from making the drive. With Laney, I have to pace myself. I can't let my heart rule my head. I've done that, and I have no intention of walking the plank again without ample reason to. But somewhere beneath all this caution is a white flag waving half-mast ready for me to simply give in. Laney isn't Nora, and I can't grudge one for the other's mistake. But if I'm forced to live by experience, I can't help but to weigh the risk. Laney has the ability to hurt me. But how much of myself do I want to invest in a woman who has to stand in the junk food aisle for ten minutes to make a simple decision. She's unsure about everything, and who's to say in a month or a day she won't feel the same about me.

Am I an asshole for thinking it?

"Aww," Courtney draws from the frame of my bedroom door, "look, Jamie, he's daydreaming about his girlfriend."

I groan, throwing my arm over my eyes as I toss the ball in the direction of my door.

"Can you two please go find some garland to strangle each other with?"

"As much as I want to Freud you, little brother, we've got to go. Yuletide is calling, and Dad's pacing downstairs."

"I'll be down in a minute."

Jamie pries my arm from my face. "Come on, do your duty and you can come back here and sulk."

"Hurry up, boy sperm," Courtney taps the door before taking her leave as Jamie lingers behind.

"What?" I feel her stare as I lift to sit, grabbing my suit jacket.

"You really like this one."

"Isn't it obvious?"

"Just be careful."

Jamie was the one who drove down when Nora dropped the bomb. For a week straight, she stayed at my side, mostly silent as I went through the motions. She'd played big brother, got me drunk for a couple of days while she cleaned out every piece of memorabilia from my life, and then forced me out of bed into the shower.

"Not too careful. I want you to take the chance again, to be happy," she says, a pensive expression flitting across her features. "I just don't ever want to see you like that—"

"I know. Don't worry."

"Can't help it."

"I got you something," I say, changing the subject.

"Oh yeah?" She lights up.

I reach into my duffle and pull out the wrapped box. "It's one more than I got Court and Brenna, so don't rat me out, okay?"

"You aren't supposed to have a favorite," she says with a light laugh.

"I think that rule is for moms, and anyway look at your competition."

She nudges me. "Courtney loves you. Brenna too."

"I know. Just open it."

She rips off the paper with enthusiasm. "Oh my God." She lifts the inscribed bar necklace and reads the scroll on both sides.

"One side means word warrior and the other, seeker of justice," I explain. I thought you could wear it your first day in court, you know, as a good luck charm."

"This is beautiful," she says, choking up.

"Don't you dare cry."

"I can't help it." She hugs me tightly to her, and I hug her back. "This is everything. Thank you."

"I'm proud of you. You worked your ass off."

"You're too cool, little brother."

"Merry Christmas."

"Merry Christmas, Teddy." She pulls away and smiles. "Come on, before Dad has a coronary."

At the foot of the stairs, we're greeted by my dad who gives us a dead stare while helping Mom into her coat. We go to the annual neighborhood Christmas party held at the clubhouse every year, but this year is different because one of Dad's new golfing buddies, who he's set on impressing, just moved into the neighborhood and mentioned stopping by.

And Dad rarely misses an opportunity to showboat his family. We take the freezing walk to the clubhouse, my sisters' heels clicking on the sidewalk as Courtney belts out "Jingle Bells" like she's one of the wicked stepsisters. My mother sighs and leans over to my dad. "I'll admit, I dropped that one."

"I knew it," he replies dryly before they share a smile.

"I heard that," Courtney says. "I'm still an improvement from the boy sperm."

We enter the clubhouse, and as usual, it's decked out. We live in one of the more exclusive neighborhoods in the Houston suburbs. My parents are socialites and make it their mission to keep their calendar full. This particular party they attend because of the few coveted awards—including best garden—passed out each year. They even give out ridiculous little glass trophies. Mom has won it twice, and I swear she shines them once a day. The whole ritual is absurd, but we humor them because appearances are important to them, and they are genuinely proud of us. I think about Laney's slice of peaceful heaven in the middle of nowhere compared to the industrial park I grew up in. It's like night and day. We come from completely different worlds, and yet I'm comfortable in hers. I wonder if she would feel the same in mine.

"There they are!"

A few neighbors greet my parents as we offspring plaster on smiles.

"And this is my son, Theo, and my daughter, Jamie. Jamie graduated last May and is with a new firm. She has her first day in court on Monday, and Theo is a junior at TGU. Music major." My dad beams with pride as Jamie and I show our teeth for inspection like prized ponies.

The man extends his hand, and I shake it.

"Nice to meet you, sir."

He grins over at me. "Call me, Jim. And I was a Grand Man myself."

My father's smile grows Grinchy big. "I didn't know that."

Jim leans forward and claps me on the back. "Loved that school. Time of my life." He gives me a knowing wink.

I nod uneasily because I get the same vibe from him that I do from Troy. And from the looks of him and his wife, he's kept his playboy appetite. He's got an arrogant type of confidence that only goes along with a lifetime of getting his way.

I play along with the humdrum of the conversation with my thoughts never two blinks away from Laney. We make our rounds until our parents get caught up in gossip and we're stuck chugging spiked nog on the sidelines.

"Maybe we can make a run for it," Brenna says with a sigh.

My mother looks over at us right at that moment and narrows her eyes.

"I think we're bugged," Jamie says. "The woman knows everything as it happens."

"We are," Courtney confirms. "No doubt. We're bugged. She's been doing it since we were young. She just knows."

"Drink up, Dad's doing that laugh."

"Oh God, not the laugh."

We all groan when we see him toss his head back and cackle like a hyena.

"Shit," Courtney says. "I can't believe we share DNA."

"They are such fakes sometimes," Brenna says as she lifts her phone, the three of them simultaneously doing duck lips before the flash goes off.

"Good one, it's going up." The girls weigh in on the picture and nod in approval.

"Oh, I almost forgot, this coworker was telling me about this crazy couple yesterday, she said they're hilarious." Brenna taps on her phone with the speed of a magician. "My real life," she frowns, searching her thoughts as I choke on my eggnog. "Crap, I forget the name. My Realest life. That's it."

"We should go make the rounds," I suggest holding out a plate of sugar cookies to the three of them like bait. Look, sugar. Sugar.

Courtney is the only one to take it.

Resorting to the phone slap tactic, I'm stopped with my own man slap to the shoulder.

"So, you're a fighting Ranger?"

"Yes, sir."

As if my dad can smell blood in the water, he saunters over to join us.

"I've got a few buddies left out that way, maybe we should make a trip down there soon." He nods towards his wife, who only bobs her head in agreement. It might be wrong for me to assume she's arm candy, but it's the only conclusion I can draw when my mom prompts her for conversation, and she gives nothing but short, clipped answers. She's probably bored and enduring this party like the rest of us. I can't help but to think of what a change in dynamic it would be if Laney were standing here. For the next half hour, I'm forced to listen to Jim's Grand Man stories. My father can't get a word in edgewise and watches me intently. I have no desire to impress this man, but I do respect Dad enough to be polite and indulge his bullshit.

"Course I had to get the hell out of there," he drains the last of his drink. "Not much to entertain there but the school."

"Oh, he's entertained," Courtney spouts.

My mother sighs in annoyance and eyes Courtney in warning.

Jim catches on because...Courtney. "Ahh, yeah. Can't

argue with *that* type of distraction. Just make sure to avoid the noose," he says, "if you know what I mean. It will only slow you down."

It's official, I'm staring at Troy's future.

"He's got a good head on his shoulders," my dad interjects with genuine pride.

Jim smiles, and it gives me pause. "Well, we have to head over to Chrissy's parents for dessert. They're holding our son hostage." He pulls out his business card, and I read the bold print and look back at Jim's profile.

Jim exchanges pleasantries with my parents, and my mother elbows me to speak up when it's my turn. Blood pulses at my temple as I nod and grit out a goodbye before I get another sound clap on the shoulder.

"Call me if you need something to get you on your feet. Us Grand Men have to stick together."

When the door closes behind them, my parents head back into the party as Jamie eyes me while I slip out the front door. I catch them down the stone path of the clubhouse.

"Your daughter is beautiful."

He pauses on the sidewalk, and they both turn to look at me in surprise.

"I'm sorry, what?"

"Your *daughter*. She's beautiful, devastatingly so. She lights up every room she walks into."

I shove my hands in my pockets to ward off the cold. "She's smart, outspoken, and can be a handful, but she can handle herself in any situation."

"Excuse me, but are you talking about Elai—"

"She's got an addiction to junk food and an odd taste in idols, but it should come as no surprise to you that they're all *women*."

He stands stunned as he reads my hostile expression.

"She could probably run a mile in her boots on the beach without breaking a sweat. She's pure country, and I'm positive that won't ever change. She's a pessimist with an optimistic heart, and I am falling madly in love with her."

I study his profile as it changes from shock to remorse.

"She's my favorite person in the world, and I can't imagine not knowing her. I can't imagine having the chance to know her and throwing it away."

I take an aggressive step forward and catch his eager gaze. He clearly wants more but is too much of a coward to ask.

"She's going to graduate soon, and I'm going to do my damnedest to be the man in her life. You don't deserve to know any of this. But you deserve to regret your decision."

"So, she's—"

"Better off." I pull his card from my pocket, rip it in half and toss in on the sidewalk between us. "Sorry, *Jim.* I'm just not *your* kind of Grand Man."

I retreat back to the party and shut the door behind me. I expect to be met with the hostile eyes of my parents; instead, I'm met with three pairs of surprised eyes.

"This is you?" Courtney says lifting her phone. "*Fifty-six thousand* followers? Are you fucking serious?"

Brenna snatches the phone away from her. "I can't believe this is you, you're famous!"

I snort. "We are not famous."

She walks up to me and shoves the phone in my face. "Fifty-six thousand people are watching your every move, Theo."

I shrug. "It's just a school project for Laney."

"A school project that's got the two of you trending as the couple to watch in 2019."

I try to ignore the small swell of pride I feel for her, for us. For what started out as a friendship and has turned into the most amazing thing to happen to me.

"Seriously, Theo?" Jamie asks with a little hurt in her voice. "Why would you keep this from us?"

"I think that's obvious," I take a step back as they circle me like vultures.

"Well, you're screwed now, little brother. We're *definitely* coming for a visit.

"Bet it up, *punk*, she's *our* new best friend."

"I still can't believe this is you, boy sperm."

Grannism—Not all men are created equal. Half of them were created due to God's sense of humor.

thirty-six

LANEY

I<small>T'S MY FIRST EVER</small> W<small>HITE</small> C<small>HRISTMAS, AND SOME PART OF ME</small> believes the credit belongs to Gran. The view of the trees from the porch is spectacular. Mom and I bundle up under the blanket on the wicker couch sipping hot cocoa mixed with coffee while watching the snow fall.

It's more ice than snow at this point, but equally as beautiful. Before I was serving coffee to the masses, gathering on the porch for morning coffee was Mom, Gran's, and my routine. Then Mom took a second shift, Gran got sick, I got the barista job, and our routine changed. It had to. I didn't like it. None of us did. There are times in your life where change is welcome, but this isn't one of them. Because for the first time in months, I'm completely at peace sitting next to my mother.

"Wow," she says, admiring our view. Stretching out a newly unwrapped off-brand Ugg, I appreciate my own view. She places a hand on my candy cane covered thigh.

"You like them?"

"I love them so much. Thank you, Santa." I kiss her cheek.

"You know your Gran would always stand guard while I put all your stuff together. If you so much as moved in your sleep, she would come running down the hall demanding I pack up and wait. As soon as I did, we'd peek in to see you were fast asleep. Drove me insane, but she did *not* want you to find out about Santa."

I grin. "Sounds like her."

"She said not to ever ruin a kid's magic. There's not enough of it in the world anymore."

"I agree."

"But I think this is pretty magical."

"I was thinking it could be her."

Mom's lips quiver. "Maybe it is."

"I think it is, Momma," I take her hand in mine and squeeze it.

Mom lifts a tear from beneath her eyes and nods. "Let's not cry. Let's smile for her today."

"Yeah. I'm with you."

"So, you seem happy these days."

"I am."

She smiles and bumps shoulders with me.

"And Theo?"

"I'm pretty sure he is too."

"Are you safe?"

"I've been on birth control since I was sixteen."

"I know but—"

"But nothing." I quirk a brow. "When is the last time you had sex?"

"I'm serious, Laney."

"So am I."

"Discussion over," my mother says, and we clink coffee mugs. A few sips later, we hear the crunch of snow.

"You expecting anyone?" Mom asks me.

"No. You?"

"Uh uh. But I have a feeling."

"Theo's in Houston."

"Sure, he is." She kisses my hair and then stands before gathering our empty mugs. "When he pulls up, invite him in. I bought him some cologne." I wince because I know it's cheap, and probably not anything he'd wear. We can't afford much, and I'm hoping he's a good sport about it. I'm already worried enough about my present. Rattling with anticipation, I look toward the road and smile when Mom's suspicions are confirmed, and his Honda comes into view.

It's unexpected and amazing as butterflies swarm around me, and I prepare my lips for the perfect Christmas kiss.

But when I see the speed at which he's traveling, alarms go off.

"Uh, Mom, he's coming in *hot*."

Just as I say it, Theo slams on his brakes, his car sliding over the ice a few feet before it fishtails and stops. Theo gets out of the car looking like he's just been electrocuted while shouting at the top of his lungs. "Great, you're awake! Of *course* you're awake!" He says, waving a hand of crazy into the air. "You should know I left at *three* a.m.! Three a.m. to take a *two*-hour drive to get to you before you woke up!"

"Mom."

"Yes, baby?"

"Pour some bourbon in Theo's coffee," I whisper-shout over my shoulder.

"Already on it," she says through a laugh as Theo continues his rant. "Do you have any *idea* what happens to Texans who get out on *icy* roads at three in the morning!?" He juts his chin out and cups his ear with his hand.

I slowly shake my head, my hands behind my back.

He rips at his hair before spreading the loose strands into the wind in front of him. "Jesus must have been celebrating his birthday *really big* last night because he sure as *hell* didn't take the wheel the two thousand times I screamed his name!"

My mother's laugh rings out behind me as I try my best not to do the same while he's in this state. I'm biting my lips so hard tears spring to my eyes.

"I-i-it was rough, huh?"

He cocks his head, his eyes bulging as if it's the dumbest question I could ask before opening his back-passenger door and carefully stacking presents in his arms. "Leave it to life to let me know that attempting to do something romantic for my girl is a foolish notion." He slaps the door closed; his arms full as he looks up to me exasperated. "So, I sure as hell hope you appreciate these blood-stained pre—"

Those are the last words he speaks before the rubbery soles of his Converse connect with a slick patch of ice.

"Oh shit, Mom! Man down! Man down!" She collapses behind me in the kitchen in hysterics.

Theo sleeps peacefully sprawled on my mattress, one foot hanging off, and I gaze on at him, watching his chest rise and fall. After breakfast, Theo and my mother exchanged presents. He'd put the cologne on the minute he opened the box, earning a bigger piece of me. And she'd thanked him profusely for the fancy cashmere scarf he'd picked, which suited her. But as soon as he drank his coffee and his breakfast started to digest, he could barely keep his eyes open, so I put him to bed. My bed. Where he rests now. With the day half gone, I decide to rouse him with a kiss to his cheek. "Merry Christmas." He groans and then reaches for me. "What time is it?"

"Six p.m."

That jars him. "Really?"

"It's okay. It's been a good day. You needed the sleep."

He pulls me to lay with him, and I snuggle close in his arms. It takes a few more minutes for him to come to.

"I don't think I've ever heard my mother laugh that hard in my entire life," I say with a giggle. "I'm sorry you busted your ass, but I have to say that was awesome."

"My ass disagrees," he says, tilting my face up and pressing a kiss to my lips.

"You are a hot mess, Houseman."

"That was the scariest drive of my life."

"I'm sorry."

He brushes the hair from my shoulder. "I'm glad I did it."

"Me too. When you wake up, I have something for you."

He moves to sit and runs a thumb down my cheek. "You didn't have to."

"Don't thank me yet."

"Oh shit."

"Don't say that yet either." I pull my laptop from my bag and open it in his lap.

"What's this?"

"Well, this is my laptop."

"Uh huh."

I click a few buttons and pull up the page. "And this is your new website."

"What?"

"Okay, don't panic, it's nothing I can't undo," I explain quickly. "Before you get mad, I got all the stuff off your drive, organized your music a little bit for both your app and the new site so you can globally start marketing whenever you feel comfortable. I also had a friend design your logo, and we can change the name if you don't like it, but I started a social page on every single platform including the two most used for this kind of application."

Theo's eyes roam the page as I try my best to weigh his expression.

"Okay, so when you're ready, all you have to do is click here." I show him where to publish the page. "And then post on the social platforms I set up in the folder, here, at your leisure. Some social presence is better than none, and I can run your pages for you, uploading samples of the music if you want. I figure you can double, if not triple your income by expanding your market overseas. If Honda is using your music here, Honda can use it elsewhere. I've drafted up an international rights license, and it's in this folder here. I also gathered a price list from other apps and created a comparable table."

Theo's silence terrifies me as he fingers the keypad and scrolls through the online library. "So, everything available here is available on your app but disappears from the site when purchased."

"Jesus, Laney."

"If you're mad, I can change everything back lickety-split. Seriously, I won't be upset."

He turns to me with such…pride in his eyes that mine water.

"You like it then?"

He grips my face in his hands and presses the gentlest of kisses to my lips. "This is incredible."

"You really like it?" I ask, searching his eyes.

"It's fucking incredible. You're incredible. I love it. I haven't had time to do this. H-h-ow have you?"

"I've been working on it for a while."

"How long?"

"A while. I bled a little for your present too," I wrinkle my nose before he takes my mouth and delivers an intoxicating kiss. When he pulls away, we just stare.

"I may need to rethink my gift."

"Don't be silly. I want what you thought I'd want."

He shakes his head and kisses me again. The look he's giving me is more than enough. Theo disappears briefly retrieving my gift from under the tree and hauling a beautifully wrapped box into my room. It's slender and stands about five-foot tall, and I can't for the life of me guess what's in it. I rip at the paper anxiously and step back when I've done enough damage to see what it is. Heart alight, I'm at a loss for words.

"It's the best two-sleeper tent out there. It's supposed to be so comfortable it'll seem more like glamping."

"Let's do it," I blurt, my eyes shining.

He nods toward the window. "Weather isn't really up to par."

"No, in here. Let's set it up right now!" I rip at the top of the box excitedly pulling the smelly new vinyl out as Theo chuckles. "Alright then, let's do it."

Staring up at the ceiling of the tent, I lay in Theo's arms as the soft light of the electric lantern he bought creates a candlelight hue in the space.

"This must have cost you a fortune."

"Don't think about that."

"Can you imagine how many stars we'll be able to see with all these skylights?"

"It's going to be awesome."

"Theo, remember how I told you I didn't camp anymore because I was scared it wouldn't be as magical."

"I do."

"That's no longer true," I say, sitting up to stare down at him. His hands are clasped behind his head. "You, sir, have single-handedly brought magic back into my life."

He lifts one of his shoulders. "I'm good like that."

"And you need some humble pie." I roll my eyes and playfully slap his chest. "But I mean it. I really do. This is the best present anyone has ever given me."

Pulling me down by my neck, he kisses me soundly on the lips.

"I'm glad you like it."

"I love it," I whisper, looking around our new fortress.

The corner of his mouth lifts. "Then I'm glad you love it."

I grin down at him.

"Merry Christmas, Theo."

"Merry Christmas, Laney."

#bestfriends #campinginthebedroom #bestpresentever
#nogummiesthankyouverymuch #whoneedsmistletoe
#hebroughtmagic #bestchristmasever #livingourrealestlife

Grannism—You should always return Tupperware. It's sentimental for some.

thirty-seven

THEO

"YOU AREN'T DOING IT RIGHT!"

"I've been manning this grill for years, back off," Laney says, snapping tongs at Devin. Chase chuckles as he steps outside, the porch door slapping shut behind him.

"They're at it again, huh?"

I grin on at Laney bundled up in a sweater, leggings, and a beanie, and briefly imagine unwrapping her later.

"I know that look," Chase hands me a beer, just as Laney swats Devin away closing the grill.

"Baby, tell this bubble-butted idiot that she has to—"

"Nope," Chase shouts from the porch. "Hell no, the last time I got in the middle of a heated discussion between you two, I barely made it out alive."

Devin huffs from where she stands. "Why did I marry you again?"

"Because I'm ridiculous hot, and I put up with your shit."

Devin smiles. "That'll do for now."

The four of us spent a quiet New Year's Eve at my abandoned house popping champagne and decided to spend the day with Deidra and Max. Laney insisted we barbecue in the freezing temperatures and no one thought to argue. The only argument that ensued was when Chase and I offered to grill, and were read the riot act from the two women currently fighting over it.

"They are something," Chase remarks fondly as they bicker back and forth. "Word of advice. Just go with it."

"When?"

"Every day. Every. Single. Day."

"Stop it!" Laney shrieks swatting at Devin's hands.

"They're currently on the same menstrual cycle," Chase says. "Please don't ask me how I know that. And if you don't want me privy to something, don't share it with Laney."

"It's like that, huh?" I say, watching them go at it.

"So very like that. They don't keep shit from each other. And they can rag on each other all damn day, but if you go after either one of them alone, they'll attack like a pack of piranhas."

"Hey Theo, have you found Laney's pause button?" Devin calls to me where I sit on the porch.

Laney whips her head around with a "don't you dare!" just as Devin's arm shoots out and she presses her fingers into the indent at Laney's collar.

Laney immediately shuts down, dropping the tongs, her entire body jerking before she goes limp while something like a snort comes out of her.

Devin grins wickedly. "Emergency shut down button. She's so ticklish when you press here that she can't fight you, but you have to press hard, see?" Devin explains as Laney speaks like the Tin Man with rusty lips.

"I'b gonna kib you!"

Devin wiggles her fingers digging them in and Laney explodes in laughter.

"See, you take it away, and you get a two-second delay before she can move again," Devin demonstrates, pulling her fingers away briefly right before she paralyzes her again. "I figure this will come in handy for you one day."

Laney is drooling a little at this point, spittle coming from her lips. "St-t-t-hap!"

Devin does it once more as tears pour down Laney's tomato-colored face when the screen door again slaps closed behind me.

"Devin, she's going to kill you," Deidra says through a laugh.

"She'll have to catch me first," Devin pulls her fingers away barely dodging Laney's first swing before she darts away with Laney charging after her.

Chase and I are hysterical as we watch the two of them run down the drive like twin female Forrest Gumps.

"You bitch! You swore you wouldn't ever tell anybody!" Laney shrieks, digging into the gravel in her boots making good time.

"Language, Elaine!" Deidra scolds.

"You're going to die, clown!" Laney declares doing an impressive leap through the trees before they disappear out of sight.

Deidra sighs. "They make me so proud. Tomboys, both of them. It's a miracle they survived this long. Come on, boys, I'll make your first plate."

"First plate?" I look to Chase for guidance.

"Go with it," he mouths before following Deidra inside. I drain the rest of my beer and hear a loud screech in the distance before all goes silent.

Laney and Devin join us a few minutes later, their hair dotted with leaves, their cheeks red from the bite of the cold, matching smiles on their faces and a fresh plate of mildly charred barbecue in their hands.

The table is full to the brim with every imaginable southern dish.

Laney hands me an empty plate before dumping a spoonful of collard greens on it. I try not to cringe. "Okay, Houseman, you ever heard of this New Year's Day tradition?"

I glance at the spoon skeptically.

"Can't say that I have."

"Alright, so you're supposed to stuff yourself full of these on New Year's Day. It's kind of a hope or wish for your fiscal year. The more you eat, the more you'll earn. Peas stand for coins, greens for bills."

Laney piles them on taking up the whole of my plate, and I try to hide my groan. "That's good. Thanks."

"Trust me, man, they look like baby shit, but they taste pretty amazing."

"Chase Hart, grown and married or not, you curse one more time at this table, all that tongue of yours is tasting is soap."

"Yes, ma'am," Chase says as Devin belly laughs.

Once we're all seated, Deidra grabs the girls' hands, and Chase and I follow suit.

"Laney, you say grace."

"Dear Lort, I just want to thank you for Dorito Tacos."

"Laney!"

"Fine. Good bread, good meat, good *God,* let's eat."

I press my lips together to keep from laughing while Deidra sighs in annoyance.

Laney shrugs. "Hey, it was good enough for Gran."

After an exhausting marathon at the table, I'm sitting on the porch with my tomboy astride me resting her head on my shoulder.

We're both in a food coma barely able to move. Patsy Cline croons through the screen door along with Max's snore. We're bundled up beneath one of Gran's old quilts, as the sun slides past the horizon between the trees highlighting a sea of bare branches.

"I like this song. Fittin' don't you think?" I grin and run my fingers through her hair. *"Crazy."*

"It's Gran's favorite. She listened to it all the time."

"Well, I like it. And I love it *here*."

"Mmm," Laney replies, her voice laced with sleep.

"I'm serious. It's like a different world."

"Yep."

"I envy you got to grow up here."

She pulls away and brings tired eyes to mine. "Really?"

"Yeah. It was so chaotic at my house."

"It is nice." She says, scanning the trees. "Thinking you might be a little bit of a country boy after all?"

"Maybe," I pull her tighter to me. The smell of freshly brewed coffee fills my nose.

"I'll be the first in the family to graduate and leave this house."

"You don't sound very excited about it."

"I don't know. What's good enough for them is for me too. I just feel like I'm expected to do great things, you know? I'm sure if I land a job somewhere else, I'll be happy not to be so damned broke all the time. It's just…"

I lift my knees to nudge her closer to me. "What?"

"Every time I think about packing up and leaving here, I don't see a destination. I've had four years to think about it, and I'm still not sure where I want to end up."

"You'll figure it out."

"I don't even have a favorite flower, Theo. I can't decide on a favorite friggin' flower. If I can't make a simple decision like that, how in the hell am I supposed to make important life-changin' decisions?"

"I'll clue you in on something," I whisper.

"What?"

"Half of the people with a degree probably hate what they majored in because they didn't know what they wanted to do either."

"I know."

"Some of them won't use a tenth of what they learned in college for their career."

"Do you think I'll be shit as a publicist?"

"Not at all, but people like you are the best example of the good kind of chaos. You thrive in the random. You shake things up and make whatever you have going *work* for you. Screw the planning and just go with your gut. Stumble your way through, wing it, and do whatever makes you happy."

"Fake it until I make it?"

"Exactly. You're a scrapper, Laney. You hustle like no one I've ever seen. You cannot fail, no matter what you decide."

"I stumbled into you."

"Glad you did."

"Me too." She's quiet for so long I assume she's asleep. I rock us back and forth, just admiring the view and the feel of the girl in my arms.

"So, you really think I'll stumble into my future too?"

"In the best way, yeah," I say before pressing a gentle kiss to her temple, "I absolutely do."

She brings her lips to mine as Deidra calls us inside for pie.

After a chaste kiss, she looks up at me with a light in her eye that warms me from within.

"Happy New Year, Houseman."

"Happy New Year, Laney."

#laidbacknewyears #happierthantwopigsinshit
#bestfriendsforeva #perfectday
#noresolutionsbutonehelluvakiss #hesallmine
#livingourrealestlife

thirty-eight

THEO

Theo: Hey.
Laney: Hey Handsome.
Theo: What are you doing?
Laney: Not much.
Theo: Good because I'm pulling up.
Laney: No!
Theo: What? Why?
Laney: Because it's not a good time.
Theo: You just said you weren't busy.

I roll up the gravel drive to see Ole Faithful, Deidra's sub-urban, Devin's Chevy, and a familiar car that has me slamming on my brakes.

Panic consumes me as I grapple for the handle staring at the front door of the house, expecting an explosion at any moment. I'm already running up the porch steps as Laney walks out closing the door behind her in full old lady garb, including her Madea wig.

"Houseman," she tries to scorn with a guilty shake in her voice. "I told you now is not a good time."

"What is Courtney's car doing here?"

Her eyes dart left and right. "Don't get mad. They just wanted to come for a visit."

"Uh huh."

"It's long overdue," she defends, her voice still unsteady. "You know. You can't keep me from them forever."

"Okay, fine. Do you want to tell me what you're doing dressed like that?"

"You wouldn't understand." She bites her lip pensively, and from inside the house, I hear a shriek.

"Oh Noooo! Nobody move! My contact!"

Laney winces.

"Was that Brenna?"

"Uh huh?"

"What wouldn't I understand?"

"Just, come back in a few hours, okay?" She drops her voice low. "I'll make it worth your while."

"Yeah, not going to work. Get out of my way."

"Houseman, turn around and go back the way you came and no one gets hurt." She thrusts a finger above my shoulder just as Courtney spouts off.

"This is football. All the people wanna hear about are touchdowns and injuries. They don't give a damn 'bout that grape shit!"

"Theo, trust me," she says as I gently push her to the side and step…into an alternate universe.

All three of my sisters sit on Laney's couch, wearing different wigs dressed like they're ready for an ice cream social. Deidra is no less guilty in the rocker, fully decked out twenty years north of her age and her dress looks like it's made mostly of yarn. All of them look up at me collectively with overdone blue-haired makeup on, margaritas in one hand and scorecards laying in their laps.

"Boy sperm," Courtney greets me with a slight slur as I trail my eyes down to Max who has the decency to look mortified in a bonnet.

I turn to Laney, utterly confused. "Live Old Maid?"

"It's Gran's birthday and the thirtieth anniversary of *Steel Magnolias*," Devin supplies, grabbing my hand to usher me into the house. "We decided to celebrate in a way that would make her proud. I'm Shelby, Brenna is Annelle, Courtney is wicked Ouiser, Deidra is M'Lynn, and Jamie is Clairee."

"That explains everything," I'm unable to hide the terror in my voice. "And who are you?" I notice the enhancement to Laney's chest.

"Truvy," she says, blowing out a breath, "played by Dolly Parton. I was going to tell you. But—"

"That's our fault," Jamie explains. "Because you would have never let it happen."

"Yes, well, I was worried it would be awkward. Imagine *that?*"

"Shut up, Theo. You're ruining our game," Courtney says, tipping back more margarita.

"Game?" I look to my girl for help.

"We, ugh," Laney's cheeks flame. "Well, we spout off our lines as they come and the one who nails the most wins."

"It's the southern bible," Devin explains as if this behavior is normal. "Any true southern woman worth their salt is going to know a line or two of this movie by heart."

"And what's the prize?"

Laney shows all her teeth looking up at me fearfully.

"The golden penis," they all say in unison.

"Courtney was in charge of that," Laney squeaks.

"Eighteen speeds, brother," my sister says, pulling a vibrator from a gift bag at her feet. "Would you like to stick around for the demonstration?"

"I think the boy may pass out," Deidra says, sipping her drink. "Someone get Drum some pork and beans."

They all burst into laughter, and I'm so lost, I may never come back.

"Walk me out?" I swallow as sweat gathers on my forehead. There is entirely too much estrogen in the room. I turn and run smack into the damned door as my sisters cackle at my back.

If there is a hell made specifically for me, I couldn't imagine a better depiction than this. "I'll see you later," I say, waving a hand behind me.

"Aww, at least give him the ass end of the armadillo cake!" That gem is yelled at my back as I take in the brisk air of the porch.

"Hey, you aren't mad, are you?" Laney says as I reach my car.

I turn to her and drag her toward me, her Dolly tits pressing against my chest and try to wrap my head around what I just walked into.

All I can do is laugh.

And she laughs with me. "I told you not to go in there."

Chuckling I look up at her as she eyes me with caution. "You."

"Me?" She asks with doe eyes.

"Are just…" I shake my head, "incredible."

"Really?"

"Crazy as hell and fucking amazing." I crush my mouth to her peach-colored lips and kiss the hell out of her. She grips my jacket and sighs into my kiss. When we pull away, I can feel the eyes through the blinds without bothering to turn my head.

"You know they're watching."

"I couldn't care less."

"So, you're not mad then?"

"No, of course not. I was fool enough to think you needed

to take them in doses. As it turns out they're going to be your greatest allies."

"I really like them a lot."

"Well, they're all yours," I say, pressing my lips to hers, "and so am I."

Her eyes flood with warmth. "I think it's going to turn into a slumber party, so I'll see you tomorrow?"

"Yes," I say, giving her one last kiss.

"Get back in here, Truvy!"

In my driver's seat, I turn the ignition and look up to see her on the other side of the hood just as she does a little Marilyn shimmy for me accentuating her puffed up chest before blowing me a kiss and running back inside.

And that's when the thud happens. There's no way I can fall any further.

I love her.

#payinghomagetoourqueens #steelmagnoliasanniversary
#southernwomansbible #southernpride #truvytits
#livingmyrealestlife

thirty-nine

THEO

I DRUM MY FINGERS ALONG MY THIGH, ITCHING TO GET OUT OF class. Spring break starts in thirty minutes, and I can't wait to have a solid week of endless Laney days. Neither of us can really afford to take off anywhere special, but both Troy and Lance left last night, which means I have a week to play house with her.

The longer the lecture goes on, the more I want to claw my hair out and curse my stupidity for not just taking the day, like half the class. If I weren't so amped about the week ahead, I would be half asleep like the rest of the dark room, due to the amount of rain cloud cover while the teacher drones on. It's when the room goes significantly darker that an ominous feeling creeps over me, drawing my attention to the window. And I'm not the only one who notices.

"Oh my God," a girl whispers next to me, "is that what I think it is?"

"Yeah, it is."

"Oh SHIT!"

Camera phones come out like guns in a gangster movie as fear temporarily paralyzes me.

"Everyone get back in your seats, please," the instructor says just as more students line up against the room-long span of windows to our left. We all jump when every phone lights up with a weather alert, including mine as I pull it from my backpack.

Theo: Drop what you're doing, get Max, get inside. Get in the tub!

Cursing my stupidity for texting, I frantically dial her number instead and get no answer watching in horror as the cloud circulates at rapid speed toward the ground. I can't be sure how far away, but I know it's in the direction of her house.

My fingers fly over the keys as a girl screams out. "It's down. It's down!"

Theo: Tornado! Get inside. Get in the bathroom! NOW!

"All of you out in the hall! Now!"

Fear like I've never known races through me as I curse my stupidity for not ever getting Devin's number. Laney said she would be home. Why isn't she answering?

Think, Theo.

Hardin Sports.

I Google the number and dial it and am connected to Devin in seconds while still frantically texting Laney.

"Devin, a tornado just touched down."

"I know. I just heard. Chase is with me."

"Good, have you talked to Laney?"

"Not since last night."

"Is there a siren near her house?"

"I think so."

"She's not answering. Please, Devin, tell me there's a siren! Have you ever heard one there?"

I can hear the panic in her voice. "I don't know."

"Jesus," I say my heart hammering, sweat collecting at my forehead. "Okay, try Deidra make sure they're safe."

"I don't know, Theo, I don't know if there's a siren!" She says in a panic.

"Devin, just call Deidra!"

"I'm on it!"

"Come on, baby, look at your phone. Look at your phone." The prayer tumbles from my lips as my stomach knots. I dial her again keeping my eye on the menacing cloud.

"Everybody out in the hall! NOW!"

What if she doesn't know? What if she's taking a nap and has no clue? Ripping at my hair, I scramble to the hall with the rest of the students. The phone rings again as I close my eyes, praying she's not stranded on the side of the road because of that fucking truck. "Pick up, please, pick up."

I damn near hit my knees when I hear her voice.

"I'm in the tub with Max and a flashlight. And emergency Doritos."

"Why didn't you answer me!" I shriek like a tween at the top of my lungs.

"I got the alert right before you texted, and I was trying to get the mattress off my bed. I couldn't do it and get Max and talk to you."

Too choked up to speak, I wipe my face, unable to form words.

"So, spring break is starting off with a bang, huh?" I can hear the fear in her voice, and it ruins me.

"Seems that way," I say hoarsely.

"I'm sorry I scared you."

"No, I'm just," I let out a harsh breath. "I'm just glad you're okay. I called Devin, she's at the store with Chase, where is your mom?"

"Mom went to pick up her paycheck, and now she's scrambling to help get all the patients out of their rooms."

"So, you're alone?"

"Yes." My heart bottoms out.

"Don't you dare hang up."

"I won't. But I'm kind of digging this bossy side of you."

"Wheels are back up," someone says from behind me. I look to see the menacing cloud has dispersed for the moment.

"Stay put until I can get to you. Don't hang up."

"Yes, sir."

"I'm on my way."

"No! Another could touch down any second! It's stupid! Houseman, don't you dare leave!"

I don't bother to argue with her, I know how damn stupid it is.

"Don't, Theo, please don't get in the car."

"It'll be fine."

"IT WILL NOT BE FINE!"

There isn't a hint of humor in her voice when she speaks next. "Remember when I told you stupid men run on impulse? This is a prime example. Do *not* leave school. Please, please, don't be a stupid man."

I break from the building and sprint toward my car, the only idiot outside, eyes like saucers as I glance in all directions.

"I can hear you breathing hard, you're running, aren't you? Houseman, don't you dare get in your car!"

Ignoring her, I turn the ignition and speed through the parking lot.

"You just started it. You just started your car! If you don't get killed by a tornado, I'm going to kill you myself!"

"Is your electricity still on?"

"Yes." I can hear the shake in her voice.

I gun my Honda onto the road from the parking lot looking in all directions.

"Houseman, park the fucking car and take cover! You know there's going to be another one! There always is!"

"Laney, it's fine. Stop yelling at me."

Bluetooth connected, I race through the streets like a madman taking every curve at warp speed as Laney screams at the top of her lungs.

"This is the dumbest damn thing you've ever done!"

"Stay in the tub!"

"I am!" She says before grumbling. "He's going to beat up hurricane-force winds for us, Max. Told you he was a keeper."

"That's enough, Laney!" I shout, as I fishtail on the road leading to hers. I still have five minutes left in the drive going a hundred miles an hour. Adrenaline spiking, I listen closely for sirens.

"There is no oxygen in that brain of yours! Pull over right now and get somewhere safe!"

"Laney, I'm going to be the first twenty-one-year-old to have a fucking heart attack in the middle of a tornado, if you don't shut the hell up!"

"Don't you tell me to shut up! You're risking your life, and for what?"

"I don't want you to be alone!"

"I can handle it!"

"I can't! I can't! I can't fucking handle it, okay? And you shouldn't be alone. Not the way you are. All. The. Time. Having to fend for yourself, and figure it out on your own because there's no one there to help you. I fucking hate it. I hate it for you, and I hate it for your mother. And I hate it that I want you to turn to me when you need me but you're so damned independent you're missing the part where I come in, so I'm going to go ahead and point out that time is *now*. This is where I come in, Laney. Right here, when it's scary, and I can be there to comfort you and ride it out *with* you. So, yeah, I would rather die in a fucking tornado than know you're scared and alone in that house without me."

A seconds-long silence ensues as I floor it, taking a turn that would make a gamer jealous.

"Theo?"

"I'm here."

"You're a stupid man."

"Thanks."

"I'm so pissed off at you right now."

"I know."

"So stupid," she says tearfully. "You're a stupid, stupid, *good* man. And my hero," her voice cracks just as I fly down her driveway.

"I'm here," I skid to a stop an inch from hitting her porch. I charge up the stairs and through the front door to see the bathroom door open. Max comes running with Laney hot on his heels. She runs full sprint behind Max in a cami and sleeper shorts, relief covering her face as tears run down her cheeks. We collide in the hall, and I lift her as she slams her mouth over mine. Gripping her close, I usher them both back in the bathroom and into the tub, our lips never parting.

"Idiot," she murmurs into my mouth as our tongues duel for dominance. She pulls away, batting a tear from her eyes as I pull her down with me to straddle my lap.

"*Stupid ass.*" She tugs on my hair, and I see the fire in her eyes as she looks me over in a daze before covering me in her kisses. My temple, my nose, my cheeks, my lips, my throat.

"Worth it," I grunt, gripping her waist as she turns on my lap, lifting Max out of the tub to the floor before turning her attention back to me.

"So stupid," she whispers, running her tongue along my

lower lip, my neck, before pushing her chest toward me. I bite into the meat of her cleavage as she cups me in my jeans before thrusting her tongue into my mouth. It's a tight fit, but she manages to get good friction. Rock fucking hard, I massage her thighs, kissing her back with equal fervor before she rips herself away, eyes hooded.

"Total dumbass," she says, resting her ass on my thighs while unbuttoning my jeans and slowly pulling the zipper down before taking my cock out and pumping it in her fist. "Moron."

"Are we having a fight?" I ask through clenched teeth.

"Yesss," she hisses, stroking the tip of my dick, her thumb brushing the pre-cum over the head. I damn near lose my shit when she begins to pump my length, eyeing my cock with hunger. Groaning, I look up to see her eyes flare, the rise and fall of her chest. She's the most beautiful thing I've ever seen.

Eyes locked on mine, she rises to position herself pushing her shorts to the side before sinking onto me and surrounding me in tight, wet heat. When she's fully seated, I see fucking stars. She grinds onto me in slow motion, and I pull off her cami, cupping her perfect tits while I drown in the feel of her.

"You win," I groan into her mouth just as she comes.

#tubbingoutthetwister #nostormcankeephimaway #inseparable #myhero #hesgotmyback #bestfriendsforlife #livingmyhappiestlife

# # # # # #

The rest of the week is drama free. There's been another shift between us since the day of the tornado. Three people died that day getting swept off the highway in their cars by one of two tornadoes that touched down. I could have very well died that day, a fact that Laney has enjoyed pointing out numerous times. My reply is always to shut her up with swift dick punishment, which she thoroughly enjoys. Last night we had Devin and Chase over for dinner. Laney cooked homemade pasta thanks to a cooking show we binged on Netflix. It was pretty damn good. We both had a lot of firsts this week.

She hosted her first dinner party.

I got to have piano sex.

She learned a few chords on my acoustic.

I mastered sixty-nine.

Some days we left the house and did mundane things, like go to Home Depot for a better shower head. It was totally domestic, and I loved every minute.

In the morning, I cooked breakfast, and my barista made the coffee, laxative-free. At night, I would read with my head in her lap while she played with my hair and watched cooking shows.

We stayed up late, wearing each other out and slept in every day waking each other up in naked and creative ways.

Every once in a while, I'd catch her looking at me, and wordlessly bring her to me for a kiss, because I knew without a doubt, when she looked at me that way, she was *with* me, and I'd made my place with her.

It was the best week of my life.

Grannism—If a man makes you smile, he's worth it. If he makes you cry, that's when you know he's worth a whole lot more to you.

forty

LANEY

TONIGHT'S THE NIGHT I CONFESS TO MY LOVE ABOUT HOW I feel. I've been patient. We've made it past every major holiday, not to mention Valentine's, the green beer of St. Patrick's Day, and Easter. So far, he's refused to be the first to utter the words. It's only in the past week that I've become obsessed with my confession. With my graduation looming I'm determined to secure my place with him as he has with me, no matter what my future entails. It's when I was in the shower this morning that I realized what's been holding him back. He doesn't want me to feel obligated to return the sentiment.

That has to be it.

And I can't hold back anymore. There's no way I can be wrong. This feeling is reciprocal. Even if it's only been mere months since we got physical, those months have changed everything for me, *inside* of me.

My gypsy heart no longer beats that beatnik way. It now thrums in a happy and monogamous rhythm, spelling out his name every four beats. Theo's carefully carved his place in my life and over my heart. It's etched all over me. At the same time, something tells me he thrives on the anticipation. He's made me wait for so much already. It's one of his talents to drive me absolutely bat shit crazy before I get to reap the rewards. But they've all been worth it.

He is worth it. While I laid myself bare, he's been spoon-feeding me pieces of himself. Layer by layer, everything he's unveiled has only made me fall harder.

A knock at the door has me running toward it, toward him. I open it to see Theo standing at my door, looking edible while holding the largest bouquet of flowers I've ever seen. It's obscene and takes both of his hands to hold it.

"Good God, man, did you buy the whole flower shop?!"

"I asked for one of each."

"So I could finally decide on one?"

"No," he leans in pressing a gentle kiss to my lips, "so you could have them all."

It's on the tip of my tongue to tell him then, but I hold back and kiss the hell out of him instead.

"Ahem," my mother says, breaking us up. "Theo, those are so beautiful."

"Hey Deidra." Theo bends down, disappearing behind the door and picks up a smaller bouquet of wildflowers. "These are for you."

"Thank you. It's been a long time since I got flowers," she murmurs appreciatively before grabbing our bouquets and heading to the kitchen.

Theo looks me over as we linger at the door. "You look beautiful."

"Thank you. Where are we going?"

"It's a surprise." He looks pleased with himself. He's wearing a long-sleeved T-shirt and dark jeans. I push up on my toes and lean in. "Heads up, Houseman, I'm in a kind of mood and when I say mood, I mean I want to suck the life out of you."

I pull back to weigh his expression, and my mom chooses

that moment to kiss us both on the cheek before darting out the door.

"I'm running late. Where are you two off to?"

"It's a surprise," Theo says, his hot gaze never leaving mine.

"Well, have fun." She calls before jetting down the steps and getting in her suburban.

When her taillights grow dim, Theo ushers me inside the door and pins me to it.

"I thought we were leaving."

"We are," he says before taking all the gloss off my lips. When he pulls away, I'm a puddle of want, and his lips are shining. Standing limply at the door, I shake my head.

"I missed you today."

"Theo—"

He cups my face rubbing his thumbs along my cheeks. "I think about you all the time. If I'm reading, I think about what you might think of the book. If I'm driving, I wonder what you'll think of the song playing. I want in that head of yours so bad, all the time."

"I'm crazy about you, too."

"Laney," he whispers softly, "this is *real* for me."

It's the perfect moment. The words are begging to be spoken, but I can't get them out. He weighs my expression carefully before lifting my hand to press a kiss to it. "Let's go."

Half an hour later, we pull up to Theo's house where we're forced to park on the other side of the street due to the number of cars in his drive.

"What's going on here?"

"Nothing we want to stick around for, I forgot something,

should only take a second." He opens his door, but I put my hand on his to stop him.

"Wait," I say, and he hesitates.

"Laney, if you—"

"This is real for me too." My fear is realized as he refuses to meet my eyes. He thinks I said it out of guilt. He leans in and kisses me. "I'll be right back."

Theo runs inside as a group of guys huddled on his porch greet him, and he gives them a quick wave. Curiosity gets the best of me and nature calls, so I decide to kill two birds. It's more a gathering than a party, and I can see why we wouldn't want to be a part of it. I've seen more ass cheeks in the last fifteen seconds than I did changing diapers at my first job. It's a grinder, and I feel like I'm walking into an episode of *Rock of Love*. This gathering is a no holds barred, titty festival fight for the biggest meat stick.

I'm so over it already.

Halfway to the house, I'm stopped by a familiar voice.

"You again. Where did you come from and where the hell have you been my whole life?" I look up to see Batman surrounded by a few Robins as he pumps a keg. "Sorry," I shake my head at his tired line and move toward the porch.

"No way, you're not getting away from me again."

"Look, you get points for persistence, but sorry to tell you, Romeo, it's *never* going to happen."

He moves to block me from the porch, his back to his friends. He shoves his hands in his jeans, his bulky frame imposing, his T-shirt strangling his biceps.

And I feel nothing but...annoyance.

"Listen. I've been chasing you for months. When are you going to finally give me a chance? There's something here," he says, dipping his head low to catch my eyes. "I know you feel it too."

I consider him, admire him briefly, and realize what a blessing it is to know the difference between attraction and true chemistry and the blessed fact that I now know *better*. Six months ago, I would've easily fallen into this trap. And it took one good man to change everything.

"You do feel it," he says with a smirk. It's then I realize I haven't replied, and I'm sending out the wrong signals.

"Maybe yo—"

"Maybe?" That voice doesn't belong to him. It belongs to the man standing to the right of us. "Did you just fucking say *maybe?*"

Theo's livid eyes meet mine and then shoot over to Batman. He reads our posture before we take a step away from each other, but it's too late. He saw intimacy, familiarity. He saw me linger too long. His eyes blaze over me and then shoot back to him.

"You've been chasing her for *months?*"

Batman shakes his head. "No, man, it's not like that."

"What's it like?" Theo spits menacingly. "Please, Troy, tell me what the fuck it's like. Because I really need to know."

Troy? Batman is Troy?!

Dread cloaks me while bile climbs up my throat.

"Oh shit." One of the guys says as Theo steps directly in front of Troy, his intent clear when he bats the full beer out of his hand, and it splashes the few guys next to him.

"What the hell," one of them spouts, wiping away the beer from his soaked arms. "You need to check yourself, Bugle Boy."

Theo's gaze doesn't waver. "Come on, tell me, *fuckboy*, because I need to know how a clueless piece of total *shit* like you gets away with this over and over."

Troy's jaw ticks and his eyes narrow. "Look, this

holier-than-thou routine is getting fucking old, man. I didn't know she belonged to you."

Theo grits his teeth, ready to pounce. "Never stopped you before, has it? You're disgusting."

Troy's eyes flare, and I shake my head, knowing he's about to go for the jugular.

"Maybe you need to ask *her* why she's sending vibes *my* way."

"Don't you dare! You bastard," I finally manage to say glaring at Troy before turning pleading eyes to Theo. "Theo, that's not true!"

"You're asking for an ass-whooping," the guy standing next to Troy says in warning. "You need to back off, Theo."

Troy lifts his hand, silencing him with a gesture. "Clear them out."

"Be a good dog, Kevin, and obey your master," Theo snarks, never tearing his eyes away from Troy.

"Fuck you, Bugle Boy," Kevin says snidely before turning to the gathering crowd. "Party's over. See yourselves out. *Now.*"

There are only a few groans before those on the lawn start to disperse. The tension is unbearable, palpable as the two stand off.

Theo is the first to speak. "You're pathetic, you know that? The worst kind of fucking man."

Troy goes rigid, his eyes icing over. "I'm the man you wish you were."

"You're a sack of shit hiding behind a pretty face, and you know it."

"Like I said, I don't know her."

Unable to handle the tension, I step between them facing Theo. "I didn't even know his name before tonight."

"You don't know her?" Theo ignores me altogether, his eyes fixed behind me as he snaps over my shoulder at Troy. He's shaking with anger.

"Theo," I say, placing a hand on his chest. He jerks his body away, glaring at me before attacking Troy again. "You don't know her, huh?"

Troy wipes a hand down his face. "No."

"Yeah, you *don't*," Theo says, swallowing. "But I know you. I've known every version of you since middle school, and I'm not impressed with the 2.0. Get your shit and get the hell out of my house, and don't fucking come back."

"Whatever, man, gladly," Troy says, stalking up toward the house.

I look back to Theo just as his turbulent eyes sweep me. "And now I know *you*, too," he says with revulsion just before he turns to stalk away.

"Don't you dare," I follow him across the yard back to his car. "I was about to turn him down. I had no idea he was your roommate. None."

He opens his driver door, and I kick it shut. Furious eyes meet mine.

"Don't go off half-cocked. This is a *huge* misunderstanding. I didn't know who he was until tonight."

"Move, Laney."

"This is ridiculous and uncalled for. I've never entertained him!"

"Get out of my way," Theo says, his voice so cold my eyes fill.

"You are making a mistake," I whisper hoarsely.

"The only fucking mistake I made is wasting more of my time and attention on another woman who didn't deserve it!"

"Don't...don't say anything else I can't forgive you for."

"Then get the hell out of my way, Laney!"

Mortified, I cover my mouth, and stumble a step back from his door just before he jerks it open, starts his car, and drives away.

forty-one

LANEY

HOURS LATER, I'M FREEZING ON HIS PORCH. TROY LEFT JUST after Theo with a few of his friends. He tried to approach me, but I'd snubbed him with the wave of my hand. He had to know how much damage he'd done with a few mere sentences. He played on Theo's insecurities while making me look guilty and all because of his arrogance.

This was a fight between two completely different with one common denominator, *pride.* Combine that five-letter word with two sets of balls and you get a mushroom cloud the size of Texas.

Gran used to tell me pride is a man's fuel source and when threatened, even the humblest of men can become a raging bull.

I'd just watched it happen. But the truth also came out as well. To Troy, I would've been another conquest. To the man I loved, I was a reason to declare war.

Except the only casualty of this war is me because neither of them was ever made abundantly clear on *my* side of things. I'm not taking the blame, but I have a part in it.

A few hours after our blow up, Theo pulls in the drive, and I smell the liquor on him before he looks up and sees me waiting. He averts his eyes and hangs his head.

"You need to go," he says, staring at the keys in his hand.

"You're being ridiculous."

"Fine. I'm ridiculous."

"Don't do this. You know how I feel about you."

"Do I?" He snaps, his eyes meeting mine. He's not drunk, but he's still angry.

My throat tightens unbearably, and it spreads to my chest. His eyes are full of a cruelty I've never seen, never thought I'd see. Not from him.

"I didn't fight it, not with you. Not a single minute. I let it happen."

He scoffs. "Guess that makes me different, huh? It's different with *me*, right?"

"You know it is." Tears fill my eyes, and I blink them away. His expression doesn't change. "I'm not her, I wouldn't hurt you that way."

"No, you definitely aren't."

The words are a lash whip against my chest.

"Please, just listen to me."

"I saw the way he looked at you." He pins me with an accusing stare. "But I *felt* the way you looked at him. I *felt* it. Tell me I imagined it."

"You have to believe me, it meant *nothing*. I'm not going to deny he's attractive, but he caught me by surprise, and when he did, I thought of how far I've come from wanting anyone like him, and I was happy about it. That's what you saw. You have to believe me."

"Maybe I would if you hadn't looked at him like *that*."

I'm shaking my head furiously. "I just told you why. It was you I was thinking about!"

His chest pumps with his sarcastic chuckle. "Right."

Stunned by his wrath, I watch him start toward his porch. Helpless, I follow.

"You're comparing butterflies to bee stings! He's not the one I feel anything for!"

He turns on a dime and glares back at me. "What?"

I stride towards him, only stopping when the space between us is too close to ignore. "I said you're comparing butterflies to bee stings."

"So, you admit you feel for him?"

"If that's what you got out of that statement, it only proves you're currently as ignorant as you are blind. It's you that I want, and you damn well *know* it's you."

I can practically taste his lips, and I feel his inclination to move toward me. His shoulders stiffen, and he inches his chin back, breaking our connection. He might as well have slapped me.

"I'm your sentence finisher, Theo, and you are mine. Deny yourself, deny me, but you'll be making a huge mistake. Maybe I gave you too much credit for being different. Because right now—you're acting like a dumbass man."

He flinches, but his gaze never warms. "Guess I am."

"Yeah, well, jealousy looks like shit on you. You're ruining everything!"

"What? What could I possibly be ruining? You looked at my fucking roommate like you wanted him."

"A split second of recognition and that's what's breaking us up?"

"Were we ever really together?"

Hot tears burn, as the rest of me stings. "How could you ask that?"

"Am I allowed to now?"

"Allowed to ask? You never had to! I just spent the last four months wrapped around you. Wake up! This is all for nothing. Fine, he's good looking, it was a second, maybe less. He took me by surprise. I admit it probably looked bad—"

"It was that second that made me no longer trust you."

The statement damns us, and I can practically hear the re-click of the worn-out armor he's just resurrected back around his heart.

"This is really how you feel?"

He shakes his head as if I'm ridiculous. "We were never going to work."

"Says you!"

"I should be able to tell the woman I'm with how I feel when I feel it, without fearing she'll run for the goddamn hills! Or worry that she feels she has to reciprocate those feelings out of obligation!"

"I never asked you to hold back!"

He snorts. "You're ridiculous if you think I did. Not with you. Not at all. The words were there even if I had to swallow them every day," his voice cracks. "Every single time I look at you. And look where it got me."

I step forward.

He steps back.

"This is in your head."

"No, it's fucked up my heart!" He pounds a fist to his chest. "How can I trust you now?"

"You would have to trust me in the first place," I say, my heart charring to ash. I choke on that revelation as he glances at the ground between us. "Oh my God, you never did trust me, did you?" I shake my head, unable to believe the truth of it. "You were expecting me to screw this up. The whole time. Weren't you?"

His silence singes me to the point I can no longer take an easy breath.

"You were waiting for me to ruin it."

"Congratulations," he says bitterly, "you succeeded."

"You don't mean any of this."

"Maybe I do. You said so yourself the night we met. Lie to me, Laney. Tell me you love me too. Isn't it my turn?"

"You're going to feel like such an idiot when you figure out how ridiculous you're acting."

"Or maybe I just saved myself a whole hell of a lot of fucking headaches."

"You're a bastard."

"Fine, I'm the bad guy, are we done here?"

"Oh yeah," my voice cracks. "we're done."

"Good, because I wouldn't want to hold you back."

I glare at him through my tears. "You're not who I thought you were."

"Funny, you're *exactly* who I thought you were."

"Go straight to hell, Houseman."

Chin quivering, I try and pull myself together from all sides as he climbs the steps to his porch. At the door, he glances at me over his shoulder, his eyes swimming with hurt.

"How could you—" he shakes his head as tears slide down his jaw and my heart stops beating.

"Theo—"

"I always knew—" he says hoarsely before swallowing, another tear sliding down his cheek. "I knew if you saw him, that would be the end of us."

"Well, that only proves how much you know," I cry with an identical tear running down my own face, "because I chose you over him months ago."

I leave him there, because nothing I say at this point will matter as much as if I'd said it before. My hesitance cost me dearly, my past caught up with me. And my words came much, much too late.

Grannism—You aren't hungry, you're bored.

forty-two

LANEY

"WHERE IS SHE?" I HEAR DEVIN SAY FROM THE PORCH. Great, an intervention. It's not like I've emptied two cans of Cheez Whiz in my mouth today. I've cut back to one. I push the empty box of Famous Amos away with my foot and bury my head under a couch pillow just as the screen door slams.

"Shit, it's worse than I thought."

I groan through the fabric. "Don't you dare. I'm just having a moment."

"You've been having a moment for the last two weeks."

"Lookie here," I say, sitting and pulling the pillow to shield the carb bulge of my belly, "I'm just bored."

Devin pushes at my feet to make room for her on the couch as I retreat to my corner. "He's hurting too, I assure you." She surveys the coffee table. "I see we're still on a strict diet of whiskey and carbs."

"And it's of no consequence to *you*."

"No, but your ass is going to pay the price."

Letting out a harsh breath, I give her a dead stare. "Always a pleasure, buddy, it's naptime. Kindly see yourself out."

"Nope, we're getting out of here. I've gotten clearance from the hubs for a girls' night, and you need it."

"I need no such thing, I'm happy here."

"Yes, I can tell by the crumbs collecting in your cleavage you're living life to the fullest. You plannin' on feastin' on that half a cookie later?"

I pull a stray piece of cookie from my chest. "Okay, maybe I could use a shower."

My mother joins us, busying herself in the kitchen, aka eavesdropping.

"You're eating your feelings. It's not healthy."

"I'm eating because these things are delicious!"

She eyes me skeptically.

"Fine," I say, clearing the contents of the table in my arms and walking them over to the trash before resting my hands on my hips. "Happy?"

"Right as rain, how are you?"

"I told you, I'm *bored*."

"You're in denial."

"I'm not. I just need to regroup."

"Regroup," Devin says nodding, "how's that working out?"

"I'm getting there."

"Uh huh," she says, turning to my mother who decides now is the perfect time to harp in.

"Your graduation is coming up and you haven't even picked out a dress."

"Yes, I have."

"No, you haven't."

"I'm planning on it," I grab the remote, "I just need—"

Devin jerks the remote from my hands. "That's it. GET UP! This is ridiculous. You got your heart broken. We gave you a decent enough grace period to lose your shit. You've spent the whole time denying it. Time to get back up."

"I'm not down or in denial," I assure them both as my mother takes the seat opposite of me.

"Excited about your trip?" Mom asks.

"Yes. Of course." *No.*

I twirl a lock of hair between my fingers. "I'm bored. I need...a change of scenery, and I'll get it on my trip. I'm just restless, I just need something..." I scrutinize the ends of my hair. "You two wouldn't understand."

"I'm pretty sure I would," my mother says through a sigh.

"You miss him," Devin declares softly.

"To hell with *him.*"

"With who?" My mom pipes in. "You can't even say his name."

"Laney," Devin says in the same maternal tone. "It's okay to admit your heart is broken. It's us."

Mom nods. "He roped you in good, baby girl. You had nothing but stars in your eyes for months."

"You're upset, maybe a little devastated and that's okay."

"For the last time, I'm *restless.* I need a change." I stare at my split-ends.

"You clearly miss him. You fell in love with him. We both saw it."

"Yeah, well, he doesn't think so. And anyway, drop it. I just need something..." I pluck at my hair, "I know exactly what I need."

I rise from the couch marching toward my bedroom and hear a collective, "Stop her!"

I'm already in my bathroom with my scissors raised when Devin tackles me like a fucking linebacker into my bathtub.

"You idiot!" I scream as we crash through the shower curtain and land at a horrible angle.

I'm gasping for air as Devin wrestles the scissors from me.

"Stop it! Damn it, Devin! You aren't supposed to even run with scissors, let alone get tackled with them!"

My mom is howling with laughter behind us as Devin manages to get them from me and stands pointing them in my direction as if *I'm* the threat.

I stand, ass bruised and back on fire, crossing my arms over my chest.

"You gonna stand guard all night, Red Rover, 'cause my mind's made up!"

"If I have to," Devin challenges, not one bit intimidated.

"I need to cut my hair! I need a change!"

Devin lifts the open tampon box on my bathroom counter and raises a brow. "You need Midol, possibly a Xanax, and to sleep on this decision for about a week. Until then, these belong to me."

I glare at my mother.

"This is funny to you?" Tears fill my eyes. "I'm a joke to you two?"

"I'm sorry, little woman, but I agree. You're a hot ass mess." She comes toward me, and I shake my head, lifting my chin defiantly to ward them off.

Devin turns back to grin at her. "Remember that time she tried to dye her hair blonde with peroxide and came out looking like a leopard?"

"I meant to do that," I snap through watery eyes. "I was going through an Animal Planet phase."

"Oh God, how about when she shaved it on one side!" My mom supplies through a light laugh of her own.

"I wanted it to look like Pink's!" I toss my hands up. "Have you seen that woman's hair? It's glorious!"

"Or the other time she tried to give herself dreads so she could be country chic," Devin says, keeping in conversation as they both completely ignore me. "She washed her hair with raw eggs!"

"That's what I read to do online! I go through hair phases. Everyone does."

Devin looks back at me, determination in her voice. "Laney, the only thing you love about your appearance lately is your hair, and you are *not* cutting it because you got your heart broken. It will break ten times worse when you wake up and realize your mistake."

I raise my wobbling chin a notch further. "What are you even doing here anyway? Didn't we marry you off? Aren't you supposed to be ironing and cooking right now?"

She rolls her eyes. "Maybe if I got married in the '50s? Chase is the one that cooks most nights. And who irons anymore? Besides, with comments like that, I know you've really lost it."

"I have not!" I defend. "I'm fine."

"You're an undeclared feminist who just told me to go play June Cleaver! You're hurting, and I won't let you take it out on your hair!"

"I-I-I-I'm not," my voice cracks, "I'm not..." sad, miserable, heartbroken, "myself," I cry out as my face falls.

"Shit," Devin murmurs, capturing me in her arms just as I break. My mom is right behind her as they both wrap around me with words of comfort. And I cry. I cry so hard I cover them both in snot. When I'm finally able to breathe, I pull away spotting Max as he walks in looking at us like the lunatics we are before scoffing and walking out.

"H-he-he won't talk to me. He's just," I hiccup, "he's done. H-h-how am I supposed to do this?"

"This is just phase one. You know all the hell hounds I went through to get to Chase. We might not put up with bullshit long, Laney, but the pain is still the same. I've been where you are. You can't force him."

"But I loved him, I loved him the best way I knew how, why wasn't that good enough?"

Both their eyes fill, and I shake my head. "Cut it out right now. Both of you."

"Shit, she finally did it," Devin whispers to my mother who gazes on at me. "I'm so proud of you. You finally opened yourself up—"

"Yeah, yeah, I get it, I've been conquered. Now how do I get him *back*?"

They exchange a long look before turning to me. I see the answer in their eyes.

I don't get him back. And I guess that realization starts phase two.

forty-three

THEO

"**H**EY YA," I HEAR FOR THE TENTH TIME SINCE I GOT TO school. At first, I wasn't sure if it was for me.

And then I was getting the official Grand Salute everywhere, on every corner of campus, by everyone, including faculty. And one brave girl had the audacity to lecture me during finals. "Hey ya, buddy, just call her. You two belong together."

I wanted to argue that all she knows is what she saw on social media and that it's misleading. But it's not. It's us. That was the whole point. And that point is constantly stabbing me.

After a hundred or so greetings, I pull up our account to see a candid of me she posted and the hashtag beneath it.

Has anyone seen my best friend? If you do, please do me a favor and give him a "Hey ya," for me.

#imissmybestfriend #livingmyloneliestlife

The sentiment doesn't ring hollow, and only hits harder as the day goes on, and one classmate after the other calls out to me from every direction. "Hey ya!" The greeting is used often enough, but I don't think it's ever been used quite like this. I'm willing to bet Laney's project outshined every other senior's this year, and all we had to do to make it happen was fall in love.

Her project might be a smashing success, but we are

currently a disaster. She'll be leaving soon. She's about to graduate. It's been weeks since we broke up. The most miserable fucking two weeks of my life.

This is where I'm supposed to admit I overreacted.

I did.

This is also the part where I'm supposed to run and tell the girl and admit what an idiot I've been.

I haven't.

Because though I credit myself for having a different mindset than most, I'm still a fucking guy. A guy who's spent more good years catering to women and getting his heart mangled in return.

Maybe nice guys do finish last. And for the first time, since I met Troy and Lance, I fully understand their philosophy.

Theodore Houseman's Colossal College Mistake #2, falling for a caged bird.

Laney was never a sure thing. She was a wild card. And I painted my glasses the perfect shade of rose to discredit any reasons why we shouldn't be together. The woman's signature characteristic is indecisiveness. She's got no map for her future. She only lives in the present with the pretense of later. And I encouraged it because I was too afraid to push her in any one set direction, including mine.

Because I'd catered to her too. No questions. No pressure to make decisions; about us, what we were, and where we were going.

But one thing is for certain. *She* is going.

"Hey ya," a voice rings out in the distance, and I pump my legs to try and escape them, but it's pointless. Another voice calls out to me, then another, and another, and eventually it's only her voice I hear, reminding me of what I'm missing. A solid lump forms in my throat as the greetings stab me from all directions while I make my way to my car. Safely inside, I white-knuckle my steering wheel. Chest battered and soul bruised from the ache of missing her, I turn over the ignition and lift my phone rereading her last text.

Laney: I trusted myself. I trusted you.

Reading the words while feeling this raw has my heart rupturing. She sent it a week ago, and then the texts stopped. What message am I sending her by ignoring it? I vowed to be the one man in her life that wouldn't abandon her. The anger was enough then to fuel my silence, but now it's the hurt and fear keeping me quiet. We met at a crossroads, and now we're at another. Trust is what we based our whole relationship on and what tore us apart. The brutal truth is, every time I think about her, I see him too, and the way she looked at him.

Music blares out of the jukebox as I sit at the bar downing another shot before drowning the aftertaste with beer.

I've been sitting here since school let out, unwilling to head home. Troy moved out the night I blew up. The house has been eerily quiet since and if I'm honest, I miss the traffic.

"Hey, man." I look over to see Lance sidle up on the barstool next to me.

Glancing over, I study the bulk of him. I observe he's the dark jock to Troy's light as he orders a beer. "What are you doing here?"

"What are *you* doing here. This isn't your scene, is it?"

I glance around the musty bar. Skeletons of longhorns hang sporadically around the place while stapled signed dollar bills pose as wallpaper.

"Not my scene, no," he says, sipping his beer. "This is where you come to hide, and it's cheap."

"Yeah."

"You look bummed."

I shrug. "Girl shit."

"Something to do with that beauty you used to bring home all the time?"

"You saw her?"

"Heard her mostly. She cracked me up."

I frown.

He shrugs. "Thin walls. Couldn't be helped."

"Sorry."

"Don't be. Seems like you had a good year." He grins and sips his beer, and I study the barbed wire tattoo around his bicep.

"Well, my good year is ending on a shitty note. Garçon!" I call to the bartender who gives me a tattooed bird before pouring more shots.

"So, what's your story?" I ask. "Seriously. I've never seen a jock be such a recluse."

"I'm a creature of my routine. I break out once in a while. But I stick to my circle, and it's small."

"I get it. Mine is dwindling."

"Yeah, be careful with that," he says, tapping the bar next to my empty shot glass. Seconds later we're raising freshly poured shots in a toast. "To the graduating class of 2019," he says before tipping it back. I inhale the liquid with him.

"So, are your parents coming to your graduation?"

He shakes his head. "Nah."

"Really, why?"

"I'm up," he says, jutting a chin over his shoulder at the guy waiting at the pool table, stick in hand. "See you, man."

"See you."

He lays a twenty on the bar, and it's when he walks away

that I realize I discovered absolutely nothing about Lance. He's moving out in a week and will forever remain a mystery to me.

I raise my finger.

"Another shot?"

"Line 'em up," I pluck my wallet of another twenty when my phone buzzes due to a slew of incoming texts.

Zach: Fucking parties everywhere man! Hit me up!

Courtney: You better not have screwed this up!

Brenna: Hey Ya? What the hell is going on?

Jamie: Call me right now!!

Sighing, I glance down at the coaster under my beer and see it's an advertisement for Laney's favorite. It doesn't matter where I look, she's there.

Just as that thought crosses my mind, the music changes, and Tim McGraw's voice fills the bar.

"Are you fucking serious!?"

"What's that?" The bartender asks.

"Mind if I unplug the jukebox?" I ask before tossing back the shots.

"Yes, I fucking mind, and you need to slow it down there."

"I'm good," I stand on shaky legs and make my way toward the source of the noise. The words of the song are like gravel scraping across my gaping chest. I pull another bill from my pocket and put it into the machine as the chorus hammers into me. "Fuck you, Tim McGraw," I flip through the music as Laney's first love tells me the story about a girl he lost because he was stupid enough to let her go and how it haunts him.

I white-knuckle grip the side of the jukebox shaking myself back and forth. "This. Is. *Not*. Happening."

Drunk and stupid, I close one eye and focus on the title "Everywhere".

"Well, isn't *that* ridiculously appropriate," I spit at the machine as I enter the song's number eight times using all my credits before I slink down onto the dirty floor next to it. Closing my eyes, I thump the back of my head against the wall memorizing every note, every single syllable of every lyric, knowing I may never play it for her.

I make it to the sixth replay before I'm slung over a shoulder and hauled out of the bar.

######

The next morning, I wake up dressed in bed with a post-it stuck to my forehead and Laney's open shampoo bottle running down my chest. The scent of orange blossoms causes my chest to re-crack just as a searing pain makes its presence known behind my eyes. Cracking one open, I spot an icy Gatorade on my nightstand. I down the liquid and squint at the words until they come into focus.

> Do yourself a favor
> and don't make the
> same mistake I made.
> Tell her.
>
> Lance

forty-four

THEO

"Yo, Theo," Dante calls from the porch.

"Sup, little man?" I say, approaching him. "What are you in for today?"

"I got in trouble at school."

"You need to take it easy on your mom."

"I know," he says, looking surprisingly guilty. "I made her cry."

"Not good, buddy."

"She didn't even tell me to come out here. I came out by myself. I told her I wouldn't make her cry no more, but she said she's tired of the men in her life letting her down."

"Oh," I say, glancing toward the door. "Look, she's going to need you to be really nice to her for a little while, okay? Think you can handle that?"

"Yeah."

"Good."

Dante grins as a familiar truck comes into view from down the street. "Mommmm, Troy is here!"

I watch his truck pull up to the curb before Troy opens his door and looks at me pensively. With a sigh, he makes his way to the bed of the truck to grab a lawn mower. Once he has it down, he walks over to the porch.

"Hey, little dude, where's your mom?"

Dante shakes his head. "She's inside, but she's crying."

Troy looks over at me, guilt covering his features.

"Tell me you didn't," I say as he sinks where he stands.

"Jesus Christ, Jenner," I say, tossing my hands up.

Dante looks between us confused. "What did he do?"

"Nothing to worry about, little man," Troy says, giving me a warning look. "Hey, Dante, do you mind letting me talk to Theo a minute?"

"Momma got that cereal you like," he supplies as Troy walks him toward the door.

"Yeah, maybe I'll have some after I do the grass. Go on inside for a second, okay?"

"If this is man talk, I'm cool. *I'm* the man of this house."

Troy grimaces. "Go on," he says, ushering him inside.

"Fine," Dante huffs. "Later, Theo."

When the door closes, Troy looks down at his feet and sighs. "I don't expect you to understand."

"Please don't confuse me for someone who cares enough about you to want to understand. It's *them* I care about."

He shakes his head and turns to me, crossing his arms. "You think I don't?"

"I don't think you care about anyone above yourself."

"Well, you're fucking wrong. Look, you hate me, and that's fine, but there's something you need to know about Laney."

"Save your breath."

"She wasn't lying. She never once gave me any reason to go after her. She wouldn't even tell me her name. Every bit of that cat and mouse was *me*. It was *all* me. She'd already told me to fuck off *twice* before you came outside and at every turn before that. I'm the one who ran up on her. I'm the one who tried to force it. I was in a fucked-up place."

I glare at him from where I stand.

"I just thought you should know."

"She already told me this herself."

"Yeah, but I'm guessing you didn't believe her."

"And I should believe you?"

"Yeah, you should because when she looked at me, she saw me the same way you do, and I think that's what attracted me to her. I wanted to prove you both wrong." He glances at Clarissa's closed door. "But I was trying to prove myself to the wrong people." He lifts his chin. "You assume so much about me, just like everyone else and I just never bothered to correct you."

"Troy! Momma won't come outside!" Dante pokes his head out of the door, and Troy winces, kneeling to whisper something to him. It's then that I see the resemblance and it's uncanny. I never looked for it, but now that I am, it's blatantly obvious. Troy closes the door and turns back to face me.

"He's yours."

Troy nods.

"And you haven't told him?"

He harrumphs. "This is messier than you could ever imagine and fuck the look on your face, Houseman. Do you think I answered your ad because I couldn't find anywhere else to live closer to campus? Half my friends wouldn't even charge me to live at their spots. Your address was my chance to be closer to *him* and look out for them both. She," he wipes a hand down his face, "she doesn't want anything to do with me." His voice turns to ice. "You think I wanted to pay rent late every month? Contrary to what you think, I wasn't getting my dick waxed every time I had a late night, I was working my fucking ass off to pay the rent for *three*. Between that and ball—" he shakes his head in aggravation, "you know what? I could fill a fucking book with what you *don't* know. You got the only explanation I owe you," he snaps before slamming the door behind him.

Stunned, I stare at the door long after it's closed. Troy is right. I'd assumed far too much about everyone close to me and used my judgments as armor, which only ended up pushing people out of my life. People I care about, people I love.

Laney's words come back to me. I did need another serving of humble pie.

And I just ate the whole fucking thing.

Grannism—Love 'em enough to let them break your heart but learn enough so they don't break your spirit.

forty-five

LANEY

"TO THE CLASS OF 2019, WE SALUTE YOU."

We all rise, tossing our hats and throwing our hands in the air. My heart's in it just enough to celebrate the moment as camera flashes go off like sparkling diamonds across the stadium. We march out in rows, and it takes me a small eternity to find my mother. And when I do, she's not happy.

"You can't just come here."

"I have a right."

"You have *no* right."

"Mom?" I ask as the man she's arguing with turns to face me.

My mom smiles and pulls me to her. "Oh baby, I'm so proud of you. Let me see this diploma." She takes the pleather folder from my hand and opens it as I study the man next to her.

"It's fake. They're going to mail the real one."

"Oh," she says, taking a step forward and blocking my view.

"Hello," I address the man behind her.

"Hi Laney," the man smiles, and it's familiar.

"Jim, right?"

His smile widens. "You remember me?"

"Not really, no." I'd looked him up a couple of years ago, but I'm not about to admit it. He has a pretty wife and a young son that looks just like him.

"I told you she wouldn't remember you."

"Please, Deidra, don't make a scene."

"Then take your ass on back to Houston," she snaps over her shoulder, carefully tugging on my hair and fussing over my gown. "You look so beautiful."

I step around her, curious.

"What are you doing here?"

"I came to see you graduate. You know this is my alma mater."

I nod. "I'm aware."

"I just wanted to be here for you, to congratulate you."

"Why?"

"Well, I was told you were graduating soon at a Christmas party."

"By who?" I look at my mother, who looks just as clueless.

"The son of one of my golfing buddies. Theo. He's not a fan of mine, and had some choice words for me and—"

"My Theo?"

"Yes, he didn't tell you we met?"

"No, he didn't," I say, tears springing to my eyes.

"Well, he made quite an impression on me and seems to care a great deal about you. Told me he was madly in love with you." My sperm donor smiles as my heart crash lands in my stomach.

"He told you this at Christmas?"

"He did, and I've been thinking about calling but—"

"What exactly did he say?"

"Laney, I'm trying to tell you about how I've—"

"I don't care about *you*," I say, letting my tears fall freely. "At *all*. I care about *him*."

Jim's features twist in defeat. "That seemed to be his exact sentiment."

"Yeah well, he could tell me exactly what was said. You know why? Because that's the type of man he is. He would know how important the conversation was to me."

"I'm sorry, I was in a bit of shock. Laney, I'd like to—"

I laugh sarcastically. "It's way too late, *Jim*. My mother did your job and hers. Thanks for the checks, we used them. We needed them. We deserved them. But this here," I gesture between us. "Ain't happenin'. *Ever*."

"Laney, please hear me out." His face is reddening from my rejection.

"No offense, Jim, but I don't want to know you. I have no hard feelings against you. None. Truly. But I don't want to know you."

I walk away, unable to hold the emotions surfacing.

Theo met my father and didn't tell me. It's too much.

"I'm going to go look for Devin," I tell my mother. "I'll be back."

I hear the faint sound of my parents arguing behind me, and I have to admit, it's odd.

"I told you."

"Fine, Deidra, you told me, I just want to be there for her."

"Well, if you're really sincere—"

I can't listen to anymore. Once I'm a safe distance away, reeling from the idea of Theo confronting my dad about being a deadbeat. Life decides to deliver another blow when the crowd parts and I see him. He's dressed in a suit, black skinny tie, and his chucks. My eyes re-fill instantly at the welcome sight of him as he searches the crowd with eager eyes, panic covering his features. I'd never been so emotional in my life as I had been while falling in love with this man and losing him. When his eyes finally land on mine, I see relief briefly as he stops his feet and stands a few yards away. His eyes roam my face, my parted robe and my new dress beneath, before trailing down to my boots and I see his lips lift at the sight of them. It's a dagger to the heart when his eyes return to mine filled with the same longing I feel. My heart calls out to his from where I stand, my eyes pleading with his to close the distance.

Swiping the tears off my cheeks, I wait while he studies me, my heart bottoming out in anticipation. Finally, he takes the few steps separating us.

"Hi."

"Hi."

"Congratulations."

"Thank you."

"You look incredible."

"So do you," I say, trying my best to keep my voice even.

"Still taking that trip?"

I nod.

"When do you leave?"

"In a few days."

He nods. "How have you been?"

"Horrible. You?"

He cups the back of his neck, guilt marring his face.

"Are you—"

"Are we really going to do small talk?"

He runs a hand down his bearded jaw and pulls it away before shaking his head and shoving his hands in his pockets. "Laney, I'm so sorry. For the things I said. For the way I acted.

I've never acted like that. Ever. I've never felt like that. It scared the shit out of me."

"Me too."

He studies me, his face filled with remorse. "I'm so sorry for a lot of things."

I nod. "I know. Me too."

"You have nothing to be sorry for." He takes a step forward, and I'm hit with the familiar scent of his cologne. The cologne my mother bought for him on one of our happiest days. He still wears it, even without her audience.

I'll never stop loving this man.

Senses reeling, I swallow all the things I want to say and let him take the lead. The ball has been in his court the whole time we've been apart. In a way, this is our moment of truth. We stand divided for endless seconds, just staring.

"I made my mistakes," I confess, "I know what they were. But you're right, you should be sorry. And you went silent on me."

He shakes his head as if to ward off emotion while we both choke on the pain radiating between us. All too clearly, I can see the battle warring in his head.

The future I've been so scared of is *now*, I'm standing in it. There are no decisions left to make. Today is the first day of the rest of the forever I have, and I want to live in it with him. With a hopeful heart, I stare on at him, willing him to believe me. Willing him to bridge the gap, because it's his to close.

It's when he remains quiet, that his lack of words rip what's left of my heart apart.

For me, today marks the beginning. For him, it means goodbye.

"I'm glad you came."

"I didn't want to miss it."

"I wanted to thank you."

"For?"

I manage a smile. "For proving to me, that I'm just a regular girl."

"You're nothing like any other girl, Laney."

"I very much am," I laugh through watery eyes. "It's a different world I'm living in now, Houseman. No going back."

He draws his brows.

"Because now I understand all these random things I didn't before, and it's been utter hell and sheer bliss. Now I can *feel* Gran's favorite song rather than just hear it. I can empathize with the poor sobbing idiot in the movie because I *am* her. In this new world, I'm capable. Capable of all of it. Capable of making big decisions that make or break me." I look directly at him. "Of ghost pains." He closes his eyes briefly, and I flick my gaze to the grass, willing myself to stay strong. "Even if I still suck at making the small decisions."

"Laney—"

I snap my tear-filled eyes to his, my voice cracking in hurt and anger. "But you cut us off at the root before we even had a chance to figure out which way we were growing. So, don't tell me you're sorry for how you acted. Tell me you're sorry that you didn't try and help save us. That you let me cry in bed every damned night for weeks wondering if you meant a word you said to me. But I guess you've said it all by saying *nothing*. But don't let me back you into a corner, Houseman. Because *I* can say plenty. I miss you. I miss your noise. I miss you all day, every day, and every second of every minute. So, until you've made your mind up about me, don't say another word to me."

And then I do the only thing I can, I let the rest of my fight go.

Lifting on my toes, I press a kiss to his cheek and hear

the breath leave him before I bring my eyes to his. "I love you, Theo Houseman. I just wish you could've trusted me enough to let me."

"Laney!" I hear Devin call out from behind me. "Where in the hell is she!?"

"You take care," I choke out before leaving him there. I don't look back, because if I do, I know I'll never stop.

Grannism—The only one you should ever try and prove yourself to, is the person you were the year before.

forty-six

LANEY

"**M**AX, YOU'RE LOOKING A LITTLE PEAKED," I WHISPER as he sloths into the kitchen behind me. "Maybe you should up your naps to ten a day."

"He's fourteen," my mother pipes in behind me as I start the coffee. "You know, we're lucky to have had him this long. His sight is only going to get worse."

Searing pain wracks through me as I stare down at him, and he seems to shrug. I'm nowhere near ready for another goodbye. It's been two days since graduation, and I'm set to leave on my trip tomorrow night. My sperm donor had done me one final solid by funding my overseas trip; courtesy of his guilt. And due to my newly-flattened heart and up in the air status, I decided not to stand on principle, take the money and run. "Don't Mom, don't even think about it, or suggest it. Not now, not ever. He's perfect."

"Okay," she says easily. "I just don't want him to suffer. Lord knows, we've seen enough of that around here."

Swallowing back my emotion, I nod.

"You've added six scoops, you plannin' on needing all that jet fuel today?"

"Shit. Sorry," I say scooping out the extra coffee. "Worst barista ever."

"Language. And maybe we could get one of those Keurig thingies."

"Gran hated the idea. Besides, we've never wasted a pot." My voice is shaking, and I know she can hear it.

"But you won't be sharing them with me anymore."

Fear runs through me at the idea of leaving my mother alone. We've never really been apart. "I don't think I should go."

"Look at me when you talk to me."

"I'm making coffee, Mom."

"Elaine Renee."

Turning to face her, I can see the worry etched on her face.

"What's wrong? And don't tell me it's Max because he's such a pain in the ass I threaten to put him down daily."

Swallowing, I shake my head.

"Spill it."

"I could postpone it for a little while. There's so much to do around here."

"No way," she says. "I'll be fine. Don't be ridiculous."

"You need me here."

"I need no such thing, busybody. You're going. Don't forget I'm the one that raised you. But don't age me so much."

"Okay," I say. "Okay."

"That's not all."

"I don't know what I want to do, Mom. I'm packed. I have a plan. I have the money. I'm ready. All signs point to go."

"But there's a man."

"Doesn't matter, he's done with me. I just don't think I can be done with him. I don't think I ever will be. I feel ruined."

"You're not."

"I couldn't convince him...I just couldn't convince him that was the truth."

"His loss."

"No, *mine*. I'll never in my life find another guy like him. I don't want to."

"Oh, baby girl," she whispers, pulling me into her arms. "I know how you love, Laney. And believe it or not, you're so transparent when you do. There is no way in the world he's clueless to that and no way in the world you would fall for any guy who couldn't see your true heart. He knows. But you know the dumbest thing a woman can do, is wait for any man to come to his senses. If he's worth a damn, and he knows you're worth it, he'll come for you. And you don't have to make it easy on him."

"No worries about that, I'll be a continent away. And the scary part is I'm not even sure I want to go anymore. I've been dreaming about it for so long, but every time I think of my future now, it's here."

"Because of him?"

"I'd hoped. Is that so wrong?"

"No, baby. It's just that you have a lot of 'what ifs' to sort. This is one of them."

"What do I do?"

"You go, you explore your heart and mind. If he ever comes calling, then you know your place with him. Until then, you find your own place in the thick of things."

I nod into her robe, inhaling her scent.

"Okay," I say, letting out a breath. "Okay."

"Come on, coffee's ready. Let's have it on the porch, and you can tell me all about your trip."

Sniffing, I pull back and wipe my face. She nods in reassurance, her eyes crinkling at the sides. "She would be so proud of you."

"Thank you."

"I miss her."

"Me too."

I pour our coffee and begin to stir in the milk when I hear thunder in the distance.

"Sounds like rain," I mumble, dumping in a spoon of sugar.

"Forecast read sunny today and tomorrow. Then again, you couldn't pay me to be a Texas weatherman. Those poor souls are doomed from day one."

We file onto the porch as the screen door slaps behind us. I'm going to miss that slap. I sip my coffee and study the scenery before me and imagine myself doing the same in a small café in Rome, which is my first stop. A slither of excitement races through me, and I consider that a good sign.

"Damn," my mother remarks of the faraway noise. "That's...what in the *hell* is that?"

Our eyes meet in confusion as we hit the edge of the steps peering down the driveway. The repetitive boom in the distance is growing closer. It's then I hear the pattern of the thunder.

"Momma, I don't think that's thunder," I whisper, just as a distant whistle blows and realization hits. "Oh *my God*."

My coffee cup bounces off the porch and into a bush as I strain to see the source of the noise.

It's only when I see the first line of Rangers march down the driveway that I screech, and turn to haul ass back inside. My retreat is cut short when the front door closes and locks. Another rapid succession of a whistle has me screaming and pounding on the door.

"Let me in! Momma! Let me in!"

"No way, you're going to face this head on, Elaine Renee. This is as good as it gets. Do you hear me?"

"I hear you, Momma, loud and clear, and that's all fine and dandy, but I'm still in my underwear!"

"Oh," she snorts, "be right back!" I can hear a burst of

excited laughter coming from her as she races down the hall. A few seconds later, the door opens, and only her hand shoots out with some sleep shorts that read *'All sass no ass.'*

"Really, Mom?"

"Hey, *you* bought them."

Jerking them from her grip, I scramble to pull them on and turn back toward the wave of percussionists closing in by the second. It sounds like a thousand of them are marching in for battle. A solid lump forms in my throat as they tap out a building rhythm as if waiting for a cue. Anticipation races through me as I tug down my fitted cami while thanking God for the built-in bra. I'm a hot mess express as I stand idle on the porch frantically running fingers through my hair.

And then I see them, the Grand Band drumline emerging from the clearing along with fifteen or more fighting Rangers. Uncontrollably shaking where I stand, I feel the warmth of my tears pool where my hand cups my mouth.

Lines form on either side of the drive declaring their imminent arrival as the rhythmic thud pounds in time with the spastic beat of my heart. It's all I can do to keep upright.

"Mom," I cry shakily back toward the door when the adrenaline catches up with me.

It's then she raises the blinds in the window directly to my right on the porch so she can get a clear view. She's with me.

Breathing easier, I turn back to the drive, heart hammering, an awareness prickling up my spine, delivering goosebumps along my neck and scalp. My senses heighten unbearably, emotions running rampant as the drums reverberate through the trees. Another ten or fifteen Rangers come into view zigzagging across our lawn in perfect formation.

Heart soaring, I take in the sight before me, tears slipping easily down my cheeks just as the drumbeat takes background to a steady bass line. It's then Theo appears in a long trailer behind a king cab along with Zach and the rest of his band. They circle the drive coming to a stop less than fifteen feet from my porch. Rangers line up on all sides of the trailer stretching down the driveway as far as the eye can see. The bass line morphs just as the screech of Theo's guitar pierces the air.

Eyes glued to Theo; I drink him in. He's dressed in a T-shirt that says "I'm with the band" underneath a black-tailed tuxedo coat that trails over plaid shorts. There's a matching plaid bowtie fastened loosely around his Adam's apple. He's strapped with a black Stratus he's wailing on, and it's the sexiest thing I've ever seen in my life. Hands over my chest, I'm doing my best to stay standing as Theo delivers the opening licks to "My Hero" by The Foo Fighters. A hysterical sob leaves me as I watch him lead the Grand Band into an epic rendition of the song while Zach begins to belt out the lyrics.

The sound reverberates through the wood beneath my feet along with the windows of my house as I stand there in awe. I'm doing everything I can not to fly to him when his eyes finally meet mine, and he winks before mouthing a, "Hi."

"Hi," I mouth back shakily as he leads them into an unbelievable crescendo shaking his head as he runs the length the guitar with precision like the rockstar he is. The star he's always been. The star he let me discover by peeling back layer after layer to let his light shine through. As surreal as the whole scene is, I can't keep my eyes off him.

His hair falls over his face as he plucks the strings rocking back and forth. Shaky sobs escape me as the song hits its peak and Zach shrieks out the lyrics. I feel every word strike me raw, bone-deep, *soul* deep. The band's brass chimes in along with the five-man crew in front of me while I completely lose my shit, enamored, in awe, and desperately in love. Drowning in adrenaline, I rock out with them, dancing on shaky limbs.

The sound of the whistle has the Rangers switching their march as the song fades into a slower, melodic rhythm that knocks the rest of the breath out of me. It's when Theo takes a seat at the waiting keyboard on the far side of the trailer and begins to play Lonestar's "Amazed" that I lose all semblance of reality. When his eyes meet mine, I'm gone. So. Fucking. Gone.

I sway on my bare feet, feeling every note, every key, every word a direct line to my starving heart.

My mother is at my back then, wrapping her arms around my chest, pulling me to her as we freely cry together, swaying back and forth. In my peripheral, I spot Devin to the left of me at the foot of the porch, tears streaming down to her smile, her phone up recording every second of what's happening.

It's then I realize this whole thing was meticulously orchestrated by a musical architect. *My* architect. My music man and the only guy on Earth that could ever possibly hold me down.

I take it all in; the music, the words, the man pouring his soul out to me.

"I love you," I mouth to him. Clearly, I can see the shine in his eyes as he keeps the melody, relief in his features while he mouths the words to me. It doesn't matter that I can't hear him, I know this song, this man, *by heart.*

"Okay, maybe you can marry him," my mom says in a tear-soaked voice, before letting me go and ushering Devin to join her.

Unable to stay planted, I take the steps down the porch two at a time and rush toward him, keeping my place at his feet attending my own private concert. Standing there, I memorize the sweat on his brow, the serene look on his face, the heart with which he plays. When the song hits a crescendo, I sing with him, *to* him. I'm pouring my heart out right back, belting it out at the top of my lungs until every note is played. When he sees the longing on my face, he lets the band take over and jumps over the edge of the trailer before capturing me in his arms, my feet already dancing on air. Instruments go up around us along with endless cheers as he effortlessly lifts me in a hug, and I wrap around him, smiling through my tears.

He's shaking as he holds me tightly to him, and I can feel the pound of his heart and count every precious beat.

And then he kisses me, deep, so deep my whole body erupts with the feel of it as thunderous applause rings out around us.

When he pulls away, we just stand and stare as the song ends and the bass line carries it to the next before the Grand Band begins to march off the way they came.

"Jesus, Houseman," I say, gripping him tightly to me. I'm plastered to him, too swept up to say anything else as Theo turns with his arm locked around me and thanks Zach and the rest of the band, giving them daps. Resting my head against his chest, I wave to the guys in thanks before I catch a glimpse of Troy standing behind the cab of his truck as the guys hop off the trailer and climb in. There's an apology in his expression, and all I can do is nod before burying my face into Theo's chest. I have no idea how much time passes. I'm too emotional, clinging to Theo's damp T-shirt, my head buried in the crook of his neck.

It's only when the truck slowly pulls away, and I hear the sound of gravel that he tilts my chin up, his brown eyes filled with love as I fight to come up with words while he wipes my tears away with gentle thumbs.

"How's that for making some noise for the girl I love?"

"I felt it *everywhere*," I sniffle.

His smile is cut in half by his apology. "I'm so sorry, Laney.

It wasn't you I didn't trust. I need you to forgive me. I'm losing my fucking mind without you. And I'll never hurt you like that again. Ever."

"I'll forgive you anything. I'm so sorry I ever made you doubt how I felt about you. I love you, too, Theo, so much."

"I know you do. I felt it every single day we were together."

I nod, and he kisses the rest of my tears away.

"So, you forgave him?" I pop my chin toward Troy's retreating truck.

"I misjudged him and he kind of owed me. He's trying to get his shit together." I nod, sensing there's a lot more to that story, but I really don't want to talk about Troy. Not now, not ever.

"That was…that was incredible. You sure set a high bar."

His smile is perfection as he eyes me, seeming to memorize my reaction to him. "Well, I hope you don't expect something that insane every time I screw up."

"Of course, I do."

He kisses my temple, my cheek, and pulls me tightly to him.

"I missed you so much."

"Same."

We stand there a mess, the new heat of the day bearing down on us as we cling to the other.

"Don't shut me out like that ever again. I almost cut my hair and agreed to therapy."

He chuckles. "I'm glad you spared your hair, but you could probably use the therapy."

I slap his chest, and he pulls me tighter.

"You never told me you met Jim."

He pulls back, his hands on my shoulders and frowns. "I didn't want to upset you. How did you find out?"

"He popped up at my graduation right before I saw you."

He weighs my expression. "Any hope there?"

"No," I deflate a little with my sigh, "I don't want to know him, and I told him as much. 'Sides it doesn't matter, I've got all the man I can handle right here."

"I love you," he whispers softly before claiming my mouth in a thirsty kiss. Wrapping my arms around him, I sink into the buzz, revel in the familiar zing in my chest, the warmth. When we pull away breathless, the excitement leaves me in a rush as I realize the clock is ticking.

"I'm supposed to leave tomorrow night."

He swallows thickly, brushing the loose hair away from my face. "And I want you to go."

"What?"

"It's a few months, a summer, Laney. Go, come back. We'll work it out. I'll be here."

"You'll wait for me?"

"I waited for the wrong girl for years. I think I can handle waiting a few months for the right one."

forty-seven

LANEY

"IT'S OVER, HOUSEMAN. YOUR GRAND MAN BAND Gesture is officially our last post."

"You're killing the page?"

"Nope. Just passin' the torch. Our legacy will live on, baby, but I'm done with it."

"Why am I suddenly afraid? Who exactly are we passing our torch to?"

"Let's just say I found someone more than capable of taking over. She's got the personality for the job."

"Laney?"

"She's, uh, well-qualified. Over-qualified if you ask me."

"Uh huh, and who is *she*?"

"Don't get mad."

"What did you do?"

Laney slowly lifts her phone as a picture of Courtney dressed in her Penn State garb complete with her bedazzled tutu comes into view.

"Are you serious? You gave this woman a hundred and six thousand people to terrorize?"

Studying the picture closely, I see Courtney is lifting a beer, in toast—*to herself*. The cherry on top is her hashtag.

#somuchbetterthanboysperm #getreadyforepic
#youaintseennothingyet #livingmyrealestlifetwopointoh
#itson #staytuned #wearepennstate

"You have got to be fucking kidding me!"

"Nope. She was all too happy to take it on, and I was all too ready to let it go."

He frowns. "Why?"

"When our posts stopped, I was made to feel like I owed everyone an explanation, and it wasn't their business. They just knew. That's why I said screw it and posted that I missed you. Some of the comments they made really hurt. But some of the support was overwhelming too. They totally fell for you."

"They fell for *us*. And I'm sorry that hurt you too."

"Well, you're a stupid man."

He scowls.

"See how that can cut both ways, like crazy does for me?"

"Yes," he says dryly. "I like it much better when you say it naked on top of me in the middle of a tornado."

"Me too, minus the tornado."

He leans in on a whisper. "We should run practice drills often, just in case."

"Mmm, we can go run one now, if you like."

"First things first. I have a date to make up to you."

"Right," I say as he threads our fingers and kisses the back of my hand.

"It's pretty ironic, a few days from now I very well could have posted a picture on the Mediterranean in a thong bikini with a glass of champagne."

He pulls his brows together in telltale annoyance, and I laugh.

"Getting to be quite the jealous guy, aren't ya?"

"Recent development. And I'm aware jealousy disguises insecurity. I'm not proud of it. I'm working on it."

"I love that you aren't so perfect. I love it that you can tell me that. We can't ever change this, okay? Promise."

"I promise."

"You know, lately you've been making me look like a saint."

He rolls his eyes before he presses a kiss to my temple. "Speaking of promises," he says, warmth lighting up his eyes. "You ready?"

He leads me down the sidewalk, and my nerves fire off, but I would follow this man anywhere. Still, I can't hide the excited tremor in my voice. "For?"

He grins. "This isn't what you think," he says, leading me past one long barricading branch after another.

"I don't care what it is, I have my answer."

He grins apologetically. "Well, I'm happy about that, but I'm not proposing. This really is a promise from me to you."

"A promise?"

"Yes," he murmurs, turning to face me once we're underneath the dark green canopy of the Era Tree. "I love how independent you are. I love it, Laney. I love that you can fill every role in your own life. But I don't want anyone to ever take mine. So, I want to make you a promise. A promise that no matter what happens between us, good or bad, I'll be the one man in your life who won't leave you, no matter what. I don't want to live a day of this life where I don't know you. I swear to you, Laney, no matter what happens personally between us, I don't ever want to know that you aren't safe in this world. This is my promise for a sense of forever with you, a promise that I will always be there for you. *Always*. No matter what."

"I don't know what to say."

"Say okay."

"Okay," I nod tearfully. "But you will marry me one day, right?"

He lifts one side of his lip in an Elvis curl. "Meh, maybe."

"You're an ass," I huff, taking a step ahead of him and dodging his outstretched hand. "You totally ruined that."

"If I was proposing, it damn sure won't be under a tree that a hundred other guys have used for lack of a better imagination."

"You just pissed all over that tradition harder than a cow on a flat rock."

He throws his head back and laughs as I narrow my eyes.

"I'm serious. This is sacred."

"As was my promise," he says, snatching my hand and threading our fingers.

I see the honesty in his eyes and melt. "You got out of that one fast."

He grins. "So, what do you want to do tonight?"

"*Rock of Love?*"

He looks away, and I gawk at him.

"You watched *all* of the last season without me?!"

"I missed you, it was a coping mechanism."

"Lies, all lies!" I proclaim, narrowing my eyes. "I can't believe you did that! Such an ass. Who wins? Who does Brett end up with? NO!" I clamp my hand over his mouth. "Don't you dare ruin it for me. Gah, I'm so going to kick your ass!"

He rips my hand from his mouth.

"Laney, I don't think anyone has cursed a man out under the tree. It's probably bad juju."

"You are a *pig* from *hell*."

"Ah," he says, pointing a finger at me. "That's an Ouiser line. I'm getting good at this."

"You watched that too?"

He grins. "Yep. *Twice*. And all of the Madea movies."

I grip his face in my hands. "You are forgiven."

"I love you, crazy Laney."

"I love you too, Grand Band Man."

Grannism—Your grandfather told me once we were moving north, so I pulled out a map and asked him, 'Where in Texas is that?'

epilogue

One year later...

I WAKE TO THE SOUND OF MISSED KEYS.

Something's off. Theo rarely ever misses notes on the piano. Playing for him is like breathing. He's already mastered another four instruments since I moved in with him after coming back from a three-month sabbatical. Hearing Theo's third attempt, I pad down the stairs past the photos I took of the landscapes on my travels and pause at the picture of the Taj Mahal. That day gave me a real sense of clarity. As much as I missed him, I cherished my trip. The first two weeks were hard. Every day I thought of an excuse to come back home, and every day, I fought with myself to see it through. After a month, I'd grown comfortable with being uncomfortable. It didn't hurt that my boyfriend FaceTimed me constantly, encouraging me to stick it out. Every day he ordered me to find our new favorite place so that one day we would return, and I wasn't allowed to come home until I did. I found out a lot about myself. I'm not a fan of foreign cuisine, like *at all*. I prefer mountains to beaches. Cold to heat, which is unfortunate because Texas is home.

The one thing I was sure of when I boarded the plane home, is that I loved my life and was satisfied with the way things were. I didn't need to go on some grand adventure to find myself and figure it out. I'd known all along that I loved being at the front line with the people closest to me. Being involved in their lives for the trials and triumphs. I wanted a life very much like those of my heroes. The funny thing about that is, I hadn't realized just how much of rocks my heroes were when it came to friends and family, until I left. I wanted to be that rock for those I cared the most for.

And a good rock rarely becomes a rolling stone.

I'm still unsure of what career I want, and the cool part is, I don't have to figure it all out anytime soon. I have my degree. It's not going anywhere, and for now, neither are we.

At the landing at the foot of the stairs, I see the obstruction we've had a million fights over since he brought the baby grand home and placed it in the center of our living room.

I walk into the room where he sits poised on the bench, his graduation gown pressed and hanging in the laundry room behind him. As it turns out, I ended up being the one to wait on Theo, and my Grand Man is graduating tomorrow *summa cum laude*.

He dug in deep this year, focusing most of his time on his music while I've been busying myself at my job at the flower shop. I hunted for it when I got home from my trip and used the rest of my time to help my mom renovate Gran's house. She joined a dating app when I moved in with Theo and started seeing someone a little younger than herself a few months ago. My mother is officially a cougar, and it's given her a little bounce back in her step. Theo gets credit for putting most of that hopeful light back in her eyes. It's his romantic antics that brought that side of her back to life.

Maybe most of the men in my family don't last, but everything inside me tells me *this man* will go the distance.

He stops the recording again, with a "Shit. *Shit.*" Another false start that has me on edge. Something is definitely wrong.

And then he begins again. The now familiar, "Three, two, one," sounding out before the recording begins.

It takes me a few seconds to place the opening to "The Luckiest" by Ben Folds and this time he's playing along with the lyrics.

I slowly make my way toward him as he presses the pedals swaying slightly back and forth, while words fly through the living room, hitting me directly in the chest. Theo's music might not be my taste, but it's his language that speaks to me. When his eyes connect with mine, I can see his intent, and I'm instantly shaking with the abundant love I feel coming from the other side of the piano.

The song tells of how fortunate we are to have found each other, in this time in our lives. Of how he's convinced his soul would recognize mine anywhere in time. Rounding the piano, I gasp when I see the small box sitting on the top of the polished wood. It's open, a beautiful solitaire sitting below the words, Marry Me?

I lose it then, crying softly as he shakily croons to the music, pledging his heart, his life, and asking me for mine.

In his favorite plaid pajama bottoms, hair askew, eyes bright, he sings off-key along with Ben, of how much he loves me, of how perfectly we belong together. Two oddballs, who aren't so odd when we're together.

Years from now, when we tell our story, I know my version.

It will be about a young girl who went from hopeful to a hopeless romantic in a few notes that only her Prince Charming could play. He didn't show up on a white horse declaring that she hops on before he gallops away. No, this prince got off his horse, fell on his ass, and stumbled in the mud with her until she could mount her own stallion. And then, in one last act of bravery, he gently trotted beside her into the unknown.

I'm sure I'll throw in a few fire-breathing dragons for drama, maybe a curse of some sort, and of course, Dave in the white Taurus, but it will be the best damn story ever.

My prince plays for me as the last of the keys echo throughout our small living room before he gathers the open box off the piano and kneels before me.

"Jesus, Houseman," I blubber, my nose running as I try to clear my face. It's a lost cause. "You keep upping your game."

"Hope so." He gently takes my hand and sets the ring around the pad of my finger.

"I thought of a thousand ways to ask you to marry me, but…"

"It's perfect. It's us."

He nods, his eyes shining with love as he looks up at me earnestly.

"I mean it, and I'll mean it every day. I swear to you. Without setting a foot outside our front door, I'm certain if I search this Earth, I'll never find anyone else I would want to spend my life with. Will you marry me, Laney?"

"Yes!"

His smile is blinding as he wraps around me, and I tug at his thick hair. He kisses me thoroughly before I pull away, admiring the ring on my finger briefly.

"Oh God, the decisions I'm going to have to make…"

"Don't you dare start," he interrupts.

"I'm just sayin'."

"Laney…"

"Okay, I'll sleep on it."

"Not quite what I was hoping for *tonight*," he says, dragging me through our living room cutting off the lights as we go.

"Oh, don't worry. You're going to get it, *so good*," I declare at the foot of the stairs. "And you'll be gettin' your graduation present early tonight too. I just need ten minutes to set up and find the batteries I bought."

"And I'm now terrified."

"First, I need to call Momma! And Devin. I bet this news will break her water!"

"They know."

"Oh," I say as he leads me up the stairs. "Well, *damn*."

"They went ring shopping with me. And it's two a.m."

"Right, that's awesome. Y'all did it together. And naturally, I wasn't in on it."

"That would defeat the purpose," Theo says, glancing back at me with a smirk.

I grunt in agreement while following him step for step. "Theo?"

He pulls me to him at the landing, wrapping me up tightly in his arms and looking down at me with amused eyes.

"Yes?"

"You know I love you, right?"

"Shhhh," he presses a slow seductive kiss to my lips, "QT, baby."

"And I think you're the most amazin', most talented man I've ever met."

Another kiss in an attempt to silence me.

"Truly. You're *my rock of love*."

He sucks my bottom lip. "Mmhmm."

I pull away and see his eyes pooling dark as he lifts my T-shirt and discards it on the floor.

"Okay," kiss, "well," kiss, "don't take this the wrong way," kiss, "but I need a promise."

He pulls back giving me his full attention. "Okay?"

"Promise me if we decide to have kids, I'll be the one to sing them to sleep."

THE END

about the author

A Texas native, Kate Stewart lives in North Carolina with her husband, Nick, and her naughty beagle, Sadie. She pens messy, sexy, angst-filled contemporary romance as well as romantic comedy and erotic suspense because it's what she loves as a reader. Kate is a lover of all things '80s and '90s, especially John Hughes films and rap. She dabbles a little in photography, can knit a simple stitch scarf for necessity, and on occasion, does very well at whisky.

Other titles available now by Kate

Room 212

Never Me

Loving the White Liar

The Fall

The Mind

The Heart

The Brave Line

Drive

The Real

Someone Else's Ocean

Heartbreak Warfare

Method

ROMANTIC COMEDY

Anything but Minor

Major Love

Sweeping the Series

Balls in Play Box Set: Anything but Minor, Major Love, Sweeping the Series, The Golden Sombrero

EROTIC SUSPENSE

Sexual Awakenings

Excess

Predator and Prey

Lust & Lies Box Set

Let's stay in touch!

Facebook
www.facebook.com/authorkatestewart

Newsletter
www.katestewartwrites.com/contact-me.html

Twitter
twitter.com/authorklstewart

Instagram
www.instagram.com/authorkatestewart/?hl=en

Book Group
www.facebook.com/groups/793483714004942

Spotify
open.spotify.com/user/authorkatestewart

Sign up for the newsletter now and get a free
eBook from Kate's Library!

Newsletter signup

www.katestewartwrites.com/contact-me.html

thank you

When I was twelve years old, my mother took me to the movie theater to see *Steel Magnolias*. Though that was over thirty years ago, I can still remember vivid details about those few hours while sitting in that seat. The popcorn was delicious, theaters were small, the seats were closer together, and the sound scared the shit out of us when it came on before dancing cats warned us to behave ourselves.

Thinking back, those precious minutes watching that movie were the first I can clearly remember experiencing the most phenomenal of emotions, laughter through tears. I remember glancing around the theater with a soaked face at the women surrounding us with tears sliding down their smiling faces and thinking we were all in it together, we're all feeling the same thing. I felt close to those strangers that day, and it was nothing short of magical.

While writing this book, I had a revelation of sorts. The first part of my epiphany is that this cast of characters made an impression on me that's lasted *thirty* years. Those fictional women became idols for me, and I haven't, not once, forgotten the impact that film had. But at the time, I had no idea how those two hours would shape my future.

The second part of my revelation is that at this point, I can honestly credit that movie for being my greatest muse in terms of the kind of stories I want to deliver, including this one. I didn't know it then, but that movie planted a seed and a hope, that one day, I would be able to write those types of moments and share them with strangers, and we would once again all be in it together.

This book is most definitely a tribute to the movie that planted the seed and has inspired me countless times over the years, both personally and professionally and will live in my head and heart forever.

So, my first thank you is to M'Lynn, Shelby, Truvy, Annelle, Clairee, and Ouiser, for showing me the true meaning of magic.

And a huge thank you to all the bloggers and readers who give me a chance to sit in the theater with you. It's so exciting to look around and see if you're laughing or crying with me, a thirty-year dream come true. I hope you know how much it means to me that you showed up.

Thank you to my incredible betas Kathy, Maïwenn, Malene, Maria, Stacy, and Rhonda for once again helping me shape this book.

Thank you to my editing team, Donna Cooksley Sanderson and Grey Ditto for lending me your expertise, and for your faith and friendship.

Thank you to my Ninja PA, Bex Kettner, for being my spotter. I love you.

Thank you, Autumn Gantz, for your friendship and unwavering support.

Thank you to my fly gal, Christy Baldwin for being the joy that you are. I adore you so much and cherish our friendship. #wellalwayshaveboston

Thank you to my proofing team, Marissa, Bethany, and Joy for the polish, and for your patience. I love you guys.

Thank you to, Amy Q of Q Designs for bringing another cover to life.

Thank you to my Asskickers who bring me so much joy, daily.

Thank you to my author friends and to my peers who continue to inspire me.

Thank you to my dear friends and family who continue to support me with unconditional love and unbelievable patience.

Thank you to my husband, Nick, who continues to be both my rock and glue. There's no way I could've done this without you.